The Whispering Wind

Montana Gold Series

The Whispering Wind

By

Janalyn Voigt

The Whispering Wind
Published by Mountain Brook Ink
White Salmon, WA U.S.A.

The website addresses shown in this book are not intended in any way to be or imply an endorsement on the part of Mountain Brook Ink, nor do we vouch for their content.

This story is a work of fiction. All characters and events are the product of the author's imagination other than those stated in the author notes as based on historical characters. Any other resemblance to any person, living or dead, is coincidental.

Scripture quotations are taken from the King James Version of the Bible. Public domain.

The Team: Miralee Ferrell, Tim Pietz, Kristen Johnson, Cindy Jackson
Cover Design: Indie Cover Design, Lynnette Bonner Designer

Mountain Brook Ink is an inspirational publisher offering fiction you can believe in.
Printed in the United States of America

Dedication

This book is for my sister, Jennifer, who rides better than me.

Acknowledgments

No book reaches readers without the efforts of an unsung group of people. Let me start by thanking my editor, proofreaders, and cover designer. I am likewise grateful to reviewers, blog hosts, and readers. Thank you, first of all, for enjoying this story, but also for helping others discover this book.

My family helped me complete this story, and indeed this series, by fending for dinner on their own and by going without my presence. Thank you.

I must express my deepest gratitude to my publisher, Miralee Ferrell, who showed herself the epitome of grace after an injury interfered with my deadline. A fast friend from the beginning, Miralee is one of my dearest mentors. I will always be grateful for her input into my writing.

CHAPTER ONE

Liberty Township, Montana Territory, June 1886

PHOEBE WALSH SHIELDED HER EYES AGAINST the morning sun and watched a large bird glide across the sky. Its wings resembled those of a red-tailed hawk, but black bars banded the creamy underside of the flight feathers. Also, compared to the impressive wingspan, the bird's head looked stubby—more like that of an owl. The wings lifted into a vee and its tail fanned as the bird adopted the characteristic posture of a marsh hawk. She caught her breath. "What a magnificent creature."

Her brother Quinn let out a low whistle. "I'll say." Seated on a black Morgan that dwarfed Nutmeg, her dainty quarter horse, Quinn presented a rather splendid figure himself. He rode with ease, and his bearing seemed nothing short of noble. He might have been one of the ancient kings of Tara.

Phoebe smiled. "Your appreciation of nature is wonderful to behold. Murphy would wish for his hunting rifle."

"You can't fault him for that." Quinn pulled off his Stetson and ran a hand through his dark mahogany hair. "He's a far better hunter than I'll ever be."

Phoebe despaired of her two brothers ever getting along, but they seemed to enjoy their never-ending rivalry. She arched her brows. "It's rare to hear you praise him."

He grinned. "Don't let on that I said that."

"Honestly, the pair of you will drive me to distraction. There's no need to best one another at everything. Murphy hunts well, and you're better at farming. So what? You both put food on the table."

The corners of his lips tilted in a sheepish grin. "Sorry, Sis. Competing with Murphy is a habit I may never break."

"I guessed that." Recognizing the futility of trying to convince Quinn otherwise, she opted to change the subject. "Thanks for riding with me today. If I tried to come so far alone, Ma would have a conniption." She shook her head. "I don't understand her sudden interest in keeping me close to home. I can ride better than ever, and I'm a crack shot, thanks to Pa."

"The Indians aren't so happy to share the land with us these days. Perhaps that's why." He plunked his hat onto his head and pulled down the brim, shading his pale blue eyes.

"Maybe." She could swear something else lay behind her mother's new attitude. Phoebe pushed her suspicions to the back of her mind. Dwelling on them would take the shine off a perfect June day.

"Race you!" Quinn lit out as he spoke, which technically was cheating. Phoebe didn't mind. She knew as well as he did that she could outride him. She could guess that he meant to cheer her. Her brother's tactic must be working, because she couldn't restrain a smile. She caught up with him easily. Instead of pulling ahead, she rode alongside her brother. She could remember a time when long stretches of bunch grass were common, but sagebrush was overtaking it. She didn't need to guess why. Pa ranted often enough that overgrazing was depleting the range's native grasses.

The horses picked along while the sun lifted higher and the shadows beneath their hooves retreated. A flock of geese passed overhead, winging towards the Bitterroot River. A straggler trailed the others, honking as if in alarm. Phoebe smiled. Sometimes she felt like that goose. She didn't fit in with the gaggle of local females eager to find a husband and settle down. She'd never had much enthusiasm for the whole business. Perhaps she should stop trying altogether.

"What's wrong with Pa?" Quinn's exclamation jerked her out of her thoughts.

Phoebe followed her brother's gaze across the grassy range. She went cold. "Something's wrong." Even from this far away, she could see Pa bending in a strange position.

She urged Nutmeg forward, grateful for the little mare's speed. This time Phoebe didn't wait for her brother but covered the ground swiftly. As she drew closer, she noticed the posts that pricked the earth at periodic intervals and the gleam of barbed wire. Where had it come from? She'd never seen such a thing in these parts. A hideous bawling reached her before she saw the bloodied calf tangled in what Pa called the "devil's wire." Her stomach knotted. No wonder her father was bent over that way. He was keeping the calf from injuring itself further.

She dismounted and rushed to help. "What can I do?"

Pa glanced up briefly. "Phoebe! I'm glad to see you." The Irish accent he'd never lost lilted his words. "Take over here, darling girl. Careful not to cut yourself."

"Sure, Pa." She hurried to the calf. It was all she could do to hold on while it struggled. Phoebe was grateful that caring for horses had increased her strength but also that Quinn would arrive in a moment. Pa panted and winced as he worked to extricate the creature. The calf showed the whites of its eyes, bleating piteously. Throaty bellows answered it. Phoebe glanced up and spotted a roan Hereford approaching. Her heart thudded. Hopefully, the mother wouldn't object to their treatment of her calf.

Hooves thudded, and then her brother flung himself down from the saddle.

"Quinn, make sure that cow doesn't come over here. I'd rather be spared a visit from an anxious mother." Pa spoke between gritted teeth. "Keep that calf still as you can, Phoebe."

"I'm trying!" Phoebe's hands were going numb, and her grip was slipping. She wasn't sure how much longer she could last.

"Easy now!" Quinn's cry rang out, followed by more bellowing.

"Don't let her bully you." Pa shouted. "Only a little longer, Phoebe. We're almost finished."

Phoebe held on for all she was worth. The frightened calf struggled anew. Phoebe's arms shook as if palsied. Pa grunted. Barbed wire flashed in the sun. The calf slid from her grasp, complaining loudly. Its mother broke past Quinn, and the pair met. The cow lowered her head and nosed her calf.

"Her care is the best medicine." A tired smile hovered on Pa's lips. "Even so, we'd better cauterize those gashes or they'll attract flies. We can't have larvae hatching in the poor fellow's wounds."

Phoebe shuddered at the thought. "I'll gather firewood." She turned away as she spoke, already searching.

Pa stomped the grass around him, and then hefted a nearby stone into the trampled circle. Phoebe had seen him build a temporary stove in this way before. Quinn hurried over and laid a second large rock beside the first. Pa nodded to him. "Thanks for the help, but I'd rather you stay with the cows, in case the pair of them wander off."

"Sure thing." Quinn strode toward the horses, which had their muzzles in the bunchgrass. He returned on horseback. "It's a crying shame that folks feel the need to fence the range."

Pa picked up his hat from where it must have fallen earlier. "If everyone does so, it will spell the end for the open range."

Phoebe dumped firewood beside the makeshift stove, then moved out of ear shot to gather more. She'd heard Pa's complaints before. If only she could think of a solution, but this was one problem that defied her optimism. Pa didn't have as much cattle as he did horses, but the current conditions affected all livestock. Greed was to blame, with more and more prospective ranchers moving to the valley. But that wasn't the worst of it. Investors from England and other countries eager to turn a profit in America were helping ruin the beef market. Even with the buffalo herd dwindling, the prairies couldn't withstand such an assault.

A chittering cry pulsed the air, and a shadow rippled over her. She'd forgotten the marsh hawk. The bird rode above the bunchgrass with sunlight picking out the white patch at the base of its tail. The marsh hawk dove into the grass and vanished. Perhaps it had captured prey or was guarding a cache of eggs. Although a fearsome bird of prey, a marsh hawk built a humble nest in the grass.

Recalling her task, Phoebe stopped gaping after the bird and went back to collecting deadfall. She carried an armload to her father, who straightened from hunching over the makeshift stove. The fledgling fire snapped and crackled in the cavity between the stones. Phoebe released her burden onto the wood pile she'd built.

"Thanks, Phoebe. That should be plenty." Pa pulled his Bowie from the sheath on his belt and bent beside the stove. The blade glinted briefly, and then flames engulfed its shining steel. "Do me a favor and hold this knife to the fire."

"Sure, Pa." Phoebe squatted and clasped the smooth, wooden handle.

Pa stood and whistled for his horse. "The first thing we'd better do is restrain the mother cow. We wouldn't want her interfering."

Phoebe watched flames curl around the blade while her father joined Quinn on horseback. After a brief discussion which Phoebe couldn't hear, her brother twirled his lariat. A flick of his wrist lassoed the roan's hind legs. The cow went down, and Quinn rode the short distance to reach their father. Pa dropped his lariat over the cow's neck, restraining her further. Quinn dismounted and wrapped a rope around her feet.

Pa roped the calf and dragged it across the grass to the fire. "Bring the knife, Phoebe." He spoke in the calm voice he always used in an emergency.

She swallowed a lump in her throat and brought the knife to him.

He paused with his hand on the hilt. "Look away, Phoebe. This won't be pretty."

She nodded and turned her head. The calf bellowed, and the stench of burnt flesh gagged her. The mother cow bawled. Phoebe clenched her fists and fought to keep her breakfast down.

"That does it." Pa's voice held relief.

Quinn jumped backward, having untied the mother. She staggered to her feet, and the freed calf bolted toward her.

Pa put his arm around Phoebe's shoulders. "There's a brave *cailín*. We couldn't have done it without you."

Phoebe wasn't so sure about that. "I wish I could have helped better. I'd like to learn more about working cattle, Pa."

He smiled. "If today wasn't enough to scare you off, I don't know what would. Still—" he rubbed the back of his neck. "I'm not sure it's a good idea."

Phoebe frowned. "Why not?"

"You're much too pretty to turn into a ranch hand." He launched into his deepest Irish brogue, a sign that the discussion made him uncomfortable.

Phoebe scowled. "What does appearance have to do with anything?"

Already walking back to his horse, her father didn't reply.

Phoebe had a sinking feeling she already knew the answer. She turned twenty-three on her next birthday. Unless she married before then, she would officially become a spinster. Ma was determined to prevent that from happening. She sighed. Pa didn't want to point out that a suitor might object to his prospective bride roping cattle.

Sharp metal pierced Phoebe's skin. "Ouch!" Her jerk wobbled the chair beneath her feet, and she flung out her arms to keep from falling.

"Stop squirming and you won't get stabbed." Ma's voice came out muffled by a mouthful of pins. "I might hem your dress straight, too."

Phoebe glanced down at the top of her mother's head. Chestnut curls scantly threaded with grey bobbed while she pinned up another section. Phoebe sighed. Yesterday, she'd held onto a struggling calf, but this might be a greater test of endurance. "I've never known you to sew a crooked hem."

"There's always a first time." Ma warned darkly, but she glanced up with a gleam in her brown eyes.

A flicker of movement outside her bedroom window caught Phoebe's attention. What had she seen? Shapes came into view, dark against the trees, as several deer stared longingly into the garden. The netting should keep them out. The small distraction quieted her mood, and she was able to speak without sounding snappish. "You shouldn't put pins in your mouth."

"I'll bear that in mind." Ma continued working without removing them.

Phoebe sighed. "What time will we leave tomorrow?"

"Early." Ma directed her attention to pinning with renewed vigor, as if spurred by Phoebe's mention of time. "Pa wants to make the trip in one day."

"I suppose that's wisest." Phoebe didn't explain why she thought so, and Ma didn't ask. There was no need to mention the tension in the valley. As more settlers arrived, the local tribes found they had less room to hunt and gather their food. Barbed wire affected more than cattle. The buffalo suffered from it also. Sometimes it cut them off from water.

"We'll stay in our old cabin at Uncle Shane and Aunt America's place, and then go on to Stevensville for the wedding."

"What you mean to say is that you and Pa will spend the night in the cabin with my two brothers."

Ma laughed. "I expect you and Liberty will sleep in her room, as usual."

Phoebe smiled. Liberty had been Phoebe's friend before Ma marrying her new Pa had turned them into cousins. Phoebe had spent many nights whispering with Liberty until sleep silenced them. Even when they shared a bedroom as grown women, they sometimes murmured together after the lights went out.

Her mother sighed. "Stop swaying or we'll be here all night."

"Sorry, Ma." Phoebe willed herself to stand motionless.

"I'll hurry." Sympathy crept into Ma's voice. "You've never been good at keeping still. Why, when you were small—"

"I know, Ma." Phoebe headed her mother off before she retreated into memory altogether. She knew by heart the many stories of her youthful adventuring. By all accounts, she'd worried her poor mother to death.

Ma's lips curved into a sentimental smile, and her face

softened. "You were an enchanting waif with golden ringlets and mischievous blue eyes."

Phoebe restrained herself from rolling her eyes. It was a mother's privilege to savor memories of her children, but she wished Ma would forget a few of her misdemeanors. "If only I remembered more from my childhood, especially the time before my birth father died." All she could recall were vague impressions of strong arms carrying her.

The old sadness came over Ma's face. "So do I, Phoebe."

"Never mind." Phoebe spoke briskly. "God saw fit to bless me with a wonderful stepfather. I couldn't be more thankful."

Her mother smiled. "I have no doubt of that. You fell in love with Rob before I did."

Phoebe glanced down at her dress. "Are we almost finished?"

"Goodness. Look at me, dreaming about the past and forgetting what I'm doing." Ma completed her task with deft speed. She stood and gazed at Phoebe. "You look like an angel. Watch that you don't outshine the bride."

Phoebe laughed. "I doubt I could."

"Analise *is* beautiful, but so are you. There's no reason you couldn't be the one getting married."

"Apart from the fact that no one has asked me?" Phoebe lifted her skirts inelegantly and jumped down from the chair. "I suppose not. "

"Be careful or you'll break your neck. And don't laugh at the possibility of marriage."

Marriage seemed no laughing matter. Phoebe plucked at the silk of her dress, feeling stifled all at once. "How do I get out of this thing?"

"Let's take it off over your head. Watch out for pins."

Phoebe raised her arms and held her breath as blue

watered silk engulfed her.

Ma stepped back at last with the dress draped over her arm.

Phoebe pulled on her blue calico dress, a much more sensible garment.

"Alton Prescott will be at the wedding." Ma spoke casually but sent her an assessing glance.

Phoebe lifted a shoulder and continued buttoning her dress. "I hope he has a wonderful time."

A line formed between her mother's eyebrows. "I've heard that he's so brokenhearted since you rejected him that he refuses to court anyone."

"I'm sorry he's taken it so badly." Phoebe bit her lip. "I never wanted to hurt him nor any of the others."

Ma cleared her throat gently. "Perhaps you should be a little less choosy. You never know when a suitor will appeal more on closer acquaintance."

Phoebe ran her fingers over the rose carved into the mahogany chair beside her. Unlike the bright blossoms nodding in the garden, this flower would never fade. Phoebe could think of no reply. Maybe Ma would never understand that she knew her own mind.

Will tilted his face heavenward and breathed deep of the night air. The quarter moon peeked from behind a cloud, and faint rays filtered downward. He caught the riffling of wings as some unseen creature, perhaps an owl on the hunt, launched into flight. The wind tugged on his hat brim, and a sudden gust licked the flames at his feet. Somewhere near but out of sight, cattle lowed. Will parted his lips in a smile. Life on the range never lost its charm.

Chatter pulsed around the campfire, subdued at this hour

but pricked by laughter. Tall tales and friendly ribbing gave way to the occasional item of interest. In the outer reaches of Montana Territory, keeping abreast of current events proved difficult. Even so, the most important news usually reached them. Everything else could wait. The present conversation involved the marriage of President Grover Cleveland to one Frances Folsom, a bride twenty-seven years his junior. Their White House wedding bestowed upon a mildly scandalized populace the youngest First Lady in history.

Will congratulated himself on avoiding the matrimonial noose. Doing so had cost him dearly, but he counted himself well out of the fray. So long as he stayed away from Miss Phoebe Walsh, that was. Why he found himself so drawn to the golden-haired vixen, he couldn't say. He didn't trust himself around her, having proven himself incapable of ignoring her on more than one occasion.

"What's your opinion of the age difference?" Con Walsh's Irish lilt broke into Will's thoughts.

Will blinked at his boss, seated next to him on a log beside the fire. Why would Con question the four years between himself and Phoebe?

"You look confused." Con smiled. "Can it be you haven't heard of the scandal? The new Missus Cleveland is but twenty-one, while her husband is forty-nine."

Heat washed over Will as he recognized his mistake. He shrugged. "I'm not qualified to judge matters of the heart, considering my own lack of success in them.".

Con laughed. "A few others might do well to adopt your attitude."

"I don't suppose they've enjoyed the benefit I have." He managed a wry smile. "Being jilted humbles a man."

"Still rankles, does it?"

Will sat a little taller. "I don't deny it."

"I'm sorry you suffered that, but don't let it color your thinking altogether. Tying the knot with the right woman is the blessing of a lifetime, as I can attest."

Unable to form a reply, Will stared into the fire. Watching the embers glow usually soothed his spirit, but it failed to comfort him tonight. Con had brought this up before—so often that Will suspected him of meddling. Con *was* Phoebe's uncle, and he might suspect Will's interest in her.

Will couldn't fathom that someone as beautiful and vivacious as Phoebe might remain on the shelf. She drew many admirers but somehow never chose a suitor. The thought of her winding up a spinster brought a small pang. It reminded him of the one he'd felt whenever he pictured her married to someone else. Will steadied himself. His conflicting emotions should warn him to give Phoebe a wide berth. He wasn't beyond becoming muddled in her presence, a fact that could lead to serious consequences.

Con fell into a good-natured verbal sparring match with Brady, the lean-faced ranch hand on his other side.

Will drew a breath of relief. His boss had cut too near the mark for comfort. He sat in silence for a time, not really listening to the voices around the fire. Together with the whistling of the wind across the grassland, they formed a soothing background. The moon cast feeble light, but that made the stars shine all the brighter. He stretched, easing his muscles after a long day in the saddle. A yawn escaped him, and he yearned all at once for the quiet of sleep. Not wanting to be the first to seek his bedroll, he decided to bide his time yet a while.

Con turned to him. "You're most welcome to attend the wedding."

Will blinked. There seemed a lot of talk of marrying

tonight.

Con grinned. "Look at you, sitting there, owl-eyed. Perhaps you should turn in. I spoke of the wedding of Analise Meier, my wife's sister, in case you wondered. You're more than welcome."

Will waited a moment before answering. Phoebe would probably be there. Besides which, he barely knew Analise. And then, weddings reminded him of his own aborted nuptials. He'd rather not go, but refusing might seem churlish. He didn't want to offend his boss, especially since the request was proof of the bond growing between them. Will could bring his troubles to Con and find a listening ear, and he could always claim a place at the family table. He didn't often avail himself of either privilege, but it was nice to know he could. Con asked for nothing in return, but having his boss's favor inspired Will to perform his duties as ranch manager with even more heart. Beyond that, Will could offer little in exchange. Con was a wealthy man in many ways, whereas Will owned next to nothing beyond his wages. Will usually ate cookhouse grub without complaint, but they dined on five-course meals at the ranch house. Compared to the family's grand meals, Cooky served plain fare indeed.

"Your wife's family might not feel the same way about me barging into the wedding." Will trotted out the weak excuse without conviction.

"Nonsense. They'd welcome you."

This was true, from what Will had observed. Elsa Walsh's family had brought their old-world hospitality with them to America. He gave a quick nod, accepting defeat. "Well then, I'm obliged to be included." That much was true, anyway. No need to burden Con with his misgivings.

"Wonderful. Brady can keep an eye on the ranch while

we're away. Count on three days. We're stopping by Shane and America's house on the way back."

"Oh? Who all will be there?" Will tried to ask the question nonchalantly, but the broadening of Con's smile hinted at his failure.

"The whole family, of course." Con winked. "We never miss an opportunity to get together."

Will let out his breath. He should have been more curious before agreeing to attend. Avoiding Phoebe at the church paled in comparison to the burden of escaping her in an intimate gathering.

CHAPTER TWO

PHOEBE BIT HER LIP AT THE sight of her friend and cousin Liberty Hayes, brushing a gloved hand across her cheek. Why did people cry at weddings? Watching two lives join before God in the presence of their friends and family seemed cause for laughter rather than weeping.

Liberty appeared to lack a handkerchief, which wasn't like her at all. Although her prim-and-proper manners had softened over time, she still cared a great deal—too much in Phoebe's opinion—about appearances. Phoebe retrieved a neatly-folded square from her reticule and pressed it into her friend's palm. Liberty awarded her a fleeting smile before dabbing at her eyes, an exercise made futile by a tide of fresh tears. She applied the linen square once again, revealing the gleam of golden letters embroidered into the cloth—*PRW* for Phoebe Rowena Walsh.

The letters were not Phoebe's handiwork. Ma plied a needle better than Phoebe ever would. She took pains to ensure her daughter was elegantly attired—at least on social occasions. After a neighbor fell from a sidesaddle and broke her arm, Ma stopped objecting to Phoebe wearing a split riding skirt at home on the ranch. Some things were worse, it seemed, than being unfashionable. Phoebe expressed her gratitude by submitting to her mother's clothing advisories with good grace. Ma knew more about such things than she ever would.

Sniffling sounds emanated from the church pew in front of them. Aunt Elsa fished in her reticule, making the plumed hat cresting her coif bob. She extracted a lacy wisp and lifted it to her eyes. Uncle Con glanced at his wife and smiled. His adoration could not be more obvious. How would it feel to be loved with such devotion? Phoebe swallowed against a lump in her throat. She would probably never know.

"Please rise." The preacher's voice broke into her thoughts. Phoebe stood as the crowd surged to its feet.

"Ladies and gentlemen, I present to you Mr. and Mrs. William Marcus Dunworthy."

Analise smiled up at her new husband. Tilting her head caused her veil to ripple all the way to the hem of her white crepe dress. The groom beamed at her, his exuberance at odds with the formality of his clothing. A starched collar cupped his neck, and the white waistcoat beneath his mulberry jacket matched the rose adorning his lapel. Their faces radiant, the new couple descended the carpeted steps and hurried down the aisle. They looked carefree and content, two emotions Phoebe hadn't felt in a while.

She jerked her thoughts from their course, refusing to dwell on her own vexations at her cousin's wedding. Phoebe rejoiced in the new couple's happiness, although it forced her to come to terms, all over again, with her own single state.

Her skin prickled. Phoebe turned her head in time to catch Will Canfield gazing at her. She averted her gaze. How annoying that whenever their eyes met, a giddy sensation weakened her knees. She drew a steadying breath. Will's interest was not serious, as he had warned her. She wished that the attraction between them would stop. He'd kissed her once, after which they'd agreed to leave one another alone. That choice had proven both wise and painful, but most of all difficult. Since Uncle Con had all but adopted Will, he had a way of cropping up at family gatherings.

Liberty nudged her. "I suppose you didn't notice Will

staring at you."

She hated it when Liberty arched her brows in that knowing way. Hopefully, no one had overheard. A quick glance around reassured her. Everyone near them was engaged in conversation. Phoebe raised her chin. "What if he did?"

"Honestly, Phoebe. You don't need to pretend—"

"If you don't mind, I'd rather talk about something else." Explaining to Liberty why Will didn't love her felt particularly odious on the heels of such a perfect wedding.

"If you ask me, Will is sweet on you."

Phoebe sighed. She could think of only one topic guaranteed to distract her friend. "Have you heard anything from Jake lately?"

Liberty narrowed her eyes. "I know what you're doing."

"Well, *have* you heard from Jake?"

Liberty frowned. "No."

"Never mind. I'm sure you will soon."

A crease formed between Liberty's eyes. "I hope so."

Phoebe opened her mouth to ask why she seemed so worried.

Liberty clutched her arm. "Oh, look. There's Fiona and Katie. Shall we join them?"

"All right." Phoebe decided to quiz Liberty about Jake later.

They caught up to their cousins near the open doorway to the fellowship hall. Fiona turned a bright smile on them. At sixteen, she looked more like her mother, Phoebe's Aunt Elsa, than ever. "Wasn't it a wonderful wedding? When I'm married, I want a wreath of white roses like Analise's."

"That won't be for a while, I hope." Liberty spoke in faintly alarmed tones.

"You sound like Ma. She's always telling me not to grow

up in a hurry." Fiona shook her head, dislodging several blonde curls from the filigree comb at her crown. She discreetly tucked them back into place. "I can hardly help getting older."

Phoebe laughed. "I'm certain that's not your fault." Despite what Aunt Elsa or anyone said, Fiona would no doubt marry early. Out of all her cousins, Fiona's forthright personality most resembled her own. However, their similarities soon ended. Fiona's expression held a softness foreign to Phoebe. She seemed a fairytale princess waiting for her prince to arrive. Phoebe's imagination might sometimes carry her away, but she never suffered illusions about any prince charming.

Katie, far too serious for a young woman of eighteen, watched them from pale eyes that contrasted with her honey-colored skin—a legacy from her father's Cheyenne heritage. Uncle Nick's skin was darker, but from spending time outside running their horse ranch. Katie's dark braids were restrained into twin coils at the back of her head. The sensible style befitted her understated manner. Katie spoke seldom but Phoebe guessed she missed nothing.

Fiona latched onto Phoebe's arm. "Did you know? In blue watered silk, and with your hair rippling in curls from behind your head, you look like a mermaid."

"Heaven forbid." Phoebe stared at her in mock horror. "Far be it from me to lure unsuspecting sailors to their doom."

"Like your suitors?" Fiona laughed at her own joke, but then sobered. "Just kidding. I didn't mean to make you frown."

Phoebe tried not to mind. Her reputation as a heartbreaker didn't seem fair, since she'd never meant to hurt anyone. She summoned a smile, for Fiona's sake. "And you're a princess in pink taffeta."

"Oh, that." Fiona smoothed the skirt of her gown. "I'm not fond of pink, but Ma insisted."

"I see four places at a table." Liberty called from the doorway.

"Come on." Fiona tugged on Phoebe's arm. "We've fallen behind."

At the table, Phoebe wedged into a chair beside Fiona, across from Katie and Liberty. "Something smells good." She glanced toward a door that must lead to the kitchen.

"That's the *Hochzeitssuppe*." Fiona giggled. "You should see your faces. I keep forgetting you don't know German. It means 'wedding soup.' Oma Wilhelmina let them use her secret recipe. I bet she's in the kitchen right now, supervising."

Phoebe scanned the gathering but failed to locate Fiona's grandmother. "Isn't she getting a bit old for such things?" She realized almost at once what she'd said. "Never mind."

Katie smirked.

Liberty laughed. "How wise of you to notice your error. Oma Wilhelmina will never grow old."

Fiona arched her brows. "I'm surprised you even said that, Phoebe. You are very like my Oma."

"Thank you." Phoebe smiled. "I consider that high praise indeed." A commotion drew her attention as the bride and groom came through a door close to the entrance with the clergyman. Much merriment followed them as they made their way to the rest of the wedding party at a long table festooned with bouquets of mulberry and white roses in crystal vases. The door from the kitchen swung open and women laden with soup tureens, bread platters, and a variety of fragrant dishes stepped through. The tantalizing aromas made Phoebe's mouth water. She'd eaten nothing since breakfast, hours ago. The wedding soup contained beef, vegetables, and a hearty egg dumpling Fiona called *eierstich* floating in clear broth. Phoebe bit into a slice of crusty sourdough bread slathered with butter. Chicken stuffed with wild rice and mushrooms followed, along with spaetzle noodles, grated red cabbage and apples, potato salad, and green salad dressed with vinaigrette.

A gust of laughter erupted from the bridal party. Phoebe couldn't hear what had caused it above the chatter in the room, but she smiled at the bride's ecstatic expression.

"I've never seen Analise look lovelier." Liberty's voice held a wistful note.

Phoebe smiled at her. "You'll make a beautiful bride, too—once Jake comes home."

Fiona giggled. "He'll whisk you to the altar." Red patches splotched Liberty's cheeks. "It's too soon to speak of a wedding. We're not even courting."

"You and Jake belong together, and everyone knows it." Fiona tilted her head inquiringly. "What about you, Katie? Has anyone come calling?"

Katie shook her head. "I've been too busy teaching school to think about such things. Maybe I won't ever marry." She glanced at Phoebe. "Some people don't, you know."

"I'm sure you'll find someone who wouldn't care—" Fiona's blush rivaled Liberty's. "Never mind."

"Go ahead and say it." Katie's gaze held steady. "I'd need a suitor willing to overlook my Cheyenne blood."

"I'm sure someone would." Fiona spoke in a rush. "You are a wonderful person, and that's what counts."

"Thank you." Katie smiled faintly. "I'm focused on my work. Teaching requires dedication."

"It does, as I can attest." Phoebe nodded. "My mother sacrificed to teach the Salish children. She didn't marry until after they closed the Indian school."

"What do your parents think about you becoming a spinster?" Fiona's shocked expression gave away her own opinion of the idea.

Katie looked away. "They don't know I'm considering it."

Fiona frowned. "You should tell them."

"I will, if it comes to that." Katie sounded unconcerned, but she'd squinted slightly. Maybe Aunt Bry and Uncle Nick would have other ideas about what was best for their daughter. That was true of Phoebe's own parents. Ma's wish for her to settle down with a suitable husband couldn't be more transparent. Pa didn't voice his thoughts out loud, but Phoebe could tell he felt the same. She jumped up, pushing her thoughts away. "I want more lemonade."

"Is that what was in your glass?" Liberty tapped her own water glass. "I missed it."

"Would you like me to bring you some?"

"Yes, if you wouldn't mind."

"Of course not." Phoebe headed toward the banquet table. She filled a glass for Liberty from the spigot of the beverage jar, and then refilled her own.

"The lemonade is very good." Her mother spoke behind her.

Phoebe nodded. "Oma Wilhelmina made it, didn't she? I can always tell."

"She adds a touch of ginger."

"So that's her secret." Phoebe stepped aside for her mother.

Ma didn't move past her. "Did you say hello to Alton Prescott yet?"

"I will, if I come across him." Phoebe kept her voice light.

Ma didn't budge. "Be sure you do."

Phoebe sighed. "Why should I?"

"To be kind, for one thing." Ma lowered her voice. "He watches you with such a hangdog expression."

"I can't help what he does. I've told him plainly that I don't want him to court me."

Ma glanced about before speaking again. "You might want to reconsider. You're past the age where you can afford to be picky."

Phoebe opened her mouth to reply, but then closed it again. She didn't harbor the faintest affection for Alton, but this was not the time nor place to point that out.

"Promise you'll think about it."

Phoebe nodded, for the sake of argument. Ma continued toward the beverage jar, and Phoebe made her escape. She would ponder the problem of Alton Prescott, all right, but not in the way her mother hoped. His interest in her wasn't the real difficulty. That lay between Ma and her.

CHAPTER THREE

PHOEBE FELT WILL'S BLUE GAZE FROM across the room but refused to turn her head his direction. The last thing she needed in this moment was to deal with her feelings about him. She reached her table and laid Liberty's lemonade before her without taking her own chair. All she wanted was to escape into her own company. She plunked her glass down on the table and gave Liberty a bright smile. "I need a breath of air."

Liberty's forehead puckered, and a question lit her eyes.

Fiona's gaze searched her face. "Aren't you going to finish your food?"

Phoebe shook her head. "I'm not hungry anymore."

"Are you coming down with something?" Liberty studied her. "You seem a bit flushed."

"I'm not ill."

"I'll go with you." Liberty pushed back her chair and started to rise.

"Please, don't." Phoebe smiled. "Thanks for offering, but I want a moment alone."

"All right, if you're sure." Liberty sank into her chair. "I saw a garden out back. You might have a look at it."

"I'll do that." Phoebe offered her a smile.

The open side doorway framed a grassy field baking in the sun. The gleam of sunlight drew Phoebe onward.

At the table closest to the door, Will was deep in conversation with her father, Uncle Con, and Uncle Nick. Ma, Aunt Bry, and Aunt Elsa also seated at the table, seemed equally engrossed in one another.

Phoebe drew up, her stomach clenching. Walking by without needing to answer questions might prove challenging. Maybe she should go out another door. A glance toward the only other door she saw—the one leading to the sanctuary—discouraged that idea. To reach it, she would have to walk by Alton Prescott at his family's table.

Maybe she should give up and go back, but she really did feel suffocated. Although hot outside, it wasn't crammed with people. She yearned to trade the noisy gathering for a moment of solitude.

Her mind made up, she steeled herself to pass Will.

She made it to the door without Will or anyone else calling after her. As she slipped through the opening, Phoebe couldn't resist the urge to look over her shoulder.

Will glanced up and broke off mid-sentence.

Uncle Con followed his gaze to her. "Phoebe! Where are you going?"

"Outside, but only for a moment." She sounded defensive to her own ears.

"The party is in here, Phoebe." Ma spoke in a soft but firm voice.

Phoebe ran a finger under her collar. "I'm overwarm." Under Will's unwavering regard, this was becoming truer by the minute.

"It would be hotter outdoors under the sun." Aunt Elsa had lost much of her accent, but the cadences of her native Germany still entered her speech.

"Why not join us?" Aunt Bry smiled. "Every so often, a breeze wafts through the doorway." She looked at Uncle Nick. "We can find you a chair."

"Oh no, please—that's not necessary." Phoebe took a step

backward. "I saw a shade tree out back. I'll be fine."

Ma shook her head. "I'm sorry, Phoebe, but it's not proper for a young, single woman to walk alone."

"But I do it all the time at home."

"That's different." Ma's smile softened her expression. "We're in the city."

Pa gave her a stern look. "Listen to your mother, Phoebe.".

Phoebe restrained the remark that Stevensville wasn't much of a city. Sometimes Ma's well-bred upbringing grated on her nerves. Phoebe didn't care a fig about the rules of polite society, but she loved her mother and wouldn't embarrass her.

Uncle Con rose and executed a courtly bow. "I'm honored to tour the churchyard with my favorite niece." He fixed his green-eyed gaze on Pa. "Provided your parents entrust you to my care."

Phoebe laughed at the exaggerated Irish brogue he'd adopted. "You call all your nieces your favorite."

"I can't choose one, now can I?" He winked.

A grin teased its way onto Pa's lips. "You've charmed the ladies your whole life." He studied Ma, and then waved a hand. "Get on with you then."

"Don't mind if I do." Uncle Con placed his Stetson on his head with an elegant air. "Come with us, Will? Despite my brother's flattery, I'm certain Phoebe would rather have the company of someone closer her age."

Phoebe's stomach clinched. Racking her brain for a way to escape yielded no results.

"As a matter of fact, I'd welcome the chance to stretch my legs after so much sitting." Will stood, his face reflecting Phoebe's own hesitancy. "That is, if Miss Walsh wouldn't mind my presence."

"Come along, if you like." Phoebe spoke in as airy a voice

as she could manage. He'd said nothing about the delights of keeping company with her. Of course not. He'd made it clear after that unfortunate kiss two years ago that a romance with her was out of the question. He should let Uncle Con in on that fact. She certainly didn't plan to enlighten him. Knowing that her uncle was aware of her private humiliation would be bad enough without having to inform him of it.

"Good idea." Uncle Con offered her his arm with a flourish. "Shall we?"

"Yes, of course." After laying her hand in the crook of his elbow, Phoebe walked into the sunshine beside him. Will's footsteps crunched the gravel path a little behind them. No need to feel piqued about him keeping his distance when it was best for both of them.

Phoebe waited until they rounded the back corner of the church to pull away from her uncle. She mustered a smile. "I hope you don't mind, but I'd rather walk unassisted."

"You're a *cailín* with a strong mind, and no mistake." Uncle Con grinned.

"So Ma tells me."

"Ach. Don't mind your mother. She wants the best for you."

"It gets a bit much, sometimes—Ma worrying about me, and well—everything."

He nodded. "I suppose that's why you felt the need for air."

He must have noticed her discussion with Ma while refilling her glass. Quick tears sprang to her eyes. Uncle Con's support bolstered her, but his sympathy ruined her composure.

He gestured Will closer. "Come and help, will you? Phoebe needs cheering, and I'm making her cry."

Phoebe laughed. "How can anyone be glum with you

around, Uncle?"

He chuckled. "Next time I'm sad, I'll remember your remark."

After Will caught up to them, Uncle Con lagged a couple of steps behind them. The path curved into a sunny patch, and the scent of grass lifted at Phoebe's every step.

Will pulled his hat brim down, shading his eyes. "What's upset you, Phoebe?" His voice held such compassion it almost convinced her he cared.

She shook her head. "I'm being silly."

He frowned. "I would never call you that. Impetuous, yes. Even—dare I say it—given too much of your own way."

"Spoiled, you mean?"

"Don't get your dander up. That's not what I said."

Phoebe jammed her hands onto her hips. "It's impossible to imagine that you meant anything else."

Uncle Con whistled. "My, but it's getting hot out here."

She half expected her uncle to suggest they return. She wouldn't blame him for cutting short their bickering.

He favored her with a brilliant smile. "Think I'll take up residence on that bench under the maple tree. May I suggest a turn in the garden for the pair of you? The scent of roses is bound to help you come to terms."

Phoebe couldn't fail to miss her uncle's matchmaking. She bestowed a sardonic glance on him, but he was already moving away. She turned and surprised a flash of humor in Will's eyes.

He tilted his head. "Shall we take his advice?"

Phoebe raised her chin. "I feel my uncle has placed you in an awkward position."

"Is it so hard to believe that I *want* to explore the garden with you?"

"Why would you?" Her face heated. "Sorry, that was

rude."

A smile touched his lips. "I happen to agree with your uncle. Let's not harbor ill feelings between us."

If Will thought a stroll in the garden could fix anything, he had no idea how much his rejection had hurt her. Well, if he didn't know, she wasn't going to tell him. She glanced at Uncle Con, who was leaning back in the bench with his eyes shut. "Some chaperone he makes. Ma would be horrified."

Will chuckled. "I promise to be on my best behavior."

Phoebe couldn't have formed a reply, even if she'd wanted too. Rather than meet his eyes, she turned toward the whitewashed garden gate.

Will reached it before she did. He held it open, but Phoebe hesitated. He offered her a smile. "I hope you won't find my company loathsome."

"Of course not." No, that wasn't the problem. He obviously hadn't worked out that walking through the narrow gate would bring her into close proximity with him. His lack of awareness reassuring her somewhat, she stepped past him into the garden. The gravel paths continued into the garden and no doubt saved work for whoever cared for it—probably the minister's wife.

Although not large, it was well tended. Forget-me-nots twined with Sweet Williams beneath the spikes of delphiniums and larkspur. Peonies sprawled beside irises in shades of purple. Their flowers buzzing with bees. Roses in shades of pink, red, and white rambled over the fence and unfurled in shrubs. Rosemary, sweet alyssum, and lavender lined the path, making every step a delight. Kissed by the sun's warmth, the blossoms released a heady fragrance.

"I'm glad." He thudded the gate shut. "I'd hate to impose on a pretty woman like you."

"Please, don't flirt with me."

"I only meant to pay you a compliment."

His voice held emotion she didn't care to analyze. Letting her imagination run away with her could persuade her that he regretted trifling with her in the past. False hope could spring up to crush her, as it had before, but she'd learned to accept reality. Will's interest in her, by his own admission, held no weight. She moved off along the path, leaving him to shut the gate.

He followed her swiftly and turned her to face him. "Has it occurred to you that this is awkward for me, too?"

"Then why did you come?" She pulled her arm from his grasp.

"Maybe I shouldn't have, but I wanted to speak with you."

Phoebe folded her arms. "Oh?"

"First, let me apologize for insulting you earlier with my careless remark."

"So, you don't think I'm spoiled?"

"Not exactly."

Phoebe waited for him to explain.

He sighed. "Strong-willed people get their way more often than they should. I believe that is true of you."

She peered at him in suspicion. Was he calling her spoiled without using the actual word? "I do know how to assert myself, but that doesn't mean I expect to have everything my way."

"I'm glad to hear that. Otherwise, you'd see a lot more sorrow in life. Speaking of which, what were you crying about today?"

"Why do you care?"

"Phoebe, Phoebe." He took her by the hands. "I'd like to think we're friends."

"I'm not so sure." She freed herself and stumbled

backward.

He took a step forward but then halted. His eyes pleaded with her. "Because of…what happened between us?"

She looked up at him, squinting against the sun's glare. "Do you mean when you kissed me?"

"Can't we put that behind us?"

She set off along the gravel path. "I thought we did."

He kept pace with her. "If that were true, you wouldn't question my concern."

Phoebe hated being pinned by logic. Time to accept the painful truth. He'd clearly recovered from the incident, whereas she couldn't let it go. That he'd kissed her wasn't so upsetting. In fact, she'd enjoyed it. It was that he'd engaged her affections. She would never have allowed his advances otherwise. How dare he remain unaffected?

He stepped in front of her, his back to the sun. "Why haven't you married, Phoebe?"

She looked up at him in the shadow he cast. "Ma says I'm too picky."

"Are you?"

"I'm particular about who to entrust with my future."

"You show remarkable wisdom." He spoke with irony.

She scanned his face but could tell nothing from his expression. "Do you speak from experience?"

"I've made my share of mistakes." A smile wisped across his face. "I don't plan to make any more."

"Then you should understand my hesitancy."

"I do, to a certain extent, but you strike me as a woman who needs a husband."

"What, to settle me down? No, thank you."

"I'd appreciate not being misinterpreted. Some women are made for marriage, that's all. I happen to think you are one of them."

She sighed. "Well, *I'd* appreciate you not worrying about my matrimonial state or lack of one. I get enough of that from Ma. In case you wonder, I'm fine with remaining single." She would rather not become a spinster, if she could help it. Honesty compelled her to admit that much to herself, if not to Will. She had some pride remaining to her.

They stopped at the far edge of the garden, where a vine blossoming with pink rose rambled over a rock wall. How improbable—even ludicrous—to see such delicate petals adorning rough stone. And yet, there the vine clung.

Will scowled down at her. "I suspect that would be a big mistake."

"So, avoiding romance is all right for you, but not for me?" Phoebe couldn't quite keep the hurt out of her voice. He seemed in a hurry for her to marry someone else. Why, when he was always watching her? She must have misunderstood his glances. Either that, or he was lying to himself. She clamped down on the hope her thought inspired. Hope could hurt, as she'd learned the hard way.

"I, at least, took a chance on love." He paced before her. "Can you say as much?"

"That's a private matter." She wasn't about to tell him that she might have once. He wouldn't want to know. Tears sprang to her eyes, but she turned away to hide them.

He sighed. "We should start back."

"Perhaps you would tell Uncle Con that I'll be there in a minute." It was no good. She sounded stilted, and her voice wobbled alarmingly, besides.

His hand slid around her elbow. "Phoebe—"

She shrugged off his touch. "Please go."

"I'm sorry to upset you. That seems a particular talent of

mine."

Phoebe gave no answer. After a moment, gravel crunched as Will walked away. She closed her eyes and drew a steadying breath. The fragrance of roses, pure and sweet, wafted to her. Despite Uncle Con's prediction, the scent had failed to foster peace between them. Phoebe sighed. Perfumed air, although heavenly, couldn't work miracles. Maybe she and Will would never come to terms.

CHAPTER FOUR

SEATED UPRIGHT AND WITH HIS ARM slung across the back of the garden bench, Uncle Con seemed wide awake for someone who, moments before, had appeared lost to slumber. He shifted sideways and gestured for Phoebe to sink down beside him. "You're wearing a long face or I'm Irish."

"Silly, you *are* Irish."

His eyes lit. "Am I, indeed?"

"I'm sure you don't need reminding."

"Well, no." A grin spread across his face. "But now you're smiling."

Phoebe couldn't help but laugh at his nonsense, but her mirth didn't last long. "I suppose you saw Will storm by."

His gaze probed hers, after which he looked out over the garden. "Care to bend my ear?"

She swallowed against a lump in her throat. "There isn't much to say. Will and I rub each other the wrong way."

Uncle Con tipped back his hat, causing an errant lock of his black hair to tumble across his forehead. "Rubbing two sticks together makes a fire. There's nothing better to warm a person."

"A fire can also burn down the forest."

He grinned. "You won't allow yourself to be cajoled, I see. What did you quibble about, anyway?"

"Will thinks I should marry."

"Oh, I see."

Why did he sound so irritatingly smug? "I don't see why it's any business of his." Phoebe sniffed. "He's hardly in a position to give that particular advice."

"Perhaps marrying you off seems less painful than deciding what to do about his feelings."

"What are you talking about?" Phoebe stared at him. "His feelings?"

Uncle Con's smile grew. "Have you no idea when a man is smitten with you, *cailín*?"

"If you think that is true of Will, I believe you must be mistaken."

He chuckled. "Time will tell, darlin'." He ran a hand down his neck. "Meanwhile, let's not pretend that you don't return his affections."

Her cheeks heated. "Is it so obvious?"

"Maybe only to me."

She shook her head. "Even if you are right about Will, it doesn't change anything." A stray gust rattled the leaves. Phoebe spotted a bright-eyed squirrel watching from a maple branch above them. The tiny creature stared back for a moment, and then scurried away.

"Maybe not, but you can't blame a devoted uncle for trying."

"I wish you wouldn't interfere. It only makes the situation more difficult."

"I don't mean to cause trouble. Life must be difficult enough for an unmarried woman of a certain age."

She blew out a breath. "I wouldn't mind so much if other people didn't. Having my lack of a husband constantly brought up is maddening."

His eyes widened. "Who would do that?"

"Well-meaning people, without even realizing." She kept all irony from her tone. She didn't blame Uncle Con, but he was one of the worst offenders. She sighed. Weddings emboldened others to overstep where she was concerned. "Uncle Con, do you think that a woman needs to marry and have a home?"

"I haven't thought much about it, to be honest." He leaned back on the bench. "The Bible states that some should remain unmarried, but others should not. The challenge is knowing which is right for you. I suspect that you fit in the married group."

"I don't know. Then I'd have children to raise, meals to get, and a house to keep. I help Ma with household chores, but I'd rather work the ranch with Pa and my brothers. Spending all day in the saddle on the open range would be wonderful."

"I can't disagree, but I think you are romanticizing a ranch hand's life. It has its share of hardship, you know."

"I'd like the chance to find out for myself."

"Would you now?" He rubbed his chin. "It's not a very feminine pursuit."

"I don't know about that. What about Margaret Borland? She drove a thousand longhorn cattle from her Texas ranch up the Chisholm Trail to Kansas."

"Perhaps you have not heard that she died of trail fever shortly afterward."

"That could have happened to any ranch hand, male or female."

Uncle Con's eyes glinted. "Reminding me of the perils hardly persuades me to hire you."

She gaped at him. "I didn't know you were considering it."

He shrugged. "You and me both."

The idea held merit, Phoebe decided. All she needed to do was convince her uncle to take it seriously. "It can't be all that difficult, if a woman in—er—a delicate condition like Hattie Cluck could accomplish it."

He shook his head. "If you ask me, she should never have

taken her children or herself on that cattle drive."

"Her husband didn't agree with you."

"She asserted herself to change his opinion, or so I've heard."

"Surely a woman can win over her without being accused of wearing the pants in the family."

"Now, did I say that?"

"Not in so many words. Just so you know, lots of people agreed with Mrs. Cluck. Fifteen years later, people still revere her as a legend."

He frowned. "There's no accounting for what folks believe."

Oh, dear. Uncle Con was turning the wrong direction. Phoebe wracked her brains. Maybe if she came up with a better example... She brightened. "So far, Calamity Jane has scouted for the army, ridden for the Pony Express, and run her own cattle ranch. They say she handles a horse better than most men and shoots better than any cowboy."

Uncle Con shook with laughter. "You've made your point, Phoebe."

"I could drive cattle. I know I could."

"Your parents would need persuading."

She brightened. "I could talk them into it." *Hopefully.*

"I have no doubt of that, with your strong mind and silver tongue." He slapped his knee. "I have half a mind to assist you."

"Please do."

He glanced sideways at her. "I do happen to be hiring."

"I'll work cheap."

"Running a cattle ranch presents challenges, but I can still afford to pay fair wages. That is, assuming I go through with this lunatic scheme."

"You're the best uncle!" She unleashed the full force of her smile on him.

He adopted a stern expression. "Don't think you can butter me up so easily."

"Of course not."

"I wouldn't give you any special consideration."

"Of course not."

"Why sound so cheerful? Are you aware that my ranch manager—namely Will—will be your boss? If I hire you, that is."

"I know." The thought put her dander up, but she refused to let it matter. This might be her only chance to break out of the mold others wanted to cast her in. Pa had already refused to let her work cattle when she'd asked. If anyone could change his mind though, it was Uncle Con. Her own gift of persuasion paled beside his. He'd kissed the Blarney Stone, as everyone who knew him could attest

He jumped to his feet and paced before the bench. "There can't be any trouble between you and Will. Otherwise, I'd have to fire you."

"I understand."

He studied her for a long time, as if probing her soul. At last, he nodded. "All right. I'll talk with your parents. Far be it from me to deny my favorite niece her heart's desire."

Phoebe glanced at him in suspicion, but nothing in his expression gave away that he was talking about anything but working cattle.

CHAPTER FIVE

WILL SLIPPED ONTO HIS SEAT AND glanced about the table. No one appeared to notice his agitation. That was best, since he didn't trust himself to explain it. He didn't fully understand Phoebe's ability to rile him. Thank goodness he'd resisted the impulse to tell her about Sophie. Once Phoebe knew that his fiancée had jilted him, she'd want to know more. Going over the details of his humiliation would be like ripping open a half-healed wound.

He took several swallows from his water glass. His hesitancy arose from more than that, he knew. Confiding in Phoebe would strengthen the tie between them. She must be aware of it, too. Why else did he catch her watching him so often? No, it was safer not to strengthen the bond between them. He had only himself to blame for forging it that time he'd kissed her. He sighed. That event had destroyed his composure for several years. Thankfully, Phoebe also preferred to set aside the feelings they'd roused in one another.

Am I sure of that? The uneasy thought niggled his mind. Will stared at the forgotten glass in his hand. He couldn't reject the possibility that he had somehow hurt her. He didn't delude himself that Phoebe cared for him deeply. She collected broken hearts like so many flowers. Perhaps he'd wounded her vanity. That would account for the anger she'd shown him today.

Phoebe had become something of a legend around the campfires he frequented. Stories of the golden-haired angel crushing prospective suitors had grown more outlandish by the day. Potential beaus went to great lengths to win the privilege of courting her, only to suffer rejection. Will's glass thunked against the table, and he watched the water slosh about inside the vessel. He hoped Phoebe didn't really enjoy breaking hearts. She would be better off marrying. What was holding her back? He could admit to mixed feelings about the idea of Phoebe marrying someone else. He shook his head. That was all the more reason to encourage her to do so.

Elsa glanced his direction. "You've come back alone."

"Phoebe wanted to linger in the garden, but I felt like coming in." Will did his best to speak in neutral tones. "Con is waiting for her." There. He hadn't lied, and he'd even given part of the truth.

A pucker formed between Elsa's brows. "Is Phoebe all right? I thought she was acting strangely."

"I thought so too." He nodded. "She does seem a little— out of sorts." His irritation drained away. Something had been bothering Phoebe before she'd ever lit into him. What had Con said to make her cry?

Light footsteps tapped behind Will. Elsa glanced past him and smiled wide. "Katerina, come and sit down. The wedding has kept us so busy we've hardly had time to visit."

"It was worth it." Elsa's youngest sister exclaimed in her German accent. She sounded out of breath, as if she'd rushed across the room. "Analise looks so happy."

Will stood to greet Elsa's youngest sister.

Katerina's blond hair, pulled back in a simple style, shone in the light from the doorway. Faint color bloomed in her cheeks, and her blue eyes gleamed. "May I?" She indicated the empty chair beside his.

"Please." He seated her, and then sank into his own chair.

"How is Oma Wilhelmina holding up?" The pucker reappeared between Elsa's eyebrows. "The cook Analise hired didn't mind her supervising, but I wondered if we'd have to carry her out of the kitchen."

Katerina smiled. "Once the food was all served, I convinced her to sit down."

"She can ride with us when we leave." Elsa spoke briskly. "I don't think she should stay to clean up."

"No." Katerina transferred her attention to Will. "It's good to see you again, Mr. Canfield."

"And you." Will gave a polite response but backed it with a smile. "I'm honored that you recall my name."

"Of course, I do. You took over as ranch manager right before I moved to Stevensville."

"Yes. How is your brother's mercantile doing?"

"Very well." She smiled. "Christoph doesn't need my support so much anymore."

"You were kind to help him establish his business."

"How could I not?" She cast a puzzled glance his way. "We are family."

"That's an admirable attitude."

"Thank you." She tilted her head. "Is your family close, Mr. Canfield?"

"We were once, but now we're scattered. My brother, Caleb, never returned from the California gold fields. One sister married and settled in Pennsylvania. The other lives with my mother in Carson City. That's where Pa settled what remained of the family before he died."

Her brow pleated. "How sad."

"It's the way of it." He shrugged. "We do get together, but rarely. The distances are too great. You are blessed to have your family near."

"That is because of Con and Elsa. Without their help, we would still live in Germany." Katerina touched the corner of her eyes with her napkin. "I might never have seen my Elsa again."

Elsa squeezed her sister's hand across the table. "That didn't happen, by God's grace."

Will cleared his throat. "Would either of you ladies care for refreshment? Lemonade, perhaps?"

"I have some, but thanks." Elsa sipped from her glass.

Katerina's smile put dimples in her cheeks. "I already drank lots of lemonade, but you are kind to offer me some."

Will leaned against his chairback, the tension leaving him. How sweetly Elsa and Katerina treated him compared to Phoebe. He knew the thought as unfair, considering that he was responsible, at least in part, for Phoebe's attitude toward him.

A prickling sensation alerted him as Phoebe and Con entered by the side door. The noise level in the fellowship hall must have hidden their footsteps. After her first, searing glance, Phoebe kept her eyes averted from his. Con seated her on Katerina's other side before returning to his chair next to Elsa. He joined Nick and Rob's conversation.

After a cursory greeting, Elsa gave her attention to Bry and Maisey. Phoebe and Katerina launched into a discussion of horse breeds. Although interested, Will didn't comment. He doubted Phoebe wanted his opinion at the moment. Besides, he was content to sit in silence. He'd never quite mastered the skill of exchanging pleasantries on social occasions.

"Are you good at breaking horses to saddle, Mr. Canfield?" Katerina's voice interrupted his musings.

Con turned his head. "He is, indeed. There's only one other who can beat him." He smiled at his sister Bry's husband. "Nick taught Will a great deal."

"I wonder—" She blinked. "No. It would be too much to ask."

"Never mind all that." Con waved a hand. "I assume

there's a horse you want broken."

"Christoph bought a mustang at auction for me to ride. We learned, afterwards, that it is only half-broken. My brother is not much of a horseman, I'm afraid." Katerina glanced at Will appealingly. "Would you be willing to work with my horse?"

Will hid his surprise. "Yes, of course." It wouldn't be a good idea to refuse his boss's sister-in-law. He didn't mind helping her, but the request struck him as odd. Why would she single him out when she could ask Nick, who had more experience? Asking this question would be less than gracious, however. "I have to wonder whether you might do better with a less spirited horse."

"Can't you break him well enough for a beginner to ride?"

He resisted the urge to smile. "I can teach him to bear a rider, but that won't change his temperament."

"I will work very hard to ride better."

Will studied her earnest face. "I have no doubt you will give it your all."

She smiled. "Thank you."

"Then it's settled. You can stable your horse at the ranch." Con exchanged glances with Elsa. "You're welcome to come stay with us, if Christoph can spare you at the store."

Her smile grew. "I'm sure he can. How long does it take to break a horse?"

"That depends on its attitude and the trainer's skill." Con stroked his chin. "Several months, maybe."

Katerina's eyes lit. "That long?"

"That would be lovely!" Elsa's smile turned into a frown. "But, won't Christoph need you at the store?"

"He couldn't have done without me in the beginning, but the children help more now that they are older. I keep finding myself at loose ends, with Christoph scaring up things for me to do. I don't think he'll mind."

"Well then, I can't wait!" Elsa clapped her hands like a delighted child. "It's been too long."

"We'll have fun." Katerina laughed. "Christoph will be pleased too. He was wondering what to do about Diablo."

Phoebe stepped into the fellowship hall beside Uncle Con, blinking after the brilliant light outside. Once her eyes adjusted, she could hardly believe what they showed her. Will was sitting beside Katerina, a bemused smile hovering about his lips. Gone was the tension he'd displayed earlier in the garden. With one arm draped across the back of his chair, he appeared more relaxed than he had in a long while. He looked altogether appealing, a fact that did not seem lost on Katerina. Elsa's sister studied Will intently, leaning toward him with her lips slightly parted.

Phoebe pulled in a painful breath. Will's restriction against female companionship apparently did not apply to Katerina. It took all her composure to slip into the spot at the table Uncle Con suggested. She would rather retreat to her cousins' table, where she could avoid the sight of Will and Katerina altogether. With Uncle Con about to intercede on her behalf, however, she stayed put. He probably wouldn't say anything to her parents today, but she wanted to be present, in case he did.

Katerina welcomed her with a sweet smile. "How lovely you look. I am jealous of those curls."

Phoebe grimaced. "If you had to suffer the snarls I do, you might not feel so envious."

Katerina's laugh tinkled. "The grass looks best on the other side of the fence, does it not?"

Phoebe smiled, charmed by her interpretation of the expression. "Well, I love that shade of blue on you." She offered Katerina a genuine compliment. *I can't hold admiring Will against her when I'm guilty of that myself.*

"Thank you. I don't get to wear formal clothing very often." Katerina smoothed the skirt of her silk dress.

"We are very different." Phoebe grinned. "I prefer, as much as possible, to avoid it."

Katerina laughed. "Perhaps I would too, if given the opportunity to wear it more. Elsa tells me that you are often found on horseback."

Phoebe nodded. "Riding is as natural to me as breathing."

"Then we have something in common, after all." Katerina clasped her hands together. "I also love horses. I don't have your experience, but I can't let that stop me. I must learn to ride well since Christoph has given me a horse of my own."

"Oh really?" Phoebe perked up. "What breed?"

"Diablo is a mustang. He's a gelding but quite—lively, even so."

Phoebe burst out laughing. "Mustangs can be lively indeed. I hope you haven't acquired too spirited a horse."

"I believe that is what Christoph did. I am grateful that Will—Mr. Canfield has agreed to train him for me."

The sensation of being watched crept over Phoebe, and she turned her head in time to catch Alton Prescott staring at her from across the room. Phoebe jerked her own gaze away. The last thing she wanted was to encourage the man. His pursuit was hopeless, and he should accept that truth. She looked his way again, and her heartbeat picked up its pace. He'd started toward her. Phoebe jumped up. "If you'll excuse me—I believe I left my reticule in the sanctuary."

This was true, although Phoebe hadn't just noticed it. She'd meant to retrieve the bagit upon leaving, but all at once the present seemed a better time.

Phoebe took her leave of Katerina, somewhat distracted by the need to flee. No doubt, she'd acted strangely. She made it into the sanctuary uninterrupted and closed the door behind her for good measure. She couldn't recall Alton understanding finer nuances, but she could hope he would take the hint.

Silence enfolded her, a welcome relief after the noise in the fellowship hall. She paused to catch her breath before retracing her steps to the place she'd occupied during the ceremony. Her hand closed on the strap of her reticule beneath the pew. She sank onto the smooth bench, loath to leave the sanctuary.

Light flooded in from twin arched windows behind the platform with its carved oak podium. No other windows graced the walls, leaving the pews in cool dimness. Now that she was alone with her thoughts, she felt a bit guilty. Running from a potential suitor was ill-mannered, no matter how richly he deserved it.

What harm could come from greeting Alton? If she'd faced him with her composure intact, she wouldn't need to hide like a frightened rabbit. Phoebe squared her shoulders, ready to return to the fellowship hall.

The door creaked open, and a man entered. With the light behind him, she could only see his outline. Phoebe recognized him and pressed a hand against the sinking sensation in her stomach.

"Miss Walsh, I hope you will excuse my intrusion." Alton murmured. "I wished to speak with you before I depart."

"Hello, Mr. Prescott." Hopefully, that would suffice. She couldn't, for the sake of truthfulness, say that he wasn't intruding.

He crossed to her, his leather shoes thumping the floorboards. "I wonder if I might stop by the ranch and speak with you. Certain matters lie heavy on my heart. I believe you may have misunderstood me, and I would hate there to be constraint between us."

She stared at him in bafflement. Was he implying that she had misinterpreted his advances? He'd been more than obvious.

"I can appreciate that, but I—I may not be home." It was the only excuse she could come up with at the moment. It also had the advantage of being true. She didn't know how long her family would stay at Liberty's house before going home.

"Then I must seize the opportunity to speak now." He smiled. "Don't look so alarmed. I only want to tell you that I know how you feel."

She stared at him for a long moment. "You do?"

"Yes." He glanced away from her. "I know I'm not your first choice."

Phoebe couldn't have formed a reply if she'd tried. He was entirely correct, but how had he guessed? Was she so transparent that everyone knew her secret longings? What a horrifying thought. But, no. He wasn't that sensitive.

"Please." He held up a hand. "Don't say anything. I don't mean to embarrass you in any way. I mention this only to make a point." His gaze locked with hers. "I'm not your first choice, but I think you'll discover that I'm your best. Grant me the privilege of courting you, and you won't regret it. I promise."

Phoebe found her tongue, rather belatedly. "Mr. Prescott, it is not appropriate for you to broach this subject with me when you haven't spoken with my pa."

"Your father gave me his permission, provided you agree."

Had Pa betrayed her? Phoebe swallowed against a lump in her throat. She recognized Ma's haste to marry her off as a mother's concern for her child's well-being, but a father should supply caution. She pulled in a steadying breath. Under the circumstances, all she could do was stall. "This is hardly the place or time—"

"You are right, of course. Please forgive my eagerness." His eyes pleaded with her. "Tell me when and where we may speak again, and I will present myself."

There would be no denying him until he had his say. "All

right. When I return home, I'll send a note to you."

"Thank you." His eyes shone. "All I want is a chance to explain myself."

No, it wasn't all he wanted, but countering his remark would only prolong an awkward situation. She walked toward him, since he was blocking her way of escape. "If you'll excuse me, I should return to my family."

"Yes, of course." Alton stepped aside. "My own is about to leave for home, so I'll say goodbye now."

Phoebe rushed past him, but then a pang at his yearning expression caught her by surprise. She knew the sorrow of unrequited affection herself. Phoebe glanced back from the doorway, but he was watching her so intently that it made her feel hunted. The parting she might have given died on her lips, but she managed to nod before fleeing.

A commotion drew her attention as soon as she stepped into the fellowship hall. Katerina was laughing and protesting even while she allowed herself to be escorted to the piano by Christoph. Elsa sat at the piano, playing beautiful music. Guests gathered round and cried out for Katerina to sing.

"Yes, please do!" Analise called from the bridal table.

Katerina nodded to her sister. "All right." She composed herself beside the piano, displaying more poise than Phoebe would have in such a situation. Katerina murmured something to Elsa that Phoebe didn't catch. Elsa smiled and rippled the keys. Sweet strains swelled from the piano.

"When I think of the days that are gone, of the spring when both flower, and tree budded forth as the sun brightly shone, it reminds me, my loved one, of thee." Katerina's clear soprano touched every note beautifully.

"When I think of the warm summer ray, of the woods where fond hearts may be free, and can roam from the worldly away, it reminds me, my loved one, of thee." Katerina sang with more fervor.

A man stepped closer, clearly enthralled. Phoebe tore her own gaze away from the admiration on Will's face.

"When I think of the pale Autumn moon, as she shines over mountain, and lea—like spring's morning or summer's bright noon, it reminds me, my loved one of thee. When I think of the long winter eve, or of friends far away over the sea, and of those for whose absence we grieve, it reminds me, my loved one, of thee."

Phoebe didn't like the feelings jangling through her. She preferred to think herself incapable of jealousy, but that clearly wasn't the case. Katerina had the voice of an angel and should be commended for the way she brought a song to life. Phoebe would focus on that and stop wishing Will didn't look quite so captivated.

"Thus all seasons, all months in the year, all I think of and all that I see—the fond smile, the affectionate tear, all reminds me, my loved one, of thee. Oh thine image forever shall dwell, in my heart, dearest fixed it will be, until death or till Heaven shall tell. 'Time! To bring back my loved one to me.'"

The aching pathos of the ending enfolded Phoebe. Others must feel the same, judging by the silence that followed. After cheers and applause, Katerina was persuaded to sing again.

"There you are." Ma nudged Phoebe's arm. "I wondered where you went. Pa and I are ready to go."

Phoebe nodded. Today had turned out badly for her, and all she wanted was to leave. Maybe then she could clamp down on her errant emotions and talk sense to her wayward heart.

CHAPTER SIX

PHOEBE, LULLED BY THE LANDAU'S RHYTHMIC motion, leaned her head on Liberty's shoulder. Liberty rested her own head on Phoebe's, and they swayed together. The leather curtains they'd unrolled at the beginning of the journey slapped against the upholstery, letting in the breeze. Phoebe nestled against her friend and let her cares slip away.

She started upright when the carriage bounced into ruts. Ma cried out across from them, as if also awakened from slumber. After a wide-eyed moment, she sighed and sagged against the seatback next to Aunt America.

Phoebe stretched out again, thankful that Quinn and Murphy had opted to ride with Liberty's brothers in their wagon—a less elegant mode of transportation. But then, that was the appeal. Pa would have been left to drive four women home alone if Uncle Con hadn't persuaded Will to ride shotgun on the driving box.

Phoebe wasn't quite sure how she felt about this turn of events. She was glad Pa had company, and she did feel a little safer knowing he was keeping watch along with her father. On the other hand, she'd hoped to escape Will, not travel with him.

The landau rocked in and out of a rut, and Liberty moaned. Phoebe settled in beside her, surrendering to the journey once more. Too uncomfortable to sleep again, Phoebe lifted the corner of the curtain beside her. The breeze riffled her hair and cooled her cheeks. Grasslands rolled to the foothills of snow-capped mountains that flung themselves toward the sky. A flock of geese arrowed toward the river and several ducks beat their wings in unison, headed the same direction. The air took on a golden cast, hinting that the day would soon give way to night.

Thank goodness the wedding was behind them. Although glad for Analise, Phoebe couldn't deny that the event had taken a toll on her. She'd played with dolls as a child, including one in full bridal regalia. Why had she never considered where the groom might be? That seemed the question on everyone's mind, when it came to her.

Phoebe would be glad to arrive at Liberty's house, where the change in surroundings might divert her. She could hope that after a night's rest, her problems would look different in the morning.

Will hung on as the carriage bucked and tilted. Rob had slowed the horses, but riding out the rough patch took a little doing. With dust hazing the bone-dry air, he had a hard time picturing the gully washer that had gouged potholes in the hard-packed road. Summer was the best time to travel, though. The rains in spring and fall softened the dirt to treacherous mud, and winter snows created their own hardships.

"Gee!" Rob called to his team of matched bays, guiding them around a corner. He glanced at Will over his shoulder. "Thanks for coming along. Having someone riding shotgun frees me to focus on driving. It's nice to know you're ready to take over the lines, also. Phoebe could manage if something happened to me, but my mind rests easier knowing she wouldn't have to."

"I can't see Phoebe agreeing with you on that point, but I'd be glad to do it."

Rob laughed. "I expect you're right. Phoebe is good with horses, and no mistake. I suspect your own skill equals hers."

Will smiled to himself. He matched her on holding strong opinions, too. That was why they so often found themselves at odds. If he and Phoebe ever came to a meeting of minds, they would become a force to reckon with.

Whoa, there! His thoughts were carrying him way too far.

He didn't mind guarding Phoebe's carriage. Should the need arise, he'd rather protect her than someone else. Hard telling when outlaws, renegades, or even wild animals might attack. And that wasn't counting the other perils that could threaten. He didn't like remembering the stories he'd heard around the campfire. Horses bolted, carriages overturned, and all manner of mishaps waited to strike travelers. He would do his best to make sure Phoebe and her family arrived safely at the Hayes' house.

As the road smoothed out, Will leaned against the seatback, cradling his rifle. Miles of grassland rolled by, studded at the edges by a mixed forest. Largely evergreen, rank upon rank of trees pointed toward the wide sky. Above the distant mountains, the heavens shone with soft light.

"Whew!" Rob mopped his brow with his bandana. "You'd think it would cool down, this late in the day."

"Yep."

Rob grinned. "I suppose, for someone used to spending his time outdoors on horseback, my complaint seems paltry."

"Not at all." Will lifted his hat and ruffled his hair to cool his own head. "I've gained a healthy respect for what too much heat can do to a person." He replaced his hat and reached for his canteen. After uncorking it, he passed it to Rob. "Water helps."

Rob tilted the canteen to his mouth, and his throat moved rhythmically. He swiped the back of his arm across his mouth. "Thanks."

Will nodded and corked his canteen. "Traveling by

carriage is a luxury for me. If Con hadn't offered me a ride to the church this morning, I'd have arrived smelling of my horse."

Rob laughed. "It's happened to the best of us. My brother can be thoughtful, except in matters where he's dense."

Will grinned. He'd noticed that as well but would never have voiced the observation. Con had seemed unaware of pressuring him to break Katerina's horse, not that Will minded. Con inviting her to stay while he did so put him in an awkward position, however. He couldn't deny that she was inviting, but he had a feeling trouble would arise from a continued association with her. At any rate, he was glad to escape the wedding and his ever-increasing involvement with her.

Perhaps he was only imagining her interest in him. He'd noticed only faint signs, but he doubted he'd mistaken them. He would hate to disappoint so sweet a person, but his heart belonged elsewhere. If he ever changed his mind about letting a woman into his life, he would call upon Phoebe.

Not that she would care. Phoebe had looked daggers at him in the garden and later refused his help into the carriage. Will tilted his hat forward to shade his eyes from the lowering sun. He needed to put Miss Phoebe Walsh out of his mind. No point dwelling on a woman who wanted nothing to do with him.

Phoebe sat up, doing her best not to wake Liberty. Her friend murmured something indistinct, and then nothing more. Gentle snores carried from the other seat, in concert with the rocking of the landau. Phoebe couldn't tell whether they came from Ma or Aunt America, but she wouldn't inquire. Something must have summoned her from slumber—perhaps the horses' slowing hoofbeats. They must be nearing their destination. She pulled aside the curtain and peered out the window beside her.

The star-dotted sky shone purple-gray. The carriage

lanterns cast golden circles over the road and gilded a passing tree. Moonlight silvered the woods around them. Everything looked strange after nightfall, but Phoebe thought she recognized the road to Liberty township. She sat back and released a sigh. They couldn't reach Liberty's house soon enough. Besides wanting to leave the day's events behind, traveling after nightfall always unnerved her. Phoebe could admit that she disliked it less with Will riding shotgun. She liked her independence, but only up to a certain point.

The landau slowed even more and turned off the road.

"Are we home?" Liberty's sleepy voice accompanied her elbow in Phoebe's side as she sat up. "Sorry, Phoebe."

A snort ended the snoring. "Wh-what's happening?" Ma sounded slightly miffed.

"Wake up, Maisey." Aunt America swept back the curtain on the other side of the landau. Moonlight touched her profile as she leaned forward, looking out. "We've arrived."

"Hurrah." Liberty stifled a yawn. "It's a long drive from Stevensville."

"We should have left sooner, but I hated to end everyone's fun." Aunt America rolled up the curtain, allowing moonlight to flood the cabin.

Too bad they hadn't, Phoebe decided. An earlier departure might have spared her that encounter with Alton. Phoebe rolled up the curtain beside her and fastened it with the leather straps attached above the window.

The landau shuddered to a stop, and Will jumped down from the driving box. He opened the door beside Aunt America and helped her down first. Ma's turn came next. Liberty collected her reticule from the seat beside her and handed Phoebe her own. Phoebe followed Liberty from the landau, grateful for Will's steady hand helping her down to the box step.

After sitting so long, she felt a little wobbly. Her foot slipped on the box, but Will caught her. His heartbeat thudded in her ears for a few delirious seconds, and then he lifted her onto solid ground.

"Thank you." She couldn't help sounding breathless.

"My pleasure."

"Is everything all right?" Ma's voice intruded.

Will stood away from Phoebe. "Yes."

"I slipped on the step, Ma. I'm not sure how."

Will smiled. "I expect you're tired."

"Mr. Canfield kept me from injury."

"I'm grateful for that." Ma put an arm around her. "Let's get you inside."

"Go ahead and take the ladies inside." Pa called back from the driving box. "If you'll open the barn, I'll put away the horses."

"No, let me." Will strode toward the barn door. "You should be the one to attend to your family."

"I can't argue on that point." Pa jumped down. "I'll come back and help."

"There's no need." Will strode toward the barn door. "After sitting so long, I'd welcome the activity."

"Well, thank you." Pa glanced down the road. "Shane and Nick's wagons can't be far behind." He hurried inside the barn and returned a short while later with a lit lantern.

Will climbed into the driving box and picked up the lines. The scrape of the brake releasing carried to Phoebe. The landau rolled into the barn behind the horses.

Her mother kept a hand on Phoebe's elbow as they followed Pa's lantern toward the house. "Ma, I'm not going to trip." Phoebe pulled away to walk alone. "I know this path by heart."

Ma laughed. "I suppose you do. You visited Liberty often enough when we lived in the cabin."

"We were glad to have her company." Aunt America spoke from Ma's other side.

Liberty giggled beside Phoebe. "That path is worn both directions, I'm sure."

Pa held the arbor gate open for them, and Phoebe passed beneath its roses. The blossoms nodded in the faint breeze, and enough of the day's heat remained to free a whisper of scent. They fell silent, their footsteps crunching gravel.

The lantern light gleamed off the varnish on the oak front door. Pa turned back to them. "Wait, and I'll check inside."

They clustered together on the dark path while the lantern light went through the house. Pa was checking mainly out of courtesy, but the old fear stirred within her. She pressed closer to Ma. An owl hooted in the cottonwoods behind the house. How strange to take comfort from the hunting call of a bird of prey, but it carried her to childhood. On hot summer nights, when they had lived in the cabin, she'd slept with her bedroom window open.

Pa reappeared and waved them inside.

Phoebe settled with her family in the parlor. Aunt America lit the oil lamps, beautiful even with her hair mussed from sleeping. She smiled. "Can I offer you anything to drink?"

"Don't worry about that, America." Ma propped her feet up. "You must be as tired as the rest of us. Come and sit down."

"I've had quite enough of sitting, thank you." Aunt America smiled. "I don't know why you want to."

Ma grinned. "This is different. My chair doesn't move."

Aunt America laughed. "You'll forgive me if I don't join you. I need to see to my guests. Con and Elsa will stay the night with her family in Stevensville, but the rest of the brood will want somewhere to sleep."

Ma nodded. "Give me a minute, and I'll help."

"Oh, all right, I'll rest." Aunt America perched on the edge of a chair.

Ma smiled. "It won't hurt you to take five minutes."

"Everything's mostly ready, anyway." Liberty sank down on the chair next to Phoebe's. "We have a cot set up for you in my room."

More childhood memories overtook Phoebe. During sleepovers, she and Liberty had stifled both laughter and tears. They'd divulged their deepest secrets and greatest hopes.

Tonight, however, they would simply sleep.

The scent of foliage crushed beneath Phoebe's feet wafted upward. Birdsong swelled from the brush and in the stand of willows lining the road. Warmth kissed her face—the lingering caress of the sun. A mourning dove sobbed in an ancient willow, its branches draping the ground. Joy, totally out of keeping with her troubles, caught hold of Phoebe. "What a glorious day."

Liberty smiled. "I never thought we would wake so early.

"Me either, but it's nice to have time for a morning stroll."

"You seem much recovered from yesterday." Liberty kicked a stone out of the road that ran past her house for several miles before reaching Liberty township. "Weddings are wonderful, but attending one wears me out."

"I'm not surprised, knowing you."

Liberty shook her head. "A preacher's daughter should be less retiring."

"There you go, worrying about being someone you're not."

"I wish I was like you."

"Why would you want to be?" Phoebe exclaimed in mock horror.

"You are quite certain who you are and what you want."

"Really?" The first part of Liberty's assessment might be true, but the second took a little thinking.

"You inspire me to see everything anew. Take our surroundings, for instance. They are so familiar to me that I sometimes miss their beauty."

"You're blessed to have spent most of your life in this place."

Liberty smiled. "So much has happened here—both good and bad."

"You never quite leave your childhood home, I don't think. At least, I haven't. Whenever we visit, it all comes rushing back."

"Remember the time I injured myself on the road to town, and you had to leave me to go for help?"

"Who could forget?" Phoebe blew out a breath. "When I met that character on the road, I feared the worst for you."

"He did look disreputable. It was hard to imagine he could be a deputy."

"I was beside myself by the time I ran into Will." Phoebe's lips curved at the memory.

"And I was glad to see Jake. He walked me all the way home on his horse." Liberty sighed. "That taught me how much my friendship with him had changed."

Phoebe hesitated, but then decided to ask. "Why haven't you heard from Jake lately?"

Liberty's brow puckered. "I'm not quite sure."

"He might be overwhelmed by his studies."

Liberty sighed. "I wish it were only that."

"What else could it be?"

"I'm afraid I've made a terrible mistake where Jake is concerned."

"It's hard to imagine you could do anything to turn him

from you."

"I pressured him to court me sooner than we planned." Liberty burst out. "I could see no reason to wait."

"But he's gone for most of the year at seminary school."

"That shouldn't matter unless—" She averted her gaze. "Unless he wants it to."

"Liberty—"

"No, don't." Liberty held up a hand. "I think Jake is staying away to avoid me."

Phoebe stared at her, aghast. "Why would he do that?"

Liberty shook her head. "I wish I knew." Phoebe watched her friend dissolve into tears with a sense of helplessness. Liberty and Jake belonged together. She believed that with all her heart. If even they couldn't find happiness, who could?

It took a while to restore Liberty's spirits. Lunch preparations were in full swing by the time they returned. Phoebe pulled a worn apron off the peg in Liberty's kitchen where it had hung since she was a child. It had reached to her knees back then, and she'd wound the ties around her waist several times to keep them from dragging on the floor. It fit much better now. "What can I do to help?"

Aunt America stopped rolling pastry, put down her rolling pin, and pushed a lock of hair off her forehead with the back of her arm. 'Stir the filling."

Aunt Elsa glanced up from kneading dough. "We were beginning to wonder what happened to you two."

"Sorry." Liberty tied on her own apron.

Phoebe picked up the wooden spoon resting on a saucer beside the stove. A glimpse into the cast-iron stew pot revealed carrots, potatoes, and green beans simmering in a golden gravy. The savory scent made her mouth water. She stirred the mixture until it thickened, careful to scrape the bottom of the pot to keep it from sticking. "I think it's ready."

Aunt America nodded. "Take it off the stove, please. Maisey, could you dress the salad?"

"Yes, of course." Ma went on tiptoe and reached into the shelves lining one wall. She pulled down jugs of vinegar and oil.

"Don't forget the salt and pepper." Aunt Bry murmured to Liberty, who was helping her set the table. "I'm glad you came back, by the way. We were about to send out a search party. It gave us quite a turn that time you returned without Phoebe."

Phoebe's face heated, and Liberty's color rose.

"That happened a long time ago, Aunt Bry," Phoebe felt compelled to mention. "Liberty and I are careful not to walk so far nowadays."

"I'm glad to hear it." Aunt Bry smiled. "Forgive me, if I embarrassed you. I forget sometimes that you are grown women."

Ma paused from whisking salad dressing. "That's understandable, Bry. I do it, too often."

Liberty stepped onto a stepstool. "How many places should we lay?"

"Let's see…there's seven of us, five in Phoebe's family, five in Bry's family, and six in Elsa's—"

"Seven, counting Will," Phoebe hefted the stew pot onto a cast-iron trivet on the counter.

"Will left for the ranch this morning." Aunt Elsa upended the bowl of dough onto the bread board.

"That's too bad, but I suppose he had to get back to work." Aunt America carried several pastry-lined shells to the counter beside the stew pot. "How long do the rest of you anticipate staying?"

"That's a question to settle with Con." Aunt Elsa applied herself to kneading dough.

Aunt Bry looked up from laying out flatware. "I'll check with Nick."

"Rob will want to get back soon." Ma tossed the salad with two forks. "We have a milk cow coming in a couple of days. Rob bought her from the dairy farm east of us."

Phoebe was looking forward to that event, but she hated leaving Liberty so soon. "That's not for a couple of days, though."

"No rush." Aunt America smiled. "You're all more than welcome. I was just wondering how much food to prepare."

Phoebe ladled filling into the pastry-lined pie plates. She added top crusts before shutting the pot pies into the oven. How she wished she could lock away thoughts of Will as easily. He must have left while she and Liberty were out walking. She tried not to mind that he'd gone without saying goodbye. Of course, after their disastrous talk in the garden, there was no reason he would want to. Phoebe told herself she didn't care. She should embrace his absence as a relief, not a disappointment.

Phoebe sighed. Where Will was concerned, her emotions seemed determined to betray her.

Phoebe nearly choked on a mouthful of beef pie. Swallowing quickly, she reached for her water glass.

Pa paused with his fork halfway to his mouth. "*What* did you say?"

"I'm sure you heard me." Uncle Con lifted a spoonful of white crystals from the salt cellar. "I want to hire Phoebe as a ranch hand."

"Phoebe?" Pa diverted his attention to Ma, who was dividing suspicious glances between Phoebe and Uncle Con. She might suspect a conspiracy, but she made no accusations.

Phoebe kept her gaze from connecting with her mother's,

but she couldn't stop warmth from climbing into her cheeks. She'd never expected her uncle to offer her employment at the kitchen table with the whole family within earshot.

"Why not?" Uncle Con sprinkled his food with salt. "She rides better than most cowboys."

Pa laughed. "I know that as well as anyone. Phoebe would be a great help to you, but of course it's out of the question."

"Oh?" Uncle Con couldn't look more guileless. "Why is that?"

"Do you have to ask?" Ma burst out. "No reputable young woman does such a thing."

"Really?" Uncle Con raised his eyebrows. "I guess Calamity Jane is unaware of that."

Color bloomed in Ma's cheeks. "*Most* young women wouldn't dream of working on a ranch,"

"Thanks for the offer, but the answer is no." Pa shook his head. "I'm afraid we let Phoebe run wild at the ranch, but she needs to think about her future."

Meaning, no doubt, that she shouldn't do anything that might turn away a potential suitor. Phoebe waited for her initial irritation to subside before speaking. "I'm an adult, Pa, capable of making my own decisions." Phoebe knew at once that her words were a mistake. Uncle Con had used gentle logic, whereas she'd thrown down a gauntlet.

Her father's jaw firmed. "So long as you live under my roof—"

Aunt Elsa laid her hand on Uncle Con's arm. "Perhaps you should discuss this privately."

"Too late for that." Aunt Bry grinned. "For what it's worth, I think Phoebe would make a good ranch hand."

Phoebe tossed her a grateful look before returning her attention to her father. "I don't know how long I'd want to do it, but I'd like to try."

Pa jutted his jaw. "Absolutely not."

Phoebe put down her fork. "May I be excused?"

Ma glanced at her plate. "You've barely touched your food."

Phoebe stared at her plate to hide the tears swimming in her eyes. "I'm no longer hungry."

"Let her go, Maisey." Pa spoke quietly.

Ma nodded. "Very well."

Phoebe pushed back her chair and hurried from the room.

Liberty followed her onto the back porch. "Never mind, Phoebe." She slipped an arm around her shoulders. "It will all work out."

Tears fell to Phoebe's cheeks. She sighed and swiped them away. "I know that God wants me to honor my parents, but it's hard sometimes."

"They're not perfect, but they do want the best for you. "

"I just wish they would realize I'm grown."

"Give them time."

Phoebe breathed in the scent of roses from the flower bed below. How sad that such a lovely smell should bring back her falling-out with Will. She curled her fingers against the rough wood of the porch rail. "This was mostly my fault. I tried to change my parents' minds through Uncle Con."

"At least you recognize what you did."

"Will pointed out that I get my way too often." She gave a shaky laugh. "He made me mad, but I should have thanked him for telling me the truth."

"I'm sure you'll get the chance."

A mourning dove flew out of the cottonwood grove behind the house. The branch where it had perched bobbed, rustling leaves and scattering light. Phoebe lifted her face to the wind and let it dry her tears. Although it didn't seem likely, she hoped Liberty's prediction would come true and life would work out for her.

The starry eyes of night watched Will through the panes above his bed. He'd forgotten to shut the curtains when he'd tucked in for the night. That had been hours ago, and he was still awake. Will knew why he couldn't sleep. He didn't feel at ease about his abrupt departure from the Hayes house this morning. Hopefully, he hadn't offended anyone. After Con informed him that he wanted to hire Phoebe, he'd needed time to adjust to the idea.

Will understood why Phoebe would want to work on the ranch. She preferred riding outdoors to sitting in a stuffy parlor, any day. What he couldn't fathom was why she would place herself under his authority. He couldn't picture such an arrangement succeeding. The way they butted heads was bound to cause trouble. On a ranch, that could be dangerous. If Con insisted on hiring Phoebe, Will might have to quit. Too bad, because he loved his job. But it was more than that. He hated to give up the place he'd found to call home, in what had been a shiftless existence.

Will put his arms behind his head and studied the stars shining through the window. He could make out the Big Dipper and North Star. Was Phoebe watching them too? Will rolled over and turned his imagination from picturing Phoebe in bed. That he desired her had not escaped his notice. He'd thought that ignoring this fact could make it go away.

He had been wrong.

Will flung himself onto his back, yet again. Such thoughts were not a prelude to a good night's sleep. He preferred to meditate on nothing more than the wind in the sagebrush and cattle lowing in the field. He always went through this after he saw her.

He sighed and flung back his covers. The floorboards felt rough beneath his feet. The screen door squeaked open and slammed closed. He stood on the porch looking out over the moon-silvered countryside. The night breeze reached to him, cooling and healing at once. He breathed deeply, letting the sweet current revive him. It seemed to him the very breath of God.

"Tell me what to do about Phoebe." His whispered prayer vanished into the darkness. Will sighed. Why hope for an answer he'd sworn not to act upon? Had he learned nothing from his past heartbreak? Did he really want to risk the betrayal of another woman? His disappointment over Sophie and his brother felt like a horrible case of flu that never went away.

Only…the pain did seem less sharp than before.

The realization made his palms sweat.

CHAPTER SEVEN

WILL OPENED HIS ACHING EYES, WHICH felt like they contained sand. The sun streamed in, too bright for morning. How long had he slept? A knock rattled the outer door. "Will? Are you awake?" Con's voice drifted to him.

Will sat up in bed. He ran a hand through his hair and scrubbed at his face. "Yes, I'm here." He pushed back the covers and thumped his feet to the floorboards.

After pulling on a pair of trousers, he stumbled to the cabin door and yanked it open. Sunlight flooded in, making him blink. Con stood on the stoop, looking more alert than a body had a right to. Will summoned the effort to speak. "Good morning."

Con frowned. "You look like a horse that's been ridden hard and put away wet."

Will nodded. "I suppose I do. Care to come in?"

"Thanks, but I won't. I just came by to invite you to supper tonight. I didn't expect to see you in such rough shape."

"I haven't slept well since returning to the ranch."

"Oh?" Con quirked an eyebrow. "This doesn't have anything to do with Phoebe, does it?"

Will eyed him. "Why would you say that?"

"No reason in particular." Con gave him a clear-eyed look. "Except that you lit out of the family gathering awfully fast."

"I felt bad about that. I hope no one took offense."

"I doubt anyone did, but your absence may have disappointed a certain party." Con winked.

"Phoebe? But I thought—"

Con shrugged. "Maybe I'm reading more into it than I should. I'd like to believe that—"

"I know you would." Will shook his head. "Even if I wanted to get involved with a woman— which I don't— Phoebe and I are wrong for each other."

"I don't know about that." Con's eyes gleamed. "You're more alike than I think you understand."

"Phoebe is too favored for her own good."

"That's hardly her fault. If that's all you have against Phoebe—"

"Whoa!" Will held up a hand. "I have nothing against Phoebe. The question was whether we are suited."

"Point taken." Con smiled. "I wonder, though, whether having been left at the altar colors your view."

"Look, if you don't mind, I'd rather not stand half-clothed in my doorway discussing my romantic life with my employer."

Con cracked a grin. "Fair enough."

Will frowned. "I *am* wondering whether Phoebe and I should work together."

"No need to concern yourself about that. Rob and Maisey won't have it, and I'm not about to cross my brother and his wife."

Will stared at him. "Do you mean to say—"

"Under the circumstances, I can't hope to hire Phoebe." He rubbed the back of his neck. "I wish I hadn't offered."

"I see." Will didn't know how to comfort him. He personally thought the whole thing rash, but there was no need to point that out. Con appeared to have learned his lesson, but that didn't mean he wouldn't rush in again where angels feared to tread. He smiled. "Thanks for the invitation. I'm happy to accept."

"Well, then. We'll expect you." Con looked back from the

doorway. "I'll leave you to your morning."

Will was only too happy to close the door after his boss. The conversation had cut close. Maybe now that he knew a crisis with Phoebe was not imminent, he could sleep at night. A curious flat feeling assailed him. He pushed it away, unwilling to believe it had anything to do with Phoebe. He should be relieved, not disappointed, that she wasn't coming to work at the ranch.

Phoebe tugged another carrot from the ground, shook off the dirt, and dropped the vegetable into the hod beside her. She stood and stretched, arching her back. Golden rays peeked over the forest canopy and painted the trees at the edge of the garden. The leaves rattled in a faint breeze, and long shadows danced at her feet. The air smelled of the river and of green, growing things.

Her cotton skirts feathered around her ankles, but something else brushed her legs. Phoebe glanced down and laughed. She bent and picked up the family cat, but Lady Guinevere squirmed to be let down.

Phoebe set the orange tabby on her feet. "Ma is the one to butter up, if you're asking for food. She's cooking breakfast."

Tail high, Lady Guinevere stalked toward the house, for all the world as if she'd understood. Her complaints caused the back door to open a short while later. Ma, outlined in morning sunlight, waved to Phoebe while the cat slipped past her into the house. Phoebe waved back as the aroma of sizzling bacon and hot coffee wafted to her on the breeze. Phoebe's mouth watered, and her stomach growled. She returned to her task with more diligence.

Phoebe pulled out the knife she'd tucked into the hod. The blade glinted as she severed a head of cabbage. She loosened the soil around the potato vines with a garden fork, and her questing fingers uncovered a crop of new potatoes. The discovery brought a smile to her lips.

Phoebe washed the vegetables and herself at the pump before going inside. Carrying the hod, she put out her elbow to prevent the screen door from slamming shut. "I got a nice cabbage, and there are enough new potatoes for supper."

Ma glanced up from breaking eggs into a bowl. "Wonderful. They will go well with Aunt Elsa's recipe for *Weisskohl*."

Phoebe nodded. She'd been present when her mother had asked Aunt Elsa how to make the German braised cabbage dish she favored. Aunt Elsa, ever generous, had sent her home with some of her handmade sausages to go with it.

She lowered the hod to the counter. "What can I do to help with breakfast?"

"Go let everyone know breakfast is ready. Your father and brothers are in the barn. Then you can lay the table." Ma spoke offhandedly, but with constraint. It had been this way between them since that ill-fated meal with Uncle Con.

"Sure, Ma." Phoebe went out the kitchen door and clanged the iron triangle with the clapper. She returned to the kitchen and reached down a stack of plates from the open shelves above the counter. After placing cutlery on top, she went through to the dining room, and her feet sank into the Persian carpet. She arranged each setting, then twitched the damask curtains open to let in a flood of morning light.

Phoebe went back into the kitchen and returned with glasses and napkins. She carried in a pitcher of juice Ma had made from the first tomatoes, and along with that a salt cellar and pepper grinder. The molasses jug followed.

Ma turned from the stove as she entered the kitchen.

"Everything is ready. Are the others coming?"

"I'll check." Phoebe let herself out the back door. As she rounded the corner of the ranch house, she caught sight of her father and brothers on the path from the barn.

She hurried into the kitchen but forgot to keep the screen door from banging. "They're almost here."

"Oh, good. Let's wait a moment for them to wash up before we bring out the food. I wanted to ask whether you had the chance to speak with Alton at the wedding."

Phoebe glanced away from the eager look on her mother's face. She had accepted that her parents did not want her working at the ranch, but that didn't mean she was ready to fall into Alton's arms.

"Yes, I spoke with him. I've been meaning to tell you about it." Somehow, she'd never found the time.

"What did he say?" Her mother waited for her to speak with hope in her face.

A pang struck Phoebe. Her annoyance fled, and an impulse of mercy took its place. She pulled in a breath. "We didn't have much time to talk. I promised to let him know when we returned home."

Phoebe didn't ask why Pa had kept his decision to let Alton court her quiet. Nor did she say that she planned to refuse him. How could she divulge such a thing when Ma ached to see her settled? She'd never really understood the depth of her mother's heartbreak over her becoming a spinster—until now.

What am I going to do?

Phoebe could have wept. Pleasing her mother might doom her to a boring life. If she sought her own way, she would crush her mother's hopes.

Why Phoebe could play the piano so well, she didn't know.

Activities requiring patience usually did not appeal to her. Thank goodness she could, because it gave her a way, however briefly, to distract Alton from his intentions. Presently, he was delivering an out-of-tune rendition of "Oh, Susanna!" A sudden image of countless evenings spent listening to Alton's tone-deaf singing rose before her. Even for her mother's sake, Phoebe wasn't certain she could endure such a cruel fate.

Maybe she was being too picky. She couldn't fault the man's looks. From the top of his well-groomed head to the tips of his polished boots, Alton Prescott displayed every appearance of a gentleman. Any woman should be honored to win his favor. Ma certainly thought so, judging by her manner toward him. She made sure to offer him the chair with the best view of the river and kept his glass of sweet tea full. Of course, with spinsterhood looming for Phoebe, Ma might give any potential suitor preferential treatment.

"Oh, Susanna!" came to a torturous end at long last. Phoebe reached to turn the page, but Alton waved his hand in front of her music book. "That was delightful, but I'd like a moment to talk before I go."

A sinking sensation went through her. Alton no doubt wanted to continue what he'd started in the sanctuary. She felt unable to keep up her end of the conversation. Not while she was wavering over whether to discourage or encourage the man. She needed time to straighten out her thinking, not a heart-to-heart with him.

"Yes, of course." Ma glanced up from her crocheting. "Why don't you two go and sit on the porch?"

"It's hot out there." Phoebe blurted the first excuse that came to mind.

"Not so you'd notice." Ma speared her with a glance. "The breeze from the river makes it cooler."

Alton turned to Phoebe. "I'm sure the porch will be pleasant, and your mother wants to visit there."

"Actually, I'm comfortable here." Ma kept her eyes trained on her crochet. "But you two go along without me."

"But it's not proper." Phoebe could hardly believe she was raising this objection, and not Ma. She seemed to have traded opinions with her mother.

Ma smiled. "I can see the chairs where you'll sit through the window, but I doubt you'll need supervising."

Ma was right about that. Phoebe had no intention of allowing Alton near her.

Alton stood taller. "Thanks for your vote of confidence, Mrs. Walsh. I'll give you no cause to regret it."

Ma nodded. "I have no doubt of that."

Phoebe took herself in hand. She was overreacting. Although imperious and boring, Alton wasn't an ogre. If he pressed for an answer, she could always admit to not having one. "All right, I suppose."

Alton beamed at her as if she were a student who had mastered a difficult lesson. "I promise that you will not regret your decision."

Unprepared for the warmth in his voice, Phoebe glanced upward. His gaze captured hers, and a moment of vertigo seized her. Phoebe clutched the back of her chair to steady herself. By stepping closer, Alton had thrown her off balance.

He held the front door, and Phoebe glanced back at her mother before going outside. As she passed him in the doorway, she caught the scent of bay. Her skin prickled with the awareness of him watching her. She kept her head down, avoiding his gaze.

Phoebe could never be in Alton's company without feeling on guard. Even so, she surprised herself by relaxing a little. It helped that the porch felt less constraining than the parlor. Alton seemed kinder than she'd given him credit for. Either that or he was good at pretending. Sorting out the truth lay beyond her abilities. When it came to affairs of the heart, she never quite knew where she stood with the other person. That was one reason for avoiding them. Alton waited while she chose her chair—a mark in his favor. He came from a good family, as Ma had pointed out, and it showed.

When he went to the railing and looked out over the ranch, she tried not to notice the broad shoulders beneath his jacket nor his trim waist.

What might marriage to Alton bring? She pictured lazy days punctuated by social gatherings, tea with friends, and long evenings by the fireside. It seemed idyllic, but a bit vacuous. Maybe she had it wrong, and there would be literary chats, deep conversations, walks at twilight, and hours spent reading together. The passage of time would bring a troop of children with rosy cheeks and fair hair to toddle after their father. She smiled at the thought. Perhaps her mother was right, and she should look no further for a husband.

"Phoebe..." Alton's voice choked off.

Her gaze snapped into focus. She realized with horror that he'd caught her staring. Her cheeks flamed. "I'm sorry. I must have been—daydreaming."

"That's quite all right." He beamed. "I'm honored that you feel comfortable enough in my presence to do so. May I ask what brought that lovely smile to your face?"

She shook her head, hoping a blush wouldn't rise to her cheeks. "I was thinking about—about something my mother said regarding—a private matter."

He sat in the bentwood chair across from her. "Have you decided whether to allow me to court you?"

"I've given it some thought." She kept her tone neutral.

"You sound so careful." He laughed. "I hope the prospect appeals to you."

Phoebe smiled, charmed by his humor despite herself. To counter her weakening, she adopted a serious tone. "I'm waiting for you to finish explaining yourself to me."

"I haven't forgotten my promise to do so." He sat forward in his chair. "Miss Walsh, I fear that my eagerness drove you away in the beginning. I was so taken with you that I lost my head. I must apologize if I made you feel hunted. I hope you will give me a chance, but I'll leave you alone if you wish."

"Thank you, Mr. Prescott. I appreciate that." Phoebe pulled in a deep breath. His ardor decided her course of action, for she found no answering spark within herself. "You honor me with your offer, but I must decline."

"Might I know why?"

His stricken expression pierced her. "I considered agreeing to a courtship, but that would be dishonest."

"Do you care nothing for me?"

He'd spoken lightly, but Phoebe heard the pain in his voice. She softened her own tone. "I've developed a certain fondness for you, but you deserve someone able to fully return your affections."

"I wondered if that was the problem—that your sympathies are engaged elsewhere."

"You mentioned that before, but I'm not sure what you meant." She held her breath, dreading what he might say.

"I have eyes in my head. I can see—" Alton stood and paced back and forth before dropping to one knee before her. "Phoebe—Miss Walsh, all I ask is the chance to change your mind."

"Mr. Prescott—"

"Don't answer me now." He stood and straightened his jacket. "Please, take all the time you need to think this over."

Phoebe wondered if Ma was watching through the window. If so, what would she make of Alton's behavior? "I don't think—"

He held up a hand. "Let me stop you from saying anything you may come to regret."

She stared at him, robbed of speech.

"Are you aware that the ladies think me something of a prize?"

A smile tugged at her lips. "I've been given to understand that." She'd already dealt the man one blow to his ego. There was no need to inform him that she'd only heard it from her mother.

"Miss Walsh, I see you as desirable in every way. However—please forgive my bluntness—some view you as past your prime."

She repressed a smile. This was no way to sweet-talk a woman. "I don't care about their opinions."

"Perhaps you should." He returned to his chair. "The person you've set your heart on has vowed to avoid matrimony. Meanwhile, your prospects dwindle."

She drew a quick breath but refrained from speaking.

"You don't deny it, I see." Alton sat forward in his chair. "I am willing to risk never gaining your love."

"That sort of courtship wouldn't be fair to either of us."

"I don't know." He arched his brows. "I like a challenge, and you must see certain advantages. You admitted to contemplating such an arrangement, yourself."

"I did?"

"Yes, but then you said I deserve to have my affections returned." A fleeting smile touched his lips. "Please allow me to decide such a matter for myself. Promise me you'll think my offer over carefully before giving me an answer."

Sudden weariness washed over Phoebe, and she nodded. How could she withstand both her mother's expectations and Alton's insistence? What had made her think that a simple refusal would deter him? The man was relentless. She'd never expected him to guess but disregard her feelings for Will. He'd outmaneuvered her.

CHAPTER EIGHT

"HOW BAD IS IT?" KATERINA CALLED over the side of the wagon.

Her brother glanced up from beside the wheel with a broken spoke. Christoph's eyes appeared very blue against his reddening skin. As a shopkeeper, he didn't spend much time in the sun. His teeth flashed in a swift smile. "Don't worry. It's nothing I can't handle."

"Can I help you in some way?"

"Not really, apart from getting out of the wagon. I need to raise it with the jack."

"Certainly." She stood and turned toward the rear.

"Better not go past that one." Christoph gestured with his head toward Diablo. The mustang snorted and showed the whites of his eyes. His mane flew as he jerked at the rope tethering him to the back of the wagon.

Katerina glanced at her brother in alarm. "What's wrong with him? He seemed fine."

"Maybe now that we're stopped, he has time to think about escaping." Christoph reached up. "Let me help you."

Katerina leaned down, and he lowered her to the ground.

Diablo thumped his hooves and began to prance.

She caught her breath. "I'm afraid he'll hurt himself."

Christoph frowned. "He's making the wagon horses nervous. Can you calm him, somehow? Maybe give him a carrot."

Katerina eyed the plunging beast. "I think he's beyond being placated."

"I'll hurry." Christoph disappeared beneath the wagon.

Katerina scanned the countryside. They'd stopped in a place where the road cut through flat land. Dry grasses rustled in the searing wind while the sun beat down, but otherwise nothing stirred.

Diablo pulled at his rope again, shaking the wagon.

Katerina's mouth went dry. Her brother had placed rocks in front of the wheels to prevent them from rolling forward. Only the old wagon's poor brakes kept them from turning backwards. "Christoph, come out from there."

"Just a minute." His voice came back muffled.

Diablo shook the wagon again.

Katerina tried to lift a large stone, but it wouldn't budge. She dropped a smaller one behind a rear wheel, then hurried to find another rock. She was wedging the second stone into place when Christoph emerged with the wagon jack and a spare spoke. "What are you doing? You'll hurt your hands."

She straightened and dusted off her scraped palms. "Saving you from an accident."

His brows drew together, but then shot upward. "Thank you."

Diablo's squeal pierced the air.

Tears gathered in Katerina's eyes. "Please—he's going to hurt himself."

"I'll see what I can do." He started toward the horse, but then swung about. "Someone's coming."

Katerina shielded her eyes against the sun. A line of dust billowed in the distance, churned by the horse and rider headed their direction. Her heartbeat picked up its pace. The rider probably wasn't anyone to worry about. Most people you met on the road were friendly, and outlaws usually didn't travel alone.

Still, she was glad when her brother moved closer as the rider approached.

The man reined in. Through the dust he brought with him, Katerina saw that he wore chaps like a cowboy. His hat mostly hid his hair, which might be brown.

"Hello." Christoph's lazy eye drooped in the bright light. "I'm Christoph Meier, and this is my sister, Miss Meier."

"Name's Matt Malone." The man removed his hat. His age was hard to tell with dust creasing his face, but the smile he turned on her made him look young. "Ma'am."

"Good afternoon." Katerina pulled her gaze away from his, where it seemed to have stuck.

"I see that you're having trouble." Matt leaned forward in the saddle. "Want me to lend a hand?"

Christoph nodded. "Thanks."

Matt swung down and pulled something that looked like a plaid cloth from his saddlebag. Rather than walking toward Christoph, as Katerina expected, he crept toward Diablo. "Whoa, there," he murmured. "Easy."

Diablo stopped prancing and pricked his ears. Katerina stared in amazement. How had the man quieted a half-wild horse with only a few words?

Matt edged toward the horse, talking all the while. Diablo backed at first, but then allowed him to come close. Moving quickly, Matt pulled what looked like a shirt over the mustang's head. He held it in place, preventing Diablo from shaking it off. "Steady, now. You're all right."

After a few moments, Diablo stopped trying to free himself.

"Well, I'll be hanged." Christoph breathed. "How did you do that?"

"It's an old trick." Matt grinned. "It's kind of hard to throw a fit when you can't see."

"I'm glad you came along." Christoph chuckled. "When it comes to horses, I barely know the mane from the tail."

Matt laughed. "I doubt you're that hopeless. Your wagon horses look well cared for. Look, I'd help fix your wheel, but you might prefer me to remain with this fellow."

Christoph waved a hand. "Yah, yah. Please stay where you are, with my thanks. If anything happened to Diablo, my sister would weep." He ducked down, and the wagon ratcheted upward. A metallic clanging punctuated his muttering.

"Diablo?" Matt narrowed his eyes. "What kind of name is that?"

Katerina lifted her chin. "We didn't give him his name, but I think he may have earned it somehow."

"Too bad." Matt shook his head. "Unless I miss my guess, this magnificent horse was running wild on the plain only a short while ago. He doesn't appear more than a couple of years old."

A smile tugged at Katerina's lips. "I have no doubt you are correct. What would you call him instead?"

"I don't know, but certainly not after the devil. When a horse proves difficult, it is often from rough handling."

"Thank you for explaining that, Mr. Malone. I'll bear it in mind when I try to ride him."

Diablo stomped and shuddered. Matt stroked his sleek brown neck, and the horse quieted. "How much experience do you have with horses, Miss Walsh?"

"Very little, but I'm learning."

"Forgive me for pointing this out, but you may not be ready to ride so fresh a horse."

She smiled. "I think you are, in the kindest way, calling me a greenhorn."

"No disrespect intended, ma'am."

"It's all right. I appreciate your honest opinion. Diablo is my horse, and I'd like to keep him. I'm taking him to the Connor Walsh ranch for training."

"Con Walsh's ranch? That's where I'm headed, too. Con just hired me."

"Really? Maybe we'll meet once in a while."

"I doubt we'll see much of each other. I'll be in the bunkhouse or out on the range. Neither is a place you're likely to venture."

She lost a little of her zeal. "Probably not. I'll be visiting my family."

He tilted his head. "Are you related to Con?"

"He had the good sense to marry my sister, Elsa. They brought much of our family over from Germany."

"I was trying to place your accent. Do you like America?"

The wagon shook and began moving downward.

"Very much. I believe Christoph has finished the repairs." Katerina told herself that it was ridiculous to feel disappointed. Of course, they needed to continue their journey, even if it meant saying goodbye to the intriguing Mr. Malone.

"So, he has." Matt spoke without enthusiasm. "I wonder—I've taken an interest in your horse. Do you already have someone to train him?"

"Yes. Will Canfield has agreed to do it."

"He has a good reputation with horses. I'm sure he'll do a good job. If you don't mind, though, I'd like to check on Diablo once in a while."

"That's fine by me."

The wagon stopped lowering. Christoph reappeared, dusty but triumphant. "I may not know what to do with horses, but by golly, I can fix a wagon wheel."

Matt removed the shirt from Diablo's eyes and stepped away quickly.

The mustang followed, looking forlorn when he reached the end of his tether.

Katerina laughed. "You must remember to visit him."

"I will." Matt returned to the mustang and stroked his neck a final time before whistling for his own horse.

Katerina sighed. "What a nice man."

"He seems to have made quite an impression." Christoph sounded smug. "What were you talking about while I was working?"

"Oh, this and that." She gave a vague reply to stifle her brother's curiosity.

Matt waved at them from astride his horse. "You should make it to the ranch in good time."

Christoph nodded. "Thanks for your help."

"My pleasure." Matt smiled at Katerina, tipped his hat, and turned his horse down the road.

Katerina watched him ride off with a curious lump in her throat. Diablo wasn't the only one reluctant to see him go. Their paths might not cross again, but she felt ridiculously comforted that today, their destination was the same.

Phoebe slipped into the coolness of the barn and turned into the tack room. In the subdued light coming through the small window, she ran her hand along the wall beside the door. Her fingers encountered cold metal threaded by leather straps. She lifted her horse's bridle from its peg and returned to the breezeway. Several horses whickered a greeting, but most of the stalls stood empty. Pa, her brothers, and the ranch hands rose earlier even than she did.

As she neared Nutmeg's stall, a whinny vibrated the air.

"Hello, sweet girl." Phoebe stroked her horse's neck and rubbed behind her ears. "Already miss me since yesterday?"

Nutmeg nudged her in reply.

Phoebe laughed. "Here I was, thinking you were glad to see me, when you're really after your carrot." She produced the morsel and took advantage of the preoccupation it caused. While her horse crunched greedily, Phoebe slipped the bridle over her head and fastened the buckles. Nutmeg's saddle rested on the sawhorse Pa had set up nearby. He'd agreed that it didn't make sense to haul a saddle from the tack room every time she rode Nutmeg, which was often. Bright light streamed through the high windows on this side of the building, splitting into rays that lit swirling dust motes. Time to air the barn again.

After saddling Nutmeg, Phoebe led her into the barnyard, careful to close the door behind her. Coyotes had started howling at night nearby. They weren't likely to attack an adult horse, but Phoebe would hate for anything to happen to Ma's appaloosa, who was about to foal.

Nothing eased Phoebe's cares better than a ride on the ranch. She took the familiar trail that crossed into the open range, feeling a little guilty that she hadn't told Ma which way she intended to go. How could she restrain herself, with the mountains lit golden and eagles diving into the meadows? She gave Nutmeg her head. The little mare's hooves beat a tattoo as together they flew into the untamed land, free as the wind. Nothing and no one could catch her out here—not even Alton.

She came to a pounding halt on a tree-lined hillside where a stream tumbled invitingly. Nutmeg lowered her muzzle and drank, and Phoebe turned her face to catch the breeze coming down the waterway. A trout jumped, its iridescent sides gleaming in rainbow colors. Her younger brother Murphy would want to catch it, but she had no desire to do so.

She gazed across the valley to the ice-capped mountains that had guarded this valley long before she ever came into the world. When she was gone, they would remain. Life might be fleeting, but she wanted hers to count for something.

Could she settle for a mundane existence with Alton? Phoebe could hardly believe she was considering it. And yet, the life she yearned for might never be possible. A woman must accept her lot and not complain. She should marry and raise children. Her existence must include boiling laundry, cooking meals, and changing diapers—not to mention satisfying a husband's needs.

Whether for Ma's sake, Alton's benefit, or her own good—could she do it? While dressed up and entertaining guests in the parlor, giving in seemed inevitable. Here in the wild, she couldn't even imagine surrendering herself.

Katerina threw back the covers, donned her wrapper, and hurried to the window. Before retiring, she'd hooked back the embroidered wool curtains and opened the window to let in the night breezes. The under-curtains were billowing, but she pushed them aside. Although she and Christoph had arrived at the ranch after dark yesterday, she'd awakened with the sun burning at the horizon. From the window, she could see scraps of mist lit by the colors of sunrise rising from the river and dancing about the barn. A man wearing a plaid shirt, dark trousers, and a wide-brimmed hat came into view. He crossed the barnyard with a loping stride that reminded her of Matt Malone. Was he an early-riser also?

She stepped sideways, not wanting to be caught gawking, although the man probably hadn't noticed her. After glancing at herself in the washstand mirror, she found the likelihood comforting. Her hair was slipping out of its plaits, and the shorter fringe that normally covered her forehead was sticking up. She unbraided her hair and brushed it with long strokes. The silver-backed mirror, brush, and comb set had been a Christmas gift from Elsa. She smiled at the memory of her sister's delight in giving it to her. Katerina braided her hair more neatly and pinned it into a coil at her crown. She tamed her unruly fringe with water.

Katerina performed her ablutions, and then dressed quickly. She arched her back and reached for the ceiling. It felt good to have no duties for once. She would pitch in to help Elsa about the house, but that was different. She cracked open her bedroom door and followed the aroma of coffee to the kitchen.

She found Christoph seated at the counter. He would probably leave for home after breakfast, preferring not to leave Anna minding the store by herself for long.

Elsa glanced up from cracking eggs into a bowl. "I thought to see you soon. Would you like coffee?"

"Yes, please." Katerina sank onto the stool beside Christoph and accepted a steaming cup. She stirred in sugar from the bowl at her brother's elbow, the spoon clinking against the thin porcelain. She wasn't surprised to find Christoph awake. By this time at his house, he would be tending to the wagon horses, a flock of chickens, several pigs, and a milk cow. After that, Christoph and Anna or one of the children would travel the short distance to town to stock shelves, sweep, and otherwise prepare the store for customers. Katerina took her turn at the mercantile, but less often now that the children were old enough to help.

Elsa sliced into a loaf of bread. "Con will be back soon. He stepped out for a moment to talk with a new hire."

Katerina smiled. "That's probably Matt Malone. He calmed my horse while Christoph fixed our wagon wheel."

"It sounds like Con chose his ranch hand well." Elsa selected a potato from a colander and reached for a knife.

Katerina plunked her cup into its saucer. "Let me do that."

"Thanks." Elsa passed the knife by its hilt. The colander and a cutting board followed.

Christoph stood and stretched. "I think I'll go out and see what's keeping Con."

"Be sure and thank Mr. Malone again for what he did." Katerina sliced into a potato.

"I'll be sure and tell him that Miss Meier wanted me to." Christoph winked.

Elsa's eyes gleamed. "I see."

"No, you don't." Katerina's cheeks warmed. "Don't pay any attention to Christoph. I'm simply grateful that, because of Mr. Malone, Diablo suffered no harm."

"I hope you won't regret becoming so attached to that horse." Christoph shook his head. "I almost wish I hadn't given him to you."

Katerina smiled. "It was kind of you and Anna."

"We wanted to thank you for helping us establish the mercantile. We couldn't have done it without you."

"Give yourself more credit. You were the driving force." Katerina picked up another potato. "I only made it easier."

Christoph looked back from the doorway. "And now you must have a change."

She fell silent, pondering Christoph's words. Her brother would never turn her out, but he might be giving her his blessing to leave.

What lies before me in life?

Katerina reined in her thoughts, not ready to think ahead so far. She must focus on learning to ride Diablo, no matter what it took. She should call him something else. Matt was right.

Giving a horse the very name of evil was an insult. Her noble mustang deserved better. Sultan might suit him, if it didn't seem too foreign for a wholly-American horse. She would give it more thought. Maybe Elsa's children could offer suggestions.

Katerina would not need prodding to study horsemanship. Someday she hoped to sail across the prairie on her horse's back, riding free. She could ask Will for pointers, but he was already breaking Diablo. Asking him for anything more seemed an imposition. Phoebe didn't live far from Uncle Con, who could be persuaded to teach her a little. Matt was close enough for regular lessons, provided his ranch duties allowed. Katerina warmed to the idea. He'd demonstrated the deep understanding and mastery of horses that she would like to gain. She'd saved most of her wages from working at the mercantile and didn't mind paying for his time.

The sharp knife sliced through the last potato like butter. It seemed a lot to expect from a near-stranger. Also, she wouldn't want him to feel obligated because of her position in the family. It might be better not to ask, but she might have little choice.

When it came to riding Diablo, she needed all the help she could get.

CHAPTER NINE

THE CLIP-CLOPPING OF THE CARRIAGE HORSE'S hooves on cobblestone alerted Phoebe of their arrival at Prescott Manor. Oak trees lifted their branches on either side of the drive. The wind-tossed leaves above them cast uncertain patterns across the landau's leather seats. The shadows gave her parents, opposite her, a strange appearance. Murphy and the coachman Ma had insisted on hiring occupied the driving seat. Although Quinn challenged him for the position, Murphy had won Pa's coin toss. Quinn sat beside her, or he would have if he wasn't leaning out the window. He kept calling out. "The house is like a castle. Look at those towers! There's a garden and a carriage house, too. I can't wait to see inside."

"Quinn, stop hanging through the window and gawking." Ma sounded higher-pitched than usual, a sign of her nervousness.

Phoebe twisted her hands in her lap. "I wish you had let me know of the invitation sooner."

"I'm sorry. I thought I did." Ma spoke airily.

Was it Phoebe's imagination, or did her mother sound disingenuous? Had Ma plotted to throw her into Alton's company, despite her reluctance? Phoebe didn't like wondering that.

Phoebe sighed. She didn't blame her mother for wanting her happiness. She just wished Ma would stop trying so hard to ensure it. If she'd known about the invitation earlier, she might have declined to go. Seeing Alton would be a strain, since she still didn't know what to say to him. With more warning, she might at least have braced herself for the trial she was about to endure. All Phoebe could do, at this late date, was steel herself for the inevitable encounter with Alton.

She hoped to avoid embarrassing her mother. Despite Pa striking it rich in the gold fields, her upbringing had been humble. She'd learned, at Ma's insistence, which fork to use and other weighty matters of interest to the upper crust. Out of it all, she'd retained only what she used.

She would never excel at idle chatter. She couldn't comprehend why others valued something that made her shudder. Her forthright way of speaking never hindered her, and it might even be an asset. She could charm a bird from the trees, according to Pa anyway.

The landau pulled up outside the entrance pillars. The coachman opened the door and let down the steps. A footman wearing a white coat embroidered in gold hurried from the house to greet them. He made a fuss over Ma as she climbed down to the cobblestones. Phoebe clasped the footman's gloved hand and descended to stand beside her mother.

Murphy joined them, ruddy-cheeked and with his already-unruly hair ravaged by the wind. His eyes shone. "That was some drive."

"I get that seat on the way home," Quinn informed him.

Phoebe frowned and shook her head.

"I'm glad you had fun," Quinn added.

Murphy gave him a suspicious glance. "Thanks."

The coachman called to the horses, and the carriage rolled forward.

Pa offered Ma his arm. "Shall we go in?"

Phoebe walked between her brothers through the open doorway and into a spacious entryway. She gained the impression of dark woodwork and shining floorboards. The footman led them up several steps, down a paneled corridor, and into a large reception room. Phoebe recognized some of the guests at this party, although they'd never attended one at the manor before. The footman stood back for them to enter. "Mr. and Mrs. Rob Walsh…" He paused to draw breath. "Miss Phoebe Walsh…Mr. Quinn Walsh…Mr. Murphy Walsh."

Alton's parents came forward to greet them. Except for his hair, which he had clearly inherited from his mother, Alton resembled his father. Both possessed the same hooded eyes, straight nose, and strong jaw. "We're delighted you could attend," Mrs. Prescott gushed while her husband pumped Pa's hand.

Phoebe clasped her hosts' hands in turn. Their enthusiasm wasn't what she'd expected. Why were they so happy to meet her? Given the trappings of wealth and prestige within view, Alton could do better. Phoebe's family had money, yes, but they'd never sought social status. Phoebe had disregarded it most of her life. Ma had too, until she'd become obsessed with Phoebe's prospects.

Mrs. Prescott beamed at her. "My dear, Alton speaks of you in such glowing terms that I've been anxious to meet you."

She smiled. "I hope he has not built up my character so far that I must surely disappoint you."

"I am certain you could not. You seem quite sweet."

Phoebe repressed the urge to state that she could be cross at times. Ma had taught her that a guest did not contradict her hostess. All at once, she yearned to go home. She belonged at a ranch house, not a cultured mansion.

"So, you've arrived at last." Alton spoke at her elbow.

Phoebe started. "Goodness! I didn't notice you there."

He grinned. "How you wound me. I fancied that you scanned the room for me as soon as you arrived."

She smiled, taken by his charm. "Your parents distracted

me."

"You looked for a moment as if you wanted to bolt. What did my mother say to you?"

She laughed. "Only good things."

"That's a relief." He glanced about them. "Look, I know it's a lot— coming to the grand manor and all."

"It wasn't that." She studied him, wondering whether to speak her mind.

"Out with it. You can't leave me hanging."

She shook her head. "It's nothing, really."

He frowned. "I hope you will tell me later. Meanwhile, come say hello to my sister."

Alton guided her to a blonde young woman engaged in laughing conversation with an older couple. If she hadn't been nearly as tall as Alton, she would have reminded Phoebe of a porcelain doll with big eyes and rosy cheeks. Her face brightened as they neared. "Alton, you must join us and introduce your friend."

The couple she'd been speaking with murmured the same invitation, the man's words lilting in a way Phoebe recognized. He must be an Irish immigrant, like Pa. The man's heavy mustache and bushy eyebrows lent him a stern appearance, but his eyes twinkled with good humor. Joy radiated from him whenever he gazed at the striking woman beside him. With expressive eyes set in a fine-boned face and flawlessly coiffed hair, she was the epitome of beauty. The woman wore a simple strand of pearls, but she needed no other ornament.

Alton smiled. "Mrs. Daly, I'm honored to introduce Miss Walsh. She is an avid horsewoman, from what I understand."

Phoebe bowed, and Mrs. Daly reciprocated. "How nice to meet you." She extended her hand.

"And you." Phoebe shook with her briefly.

Mrs. Daly's smile lit her face. "We share an interest. I, too, enjoy taking a turn on a horse."

Phoebe tried to picture the delicate woman riding. She would no doubt perch on a sidesaddle and make it look easy.

"Miss Prescott, may I present Miss Walsh?"

"You may, indeed." She laughed. "I've been waiting for the longest time to meet her. Welcome, my dear. None of this 'Miss Prescott' business, by the way. You must call me Isobel."

"Thank you." Phoebe seemed to have met someone as forthright as herself. She shook hands with Isobel but didn't volunteer her given name. She hadn't yet allowed Alton to use it. Affording his sister that privilege would be awkward.

"Miss Walsh, allow me to introduce Mr. Daly." Alton's request relieved her from any further reply.

"Pleased to meet you." Phoebe smiled with genuine warmth.

"Delighted, my dear." He bowed.

"Miss Walsh's father is also Irish."

"Is that so?" Mr. Daly beamed. "What county is he from?"

"Kilkenny. His parents brought him to America when he was a boy."

"Ah, yes. The Great Hunger sent many of the Irish across the water." He shook his head. "What a horrible loss of life. I was but a young child myself, when my parents brought me over."

"I'm sorry if I reminded you of bad memories."

"As I said, I was only small."

Although he shrugged, Phoebe thought she saw shadows chase across his face. She nodded. "My father remembers very little about Ireland, but he vividly recalls the sea passage. That's when he lost his mother and younger brother."

He shook his head, his expression grave. "How tragic."

"Yes." Phoebe recalled where she was. "What am I thinking, unburdening myself on you?"

His eyes softened. "I was interested."

"That's kind of you, but I shouldn't bring up such a topic at a party. I'm not very good at light chatter, I'm afraid."

He smiled. "That makes two of us."

Alton turned to Phoebe. "It's time to go in to dine. May I accompany you?"

"Yes, thank you." How ironic that the man she'd avoided now seemed a refuge.

She allowed him to lead her into the dining room, where dark paneling and cut crystal gleamed in the candlelight.

"Mother placed you beside me." His expression informed her that the arrangement suited him fine.

Alton's attentiveness during the meal shielded Phoebe in a situation she would have otherwise found uncomfortable. Her mother's training also helped her hold her own. Isobel occupied the chair on her other side, which proved a great benefit. The woman could carry an entire conversation by herself. Phoebe only needed to smile and acknowledge a comment once in a while.

"How nice that you hit it off with Mr. Daly and his wife." Isobel raised her water glass as if in tribute.

Phoebe smiled. "I enjoyed meeting them."

"They are among my favorite people."

"I can understand why." Phoebe glanced down the table. The Dalys, seated beside her parents, laughed at something her father had said.

"They are the salt of the earth." Isobel sipped from her water glass. "You would never guess how important they are."

"Important?"

"Yes, of course. Mr. Daly has quite a head for business. He salvaged a failing silver mine, produced a fortune in copper, and founded the town of Anaconda for the miners. Not bad for someone who started as a paper boy."

"He seems so humble."

"Doesn't he? It must be his Irish roots." Isobel lifted a bite of crème brûlée to her mouth.

Alton leaned toward Phoebe, on her other side. "I'm glad you and my sister are enjoying one another's company. Would you like me to invite her to accompany us on a tour of the garden after supper?"

"That would be wonderful." Alton was unlikely to press her for an answer with his sister present. Phoebe would welcome a respite from the social gathering, although she was enjoying it more than she'd anticipated.

Alton repeated his invitation to Isobel.

She smiled. "That sounds nice."

Servants cleared the dessert dishes away and brought a tray bearing gold-edged demitasse cups and an elaborate coffee carafe. Phoebe sipped the spiced and sweetened beverage, and warmth uncurled within her.

Isobel launched into conversation with the man on her other side, leaving Phoebe momentarily adrift. Alton turned to her. "Tell me, what do you think of Prescott Manor?"

She chose a neutral response, rather than saying that its elegance felt suffocating. "A person could get lost in it."

He laughed. "That happens sometimes. The manor might seem imposing, but it's a home like any other."

"It's beautiful."

"My parents would be gratified you think so. Building and furnishing it was a labor of love for them." He drained his cup. "If you are finished, we should take that walk. I'm afraid we've missed the sunset."

"That's all right. I like gardens at night."

"They have their appeal." His gaze lingered on her face. "However, we must invite you over to see it properly by daylight."

After they made their excuses, Alton led Phoebe and Isobel

from the dining room. They left the manor by a side door and followed a stone path to the garden. Isobel, ephemeral in her white taffeta gown, walked a little ahead of them. The wind had risen, making the trees hiss, but a stone wall sheltered the beds. Light from the windows merged with the glow of the oil lamp Alton held. Irises and snapdragons stood at attention. Rose bushes nodded beside the path, but another scent overlaid their musky fragrance. Phoebe breathed deeply. "What is that heavenly smell?"

Isobel laughed. "Everyone asks." She waved toward a vine with trumpet-shaped blossoms glowing iridescent white. "It's moonflower. The blossoms open all night and close during the day. Winter kills the plants, but they come back each spring. It wouldn't be summer without them."

Alton bent his head toward Phoebe. "Do you have a favorite flower?"

"I've never wanted to choose one." The sight of wild roses made her catch her breath. She loved seeing blue flags wave in the wind. Cheery yellow bells never failed to make her smile. The butter-and-egg flower fascinated her. She adored the shy violets and the pink bitterroot faces peeping from among the grasses. Phoebe thought of the many other blossoms she'd noticed while riding and shook her head. "How can anyone decide between them all?"

Alton stepped in front of her. "You will hold a mixed bouquet, I suppose."

Although he spoke lightly, Phoebe caught the serious note in his voice. Maybe coming out with him had been a bad idea. She'd imagined that Alton's sister would walk closer and talk more. Isobel had fallen silent, however, and she'd moved farther ahead on the path.

Unwilling to discuss weddings or their trappings with Alton, Phoebe said nothing. With shadows hiding his face, she couldn't read his reaction. He sighed, and after a moment, shifted out of her way. They continued along the path.

"My parents will want to leave soon." Phoebe made the polite disclaimer, although her parents hadn't shown any inclination to depart. "We should go back."

"Of course." He turned at once.

Phoebe realized with a sense of shock that she had misjudged Alton. He hadn't pressed her over his remark about a bouquet. Nor had he taken advantage of the situation, although his sister had given him ample opportunity to do so.

As if suddenly aware of the need to act as a chaperone, Isobel hurried to catch up to them. Alton held the side door open, and she went inside first.

Alton, holding the door with one hand and the oil lamp with the other, watched Phoebe draw near to him. "With the moonlight haloing your hair, you look like an angel."

She smiled. "That's kind of you to say, but I am a mere mortal." She had to admit, after Will's mixed signals, being with a man who knew his own mind felt better. She was the one who didn't know what she wanted. Alton's interest in her, so annoying before, now soothed the heartache of Will's rejection.

Would it be so terrible to allow Alton to court her? Maybe that would help her decide whether to marry him or not. Words leaped to the tip of her tongue, but she retained enough sense to hold them back. No woman should make such a decision under the influence of starlight.

She passed close to him in the doorway, aware of his intense regard.

"May I call on you soon?" he murmured.

"That would be fun." Phoebe kept her tone casual. She didn't dare look at him, in case he read her face. What might he see there? Confusion would peer out at him, certainly, but also a half-acknowledged longing ready to betray her.

CHAPTER TEN

WILL HELD UP THE SEVERED END of a length of barbed wire, his hands protected by thick leather gloves "What do you make of this?" He squinted from the glare behind Matt, crouched beside him in the bunchgrass.

Matt whistled. "Maybe certain ranchers object to fencing the range."

"Some do, but folks hereabouts are law-abiding." He'd rather not come across a cow sliced up from tangling with the wire. Will coiled the strand he held and slung it over the nearest fence post.

"Give me a minute, and I'll help you." Matt rummaged in his saddlebag and pulled out a pair of leather gloves.

"Thanks." Will took up another cut strand, careful to avoid the barbs. "Only yesterday, Con mentioned reports of rustlers in the area. I'm more inclined to think it's their work."

Matt followed behind him, rolling up a third wire. "Supposing you're right, what do we do about it?"

"Pray we catch them in the act, but not if they outnumber us." Will draped another coil over the fence post.

The corners of Matt's lips ticked upward. "Agreed."

"Other than that, we can double the number of men riding herd." Will rubbed his chin. "I hate to do it, but it might become necessary."

"I wouldn't mind standing an extra watch with you." Matt chuckled. "Just so long as you're not taken by the urge to hum."

Will laughed. There was no need to explain. "Davis's

humming wouldn't be so bad if he could carry a tune in a bucket."

Matt dissolved into laughter. "He does it without thinking, which makes it somehow worse. How can you be mad at a person when he doesn't know he's afflicting you?"

Will sobered. "It wouldn't be easy. As for taking extra shifts, everyone works hard enough already."

"You won't see me complaining." Matt dropped his wound-up wire over the others. They started back together for the last two. "This is the best job I've ever landed."

"You have a good attitude."

"It's not too tough. Con's a fair man, and he runs a good operation."

"That's my assessment, too." Will glanced sideways at him. "Ranching is steady work. In my book, that beats mining all hollow."

"I can't argue with you on that head, either." Matt narrowed his eyes, as if caught by memory. "There's a draw to mining, but it wears off quick enough if things don't go your way."

"That sounds like the voice of experience." The task completed, Will headed for the wire on the other side of the cut.

Matt kept pace. "Let's just say I'm a better ranch hand than miner."

"I'd love to hear the tale, someday."

Matt's eyes gleamed. "I hope you have a high tolerance for boredom."

"I'll take my chances."

"I never took you for a rash man."

Will laughed. "Mining must be more interesting than that."

Matt tilted his head. "Colorful is a better word."

Will reached the second fence post and looped the wire in

his hands over it. "I don't expect you to reveal all your secrets."

"I bet I could trust you not to condemn me for them."

"I'm the last person qualified to throw stones at others." Will pushed his guilt over kissing Phoebe, only to reject her, out of his mind. "We'd better head back. Cooky waits supper for no man."

Phoebe stopped her horse in a hilltop meadow, pausing to take in the view. Lupines waved above the green grass all around her. Gentle swells fell away below her, dipping where a gulch cut through them. She could see across the valley, where a rise bumped upward into foothills. The sky rolled out fleecy clouds but sporadic rays glistened on the snow remaining on the mountains. The sun stood high in the sky, warning Phoebe that she'd stayed out too long. Ma worried about her on the open range, but while riding Nutmeg, Phoebe felt safe. The sure-footed mare never gave her cause for alarm, even on the narrowest of paths, and could outrun the other horses on the ranch. Phoebe trusted her own skill at riding to protect her. She could see a long way out here, which would make it hard for anyone to creep up.

Now and again, Phoebe felt someone watching while she stayed close to home. Her hackles might rise even in the safety of the barn. She had no control of when the old fear would crop up, but she couldn't let it control her. Ma considered riding along the road safer, but Phoebe tried not to do it alone. In her opinion, a person with evil intent would more likely frequent the road than the open range.

Ma knew all this, but fear still gripped her whenever Phoebe ventured off the ranch. Phoebe preferred not to cause her mother concern. After years of roaming where she wished, however, confining her riding to the ranch would be too hard.

Phoebe and her mother had reached an unspoken compromise. Her mother wouldn't worry about her as long as she didn't remain gone so long that it forced Ma to inquire after her.

Phoebe stroked Nutmeg's shoulder. "Come on, girl. Time to go home."

Needing no further instructions, the mare swung in the direction of the ranch and set off at a brisk trot. Phoebe smiled, knowing that her horse was anticipating the usual treat at the end of a ride. Nutmeg possessed a sweet tooth. She preferred apples and sugar cubes, but she would accept carrots and oats.

Phoebe's stomach grumbled that she'd missed the midday meal. Ma would worry. Phoebe put Nutmeg through her paces and into a gallop. The wind snatched Phoebe's breath away and tugged strands of her hair free. As they neared the ranch, she slowed her horse and shaded her eyes. A rider had turned off the road onto their drive. Phoebe couldn't identify their visitor at this distance, but she could guess it was Alton. Her stomach sank. They would arrive at the house around the same time. If she hurried, she might slip into the barn before he caught sight of her. She would rather not meet company—no matter how annoying—with her hair flying wild like some hoyden. Feeling slovenly did nothing for a woman's confidence, and she would need to rely on hers when meeting with Alton.

She gave Nutmeg her head, and the mare's hooves struck out at a fast clip. The ground sped past in a dizzying rush. The rider picked up speed, also. It seemed he meant to race her. Aware that he would win, Phoebe slowed her horse.

Alton hailed her from astride his horse as she arrived at the barn. Impeccable in a tweed riding jacket, breeches, and shiny boots, he stared at her. "Miss Walsh? I can hardly believe my eyes. Is that really you?"

"Yes, of course it is." Phoebe couldn't restrain her irritation at the disdain in his voice. She drew a deep breath. "Hello, Mr. Prescott. We didn't expect you today."

"Sorry I stopped by without warning, but maybe it's for the best."

"Why do you say that?"

"Otherwise, I wouldn't have seen you riding astride, and in *that outfit*."

Phoebe gazed at him in horror. How could she have thought she'd misjudged him? Staring at her with that judgmental expression made him look every bit as insufferable as she'd imagined. "There's nothing wrong with my clothes."

"You can't be serious. No decent woman would sit on a horse like that. Nor would she compromise her femininity in a split skirt."

With an effort, Phoebe held onto her temper. "A regular skirt would be immodest. As for riding astride, that is safer than using a sidesaddle."

"Such a posture is indelicate for a woman." He continued smiling, but his snippy tone gave him away.

"I beg to disagree." Phoebe lifted her chin.

"You have strong opinions, but I'm sure you'll see reason."

"It's not unreasonable for a woman to want to sit securely on a horse. No man would put up with a sidesaddle for so much as an hour. I'm on horseback a great deal more than that."

"You ride too often. It gives you strange ideas."

Phoebe waited to reply until she could do so in an even voice. "I'm sorry you think so."

"Let's not argue." Alton belatedly removed his hat. "I came to see you because I couldn't stay away."

Phoebe restrained a laugh. "From your greeting, that's hard to imagine."

"Consider this from my point of view. No man wants a

woman he's courting to parade about in such a wanton manner."

"We aren't courting." She emphasized every word.

"We are near to it." He shook his head. "I must insist that you use a sidesaddle and spend more time in feminine pursuits, if we are to court."

Phoebe lifted her chin. "I have an answer for you."

"Oh really?" His eyes gleamed. "Perhaps you should wait to give it until you've thought a little longer."

"There's no need."

"I have a lot to offer." He displayed his even teeth in what might pass for a smile. "Turn me down this time, and I won't return again."

"I am honored by your interest but must regretfully decline." Phoebe trotted out the polite wording she knew by heart. "It's become quite clear that we would never suit."

He winced. "You've refused me. No need to drive it home."

"I'm sorry to hurt you, but—"

"Say no more." He held up a hand. "I'll be on my way."

Phoebe nodded, tears springing to her eyes. Before he could see them, she turned her horse and began circling the barnyard. Nutmeg needed to cool down, and so did she. Alton might misinterpret her tears, if he saw them. She cried mainly for herself, since this would probably be her last admirer.

His retreating hoofbeats drove home the truth. She'd wondered while the moon was shining if settling down with Alton would be all that bad. In the harsh light of day, she could see that living with him would have made her miserable. He wouldn't have been happy either. Thank goodness that she'd shattered his dream of her, simply by being herself.

"Phoebe, is something wrong?" Ma's voice broke into her thoughts. She sounded winded, as if she'd rushed from the house.

"No, Ma. Everything is as it should be."

"I saw Mr. Prescott and you talking, and then he rode off."

"I'll come in after I take care of Nutmeg." Phoebe sighed. "Let's talk then."

Not excited about explaining to her mother, she lingered longer than necessary over cooling Nutmeg down. Afterwards, Phoebe groomed her horse thoroughly. When she could delay no more, she headed for the house.

In the kitchen, Ma glanced up from pouring tea. "Care for a cup?"

"Thank you." Phoebe carried her cup to the scrubbed oak table in the center of the room.

After a moment, her mother set the tea tray between them. Ma lowered herself into a ladder-back chair across from Phoebe. "What happened?"

"I refused him." Phoebe went straight to the point.

Ma's shoulders sagged. "How disappointing."

"I know, Ma. I tried." Tears sprang to her eyes. "I wanted to make it work, but I just couldn't."

"What happened?"

Phoebe dabbed at her eyes. "Alton didn't want me to ride as much, and only with a sidesaddle."

Ma stared at her. "He said that?"

She nodded. "Oh, and he thinks that a split skirt isn't respectable."

"I did warn you not to wear one anywhere but our ranch."

"That's where I was." Phoebe sniffed. "Can I help it that he showed up without notifying us first? And a split skirt is more modest than bloomers."

Ma frowned. "I hope you won't take up wearing those outlandish garments. That aside, Mr. Prescott overstepped by addressing you on personal matters. He doesn't have the right."

"I answered him back, and I'm not sorry." Phoebe swallowed a mouthful of warm tea, letting it soothe her.

"Good for you. If I'd been present, he'd have gotten an earful."

Phoebe stared at her mother. "Really?"

"Why do you even ask?" Ma looked shocked. "Of course, I'd have defended you."

"Even if it meant driving away a potential husband?"

Ma gazed at her in silence. "Forgive me, Phoebe. I've pressured you to find a man to marry when I should have trusted God to provide for you."

"It's all right, Ma. I'm just glad you can see that."

"I know why I did it. I've been feeling guilty about cutting you off from your heritage."

"That wasn't your fault. You didn't turn away from your parents. They turned away from you."

"I know, but I can't help feeling to blame. If I hadn't run off with your father, they wouldn't have disowned me. I wanted you to have the lifestyle you lost before you were born."

"I don't care about wealth or status."

"Obviously not, since you refused Alton Prescott."

"I had to, Ma." Phoebe took her mother's hand. "I know you want only good for me, but please let me live my own life."

"I'll try my best." Ma smiled. "Although, I doubt I'm ready for what that will look like."

Phoebe climbed into the landau with her parents and brothers. No clouds marred the clear sky, and it was only a couple of miles to Uncle Con's ranch. They didn't really need the carriage, but her parents liked to use it on special occasions. Pa enjoyed taking it out, anyway. Phoebe suspected that this was one of the endearing ways he pampered her mother. The beatific smile that spread over his face as he handed Ma into the carriage gave him away.

Pa had put the top down, which meant that her brothers couldn't quarrel over who rode outside in the jump seat. They proceeded to vie for the unoccupied seat in the driving box. Pa ended the contest by declaring it Quinn's turn. Murphy crowded into the landau and plunked into the empty spot beside Phoebe. He folded his arms with a huff. "It's my turn."

Phoebe hid a smile. Tufts of ginger hair escaping from beneath Murphy's bowler gave him the appearance of an incensed squirrel in fancy dress.

Ma stared out the window as if fascinated by the rolling grassland she saw every day, but her lips twitched. "Be that as it may, I'm certain you will be happy for your brother."

Murphy looked anything but joyful, but he was wise enough to say nothing.

"Cheer up, Murph." Phoebe nudged her youngest brother. "It will be your turn on the way back."

"Only if his attitude improves." Ma awarded Murphy the glare she reserved for such moments.

Murphy subsided against the back rest.

Pa called to the horses, and the landau lurched into motion.

Quinn twisted and looked down from the driving seat at his brother. Triumph stamped his features. He opened his mouth, but Phoebe shook her head before he could speak.

Quinn closed his mouth and faced forward again.

Phoebe released her pent breath. Listening to her brothers fuss at one another did not appeal in the least. Her nerves were too raw after yesterday's confrontation with Alton. Thank goodness that Ma understood why she'd rejected him. Otherwise, Phoebe would have been in a worse state today.

Ma raised her field glasses, a cherished gift from Pa. She peered out the window, exclaiming with enthusiasm. Phoebe leaned against the leather seat back, letting the flow of words wash over her. "What beautiful markings! How lucky to spot an owl at this hour. I've never seen a hummingbird with such intense colors."

The creak and sway of the carriage in concert with the clopping of hooves lulled Phoebe. She drifted in and out of a curious dream. She was attending a party at Prescott Manor. Alton, at first solicitous, began mocking her before his guests. The landau lurched, jerking her into wakefulness. Phoebe sat upright, determined not to doze off again. The incident with Alton must have upset her more than she'd known. To be misunderstood and mischaracterized cut to the core. Alton had all but accused her of being disreputable. How dare he tell her how to ride, what to wear, and the way to occupy her time.

She'd had a lucky escape, Phoebe felt certain. Remembering how close she'd come to accepting Alton's suit made her heart race. She'd always considered herself strong, but some weakness must have swayed her thinking. It felt like loneliness. How ridiculous. She lived with her family. Unless… Maybe she felt a different kind of loneliness. By Uncle Con's assessment, she numbered among those who should marry. Could he be right?

She pulled her thoughts from their course and focused on the present moment with Murphy slumbering beside her. His face, tender in sleep, had lost the roundness of childhood. He resembled their mother but also had a look of Pa about him. His lips moved in silent speech. She smiled. He was probably arguing with Quinn in his dreams.

Outside the window, a herd of antelope displayed their white hindquarters as they bounded away from the carriage.

Phoebe never tired of seeing the graceful creatures run at what seemed impossible speeds. The day was young, but already heat shimmered above the plain. Thank goodness they were going to Uncle Con's place, which was cooler than their own. His ranch house sat close to the Bitterroot River with windows situated to catch the wind off the water.

Would Will come to Uncle Con's birthday dinner? It seemed likely. The expectation of seeing him again stirred a familiar ache that no river breeze could cool.

CHAPTER ELEVEN

THE CARRIAGE VEERED OFF THE ROAD and rolled down the long drive. The two-story ranch house Uncle Con had built came into view. The clapboard siding shone white in the sun. Green shutters folded back from casement windows that looked out toward the river. Phoebe spotted Fiona on the balcony above the porch. She waved, spun about, and hurried inside. Phoebe pictured her cousin running through the house as she called out that their guests had arrived.

The landau rolled to a stop in front of the porch. The front door burst open, and the whole family poured out. Fiona beamed and met Phoebe's eyes as she hurried down the steps. Her brother, Richard, followed right behind her. At fourteen, he'd already surpassed Fiona in height. Eight-year-old Wilhelmina, whom everyone called Willie, helped her younger brother, Otto, down the steps. Aunt Elsa waited in the shade beside the porch pillar Uncle Con was leaning against.

After yesterday's upset, Phoebe hadn't felt like attending Uncle Con's birthday dinner, but she'd come for his sake. Gazing into the smiling faces before her, Phoebe was glad she'd pushed past her reluctance.

Pa called to the horses, and the landau shuddered to a halt. Ma debarked first, and then it was Phoebe's turn.

Fiona rushed to greet her. "It feels like ages since I've seen you."

Phoebe laughed. "I've missed you, too." She fielded Richard's embrace, and then Willie's before bending down to listen to Otto, who kept tugging her skirt.

His eyes gleamed. "It's Pa's birthday today!"

"Yes, it is." Phoebe smiled. Otto's sweet reminder was enough to restore her balance. She picked him up. "Oomph!"

He giggled.

"You're getting too big to carry, little man."

His forehead creased. "But I'm only five."

Phoebe held back a smile. "I'm sure I can lift you for another year."

"Come inside, everyone." Aunt Elsa waved them toward the door. "It's hot out here."

Pa and Uncle Con drove away in the carriage while everyone else went inside. Pa could afford to hire a coachman and groom, but he enjoyed driving and looking after the horses and carriage himself. Phoebe could guess that he also relished the chance to talk in the barn with Uncle Con. Smiling, she started up the steps with Otto in her arms.

Fiona fell in beside her. "You're the first to arrive."

"Who else is coming?"

"Kate's family should arrive soon. Uncle Christoph is bringing Oma Wilhelmina and some of my relatives on my mother's side. Several of the neighbors will also attend."

"What about Liberty's family?"

Fiona frowned. "They can't make it this year. Uncle Shane is officiating at a wedding, and one of Liberty's friends is the bride."

Uncle Con's birthday always drew a large gathering. Thank goodness that Phoebe's parents had insisted on turning out early. She would have time to adjust to the crowd before the noise level grew. In the parlor, Phoebe surrendered Otto to Willie, who occupied her brother with a set of building blocks.

Phoebe settled on the sofa. "I see that our brothers have

vanished, as usual."

Fiona smiled. "They'll show up for supper. I hope you're hungry. We're having beef roulade with potato dumplings and red cabbage, and there's chocolate cake."

"That sounds wonderful." Phoebe's stomach kept informing her that she'd skipped the midday meal. The ambitious menu explained why Aunt Elsa had hurried toward the kitchen. Ma had gone with her, carrying three-year-old Meg. Ma liked entertaining Fiona's youngest sister, which freed Aunt Elsa to cook. Phoebe would offer to help soon, but she needed to catch her breath before she entered the fray.

"Would you like iced tea, and maybe a bite to eat?"

Phoebe smiled at Fiona's perfect manners. They came naturally. "Yes, please."

"I'll be right back."

"You don't need to wait on me." Phoebe sat forward, ready to stand.

"Yes, I do. "Fiona waved her back down. "You look pale."

Phoebe subsided. "Riding in the carriage always gives me a strange sensation of movement afterwards. At least I'm not given to travel sickness."

Fiona made a face. "Don't remind me about that. Motion sickness was the bane of my existence when I was little."

"I'm glad you've outgrown it."

"Mostly, anyway. I wouldn't guarantee how I'd pass a rough journey."

"Step aside." Katerina appeared behind her in the doorway. "If you'd like food and drink."

"You startled me." Fiona stepped out of the way.

Katerina carried in a tray laden with tall glasses of tea. Wearing a blue apron that matched the color of her eyes, she looked fresh and lovely. "Hello, Phoebe. I'd have greeted you with everyone else, but I was stirring something on the stove."

Phoebe wasn't surprised to hear that. She shared Aunt Elsa's passion for cooking. "It's good to see you. How are you doing?"

"Very well." Dimples peeked from Katerina's cheeks. "I'm here while Mr. Canfield works with my horse."

The news brought a spark of jealousy that Phoebe immediately doused. "Is he making progress?"

"I don't think he's started yet." Katerina extended a glass of tea to Phoebe. "We only arrived a week ago."

"Thank you." Phoebe accepted the glass and took a long drink of the sweetened tea. The whole family went to a lot of trouble for the chunks of ice tinkling in the amber liquid. Whenever the river froze over during the winter, the men gathered to cut blocks from the surface. She helped to salt the slabs and store them in the ice house. Packed in straw, they lasted through the summer.

Katerina offered a glass to Fiona. "Where are the boys? I brought tea for them."

"I'm sorry you bothered." Fiona lowered her glass to the porcelain coaster embellished with roses on the table beside her. "They always take off together. I have no idea what they get up to. We won't see them until supper time."

"I should have known. My brothers were the same with their cousins." Katerina placed a plate of sausage strudel with mustard sauce on the table beside Phoebe. "Elsa thought you might need a little something to tide you over."

Phoebe did her best not to salivate. "Please thank her for me."

"I will." Katerina smiled. "I wonder—would you show me sometime how you ride so well?"

Phoebe chose her words carefully. "A lot of my skill comes

from time in the saddle, and there's no way to demonstrate that."

"Oh." Katerina looked crestfallen. "I hoped you could help me."

"I can watch you ride and give you advice, if you like."

Katerina brightened. "That would be wonderful."

"It's settled, then. We're going home tomorrow, but not until later in the day. Do you want to ride out early? That's when it's coolest."

"Yes, let's." Katerina smiled. "That way, we'll have plenty of time."

"Do you care if I invite myself along?" Fiona asked.

"You're more than welcome." Phoebe and Katerina spoke at the same time.

They all broke into laughter.

"Thanks so much." Katerina picked up the tray with its extra glasses and left the room.

Phoebe bit into a buttery crust filled with sausage, apples, and onions. She sighed.

Fiona chuckled. "You look pleased with yourself."

"I am, for having such a wonderful cook for an aunt."

"Ma makes wonderful food. Your own mother is skillful in the kitchen, also."

"That's how she won Pa over." Phoebe laughed. "According to Ma, anyway. Pa tells a different story."

"He adores your mother. I don't think he'd care if she cooked like Aunt Bry."

Phoebe giggled. "That's a naughty comparison."

"But it's true, right?" Fiona grinned. "Aunt Bry would be the first to confess that she's a terrible cook."

Phoebe reached for another delicious morsel. "I suspect that Aunt Bry does better in the kitchen than she lets on."

"Maybe, but she's quite convincing. How well do you

cook?"

"Ma is better at that sort of thing than me, but I can scramble eggs or boil potatoes when called upon."

Fiona nodded. "My mother teaches me what she knows, but Willie is the one who inherited her knack. I want to marry someone with buckets of money so we can hire a cook."

"You must interview all your admirers to make sure."

"I can see me now." Fiona snickered. "Sir, I'm honored by your offer, but I simply cannot accept anyone who lacks sufficient money to avoid burnt bacon and underdone potatoes."

"Hmm…I wonder what sort of response you'd receive." Phoebe stood, smiling. "I'm going to offer my help in the kitchen."

"You're removing my excuse to linger." Fiona jumped to her feet. "I'd better come along."

They'd reached the entryway when Fiona clutched Phoebe's arm. "Wait! I hear hoofbeats." Fiona rushed to the front door and threw it open.

Phoebe caught up with her on the porch, where she was waving madly.

Uncle Nick's wagon rattled down the drive behind the sweetest team of matched black Morgan horses Phoebe had ever laid eyes on. Pa and Uncle Con strode from the barn. Aunt Elsa emerged from the house with Meg still on her hip. Ma and Katerina trailed behind her.

The wagon drew up, and Katie piled out with her family. After a round of greetings, the men turned toward the barn. The women and children followed Aunt Elsa into the house. They'd barely gone inside, when Christoph's wagon rolled up.

In the chaos that ensued, Phoebe retreated to the kitchen. When Aunt Elsa returned, she put her to work mixing the potato dumplings. Fiona assembled a salad and Katie set the table. No one but Aunt Elsa was allowed to touch the beef roulade, as Uncle Con's favorite dish must be exactly the way he liked it. Oma Wilhelmina, with Ma her willing helper, added loving touches to the chocolate cake. The frosting could not be plain but must wear a crown of whipped cream, glazed cherries, and chocolate shavings. The confection emerged a masterpiece, as all present agreed.

Surrounded by her family and immersed in the task of celebrating her uncle, Phoebe lost the angst that had dogged her. Alton's insults fell away, and even her heartache over Will slipped from her. She was laughing when she ran into him in the parlor.

<hr>

"Careful!" Will caught Phoebe against him, preventing her fall. They rocked together for a long moment. Restraining the impulse to keep on holding her, he loosened his grasp. "Sorry for stepping into your path."

She straightened away from him. "It wasn't your fault. I should have looked where I was going."

"No harm done." He wouldn't count damage to his equilibrium. The change in her appearance rivetted his attention. The woman before him couldn't look more vibrant. The careworn and cautious Phoebe he normally saw was nowhere in evidence. A suspicion niggled at him, and he couldn't gainsay it. Maybe she only looked that way around him. "Where were you going in such a hurry?"

"Only to retrieve the dishes Fiona and I forgot to remove earlier. Here they are." She gestured toward two empty glasses and a plate holding a tiny, footed bowl. "I was trying to remove them before anyone came in."

"You would have made it, if not for me."

"Why aren't you with Uncle Con?"

He shrugged. "I don't need a ranch tour, and your uncle

was doing fine without me."

She laughed. "That sounds like Uncle Con, all right."

When had he last seen that mischievous light in Phoebe's eyes? He couldn't remember. Will forced his mind back to the topic of discussion. "I thought I'd wait inside. Con and Elsa don't expect me to knock, but I like to do it anyway. No one came when I did, though."

"I didn't hear you. We were making a lot of noise in the kitchen."

"So I gathered." He smiled. "Since the door was standing open, I walked in and headed for the parlor, only to collide with you."

Phoebe's cheeks turned a becoming shade of pink. "I was in a hurry. I still am, for that matter. Dinner is almost ready."

"Before you rush off—is there anything I can do?"

Her eyes widened. "You're offering to help?"

"Is that so unusual?"

"You surprised me, that's all. Tell Aunt Elsa, if you want to help. I don't know what else she needs."

"I imagine she's still in the kitchen?"

She nodded, a bemused look on her face.

Did he chip in so rarely? Maybe she looked so startled because kitchen work normally fell to women. Will couldn't shake the uncomfortable suspicion that he'd been entirely too self-absorbed.

Katerina looked in from the doorway. "Did I hear someone offering assistance?"

Will studied her, never quite sure what he was getting into with Katerina. "I did."

She offered him a wide smile. "We're a couple of chairs short in the dining room. Would you mind carrying two in from the library?"

"Not at all." He turned to Phoebe. "If you'll excuse me…"

"Of course." The guarded expression had returned to her face.

Will paused before turning away. The light in Phoebe's eyes had died, and she'd lost the spring to her step. What could have caused such a drastic transformation in her? This was neither the time nor place to delve into the matter, but Will wouldn't let it go. Something was wrong with Phoebe, and he couldn't ignore the horrifying suspicion it had to do with him.

Phoebe tried to muster her lost joy. She didn't want to detract from the festive atmosphere in the kitchen. She could swear Will had gazed at Katerina as if besotted. Maybe she'd imagined it. Possessing a fertile imagination had led her astray before. If her suspicions proved true, it would be hard to bear, but Phoebe would wish them well.

Aunt Elsa glanced at Phoebe, and her forehead puckered, but she didn't ask if anything was amiss, thankfully. Aunt Elsa picked up a potholder and lifted the lid of the cast-iron pot in the warming oven at the back of the stove. She waited for the cloud of steam to escape before plunging a wooden spoon into the pot. "Phoebe, please let everyone know that it's time to eat." She spoke without turning her head.

Phoebe escaped from the confines of the kitchen and into the fresh air through the back door. She followed the path past the garden, with its neat rows fenced in to keep the deer out. Following the sound of voices led her to the riverbank, where Uncle Con was pointing out the fish traps Uncle Nick had taught him to make. "It's ingenious, really. The fish swim into the opening but can't figure out how to escape."

Phoebe waved to him. "Supper is ready."

Uncle Con's gaze rested on her for a long moment.

Phoebe started back to the house, feeling like the Pied Piper leading the small crowd behind her.

Uncle Con caught up to her. "Is something ailing you, *cailín*?"

"This is no time to trouble yourself about me."

He huffed, sounding exactly like Murphy. "Perhaps you think I become less of an uncle on my birthday."

Phoebe smiled. "It's not important."

"Then you won't mind telling me why you are so sad."

She let out an impatient sigh. "You're impossible, did you know that?"

He quirked an eyebrow. "Others may have informed me of that before."

"Since you insist on intruding into personal matters, I had a falling out with Alton Prescott." Phoebe fobbed him off with a half-truth. Her conscience pained her, but admitting her worries about Will and Katerina was unthinkable.

He stopped and turned her to face him. "Alton Prescott—is he the fellow, I noticed hanging around you at the wedding?"

"Oh, my." Phoebe touched her warm cheeks. Had he seen Alton follow her into the sanctuary? "That's the one."

"He's too much of a precious pearl for you, Phoebe. You need a man who knows how to work with his hands."

"You don't need to persuade me that Alton and I are wrong for one another. I'll admit I wasn't entirely convinced at first."

"What soured you on the idea?"

"He proved that he's not really interested in me. He only wanted the person he imagined me to be."

"I see." Uncle Con's arm encircled her shoulder. "Never mind, darlin'. You'll find someone who appreciates the treasure you are."

Phoebe smiled, her spirits lifting. "You do have the gift of blarney."

He tapped her under the chin. "I'm entirely serious."

Phoebe returned to the house with a better mindset. The

dining room was transformed from its earlier chaotic state. The long table fairly groaned under the weight of numerous plates, cutlery, drinking vessels, and serving dishes. Daylight filtered through voile curtains at the tall windows. Candelabras on either end waited to be lit, should the festivities carry on into evening.

The excitement of the guests was contagious. Phoebe succumbed to it once more, despite the sight of Will deep in conversation with Katerina. He talked to Katerina so easily, yet chose his words with Phoebe.

What if the haranguing Phoebe sometimes gave him was to blame? She hadn't held back in the church garden.

Phoebe pushed the riddle away and set her mind on honoring her uncle. That's what she was there to do, not obsess over Will.

"Phoebe, allow me to introduce Matt Malone, our newest ranch hand." Aunt Elsa's voice interrupted her thoughts. "Mr. Malone, this is my niece, Miss Phoebe Walsh. I've placed you beside one another at the table."

Phoebe looked up into hazel eyes rimmed by dark eyelashes. She didn't feel particularly interested in men at the moment, but she couldn't help noticing his handsomeness. "It's nice to meet you, Mr. Malone."

He smiled. "My pleasure."

"I thought you might want to discuss horses, cows, or..." Aunt Elsa waved her hand in a vague gesture that could have encompassed all manner of beasts. "If you'll pardon me, I'm needed in the kitchen."

Phoebe watched her aunt rush off while holding back her mirth. She didn't blame her for not knowing what a ranch hand would want to talk about. Apart from Will, who had a special place in Uncle Con's heart, she probably didn't see many of them. The ranch hands mostly kept to the barn, the outbuildings, or the bunkhouse, unless they were out on the range.

Matt's eyes gleamed. "Was your aunt joking, or are you actually interested in livestock?"

"Is it so unusual for a woman?"

He laughed. "I've never inquired on the matter."

Phoebe raised her chin. "Well, this one is."

"Good for you, speaking up for yourself."

Detecting no sarcasm in his tone, she glanced at him in surprise. His expression held admiration. "Thank you. I prefer horses but have an affinity for most animals."

"That's to your credit." He laid a hand on the ladderback chair at the place Aunt Elsa had indicated for her. "May I seat you?"

She smiled. "Yes, thank you."

Matt settled her at the table, and then claimed the place beside her.

She waited a moment before speaking. "How new are you to the ranch?"

"I've only been here a couple of weeks."

His reply confirmed her suspicions. Uncle Con must have taken Matt on when he couldn't hire her. She found it impossible to resent so nice a person for landing the job she'd wanted, though. If a man's character could be measured by his manners, Uncle Con had made a good choice.

Phoebe's skin prickled with the awareness of someone watching. She turned her head and collided with Will's gaze. The room receded, the voices around her fading for a timeless moment. Something passed between them, no less real for being intangible.

Katerina murmured to Will, and he returned his attention to her.

Phoebe dragged her own gaze back to Matt. "How do you like working on the ranch?"

His eyes lit. "It's a dream come true."

"Didn't you work with cattle before this?"

"Off and on, but not at such a well-run spread." He unfolded his napkin. "After failing at gold mining, I was grateful for a steady job."

"I can imagine. My uncles tried their hands at mining early on, when it was easier. Gold miners can still come by a fortune nowadays, but those who search for other metals might do better. Take Marcus Daly, for instance."

A grin spread across his face. "That's no doubt true, but I lack the necessary talent for mining."

She laughed. "At least you're aware of your failing."

"Oh, yes, ma'am." He shook his head. "I learned the painful truth rather thoroughly."

Phoebe's cousin, Richard, dropped into the chair on her other side and leaned toward her. "We're not late, are we?"

Phoebe glanced across the table at her brothers, who were also slipping into chairs. "Almost."

Richard's eyes gleamed with humor. "If we were, it would have been Quinn and Murphy's fault."

Phoebe frowned. "I'm sure I don't want to know why."

"I wouldn't tell you anyway." Richard bent his head toward his sister, Willie, who began chattering on his other side.

Phoebe turned toward Matt, but her gaze snagged on Will's. The seating arrangement was going to be a problem. She glanced away and kept herself from looking back. She couldn't stop his voice, however. She seemed curiously attuned to its cadences. Although Phoebe found Matt interesting, she wasn't sorry when the meal ended. Phoebe waited until the cake plates contained only crumbs before excusing herself. She helped Fiona and Katie clear away dishes, after which she gladly escaped from the party.

Fiona returned to the dining room, but Phoebe opened the

back door and stepped outside for a breath of air. She wouldn't linger long. The fragrance of warmed earth, pine, and lavender drew her to the garden. Phoebe walked between neat beds filled with the feathery fronds of carrots, frilly patches of leaf lettuce, and the spikes of onions. She broke off a lavender wand and rubbed it between her fingers. The scent soothed her, although she'd bruised the flowers to release it. The sun hung low and would soon sink below the mountains. A breeze stirred the leaves in the forest beyond the garden fence, and frogs croaked in the river.

Phoebe retraced her steps to the house with reluctance. She loved her relatives, but lingering in the quiet of nature invigorated her more than celebrating in a noisy room. She reached for the back-door screen but couldn't resist a last glance at the garden.

A figure strode around the corner of the house and turned onto the path toward the barn.

"Will?" Why wasn't he in the dining room, where she'd left him?

He spun about, looking as surprised as she felt. "Phoebe? What are you doing there?"

She started toward him. "I was going to ask you the same thing."

"I'm headed home."

"You're leaving? But the party is in full swing."

He smiled. "That's the best time to go. It's better not to wait until your host is wondering when you'll ever leave."

"You know that wouldn't happen with Uncle Con and Aunt Elsa. They love company, especially yours."

He stopped before her. "I can only abide a party so long. Con knows that."

She nodded. "I'm much the same, which is why I'm out here."

"I hope it doesn't go on too long, for your sake."

"I have an excuse to retire early. I'm taking Katerina riding in the morning."

"I'm not sure that's a good idea." He shook his head. "The neighbors have seen rustlers about lately. If you insist on going out, I'd feel better accompanying you."

Phoebe opened her mouth to argue, but then closed it again. Will was not Alton. Rather than demeaning her as a woman, he could be expressing real concern. Their falling out in the church garden still haunted her. She should watch how she answered, since she didn't want anything else to regret. "If you would like to come along, I'd appreciate it."

"I'll meet you before breakfast, if that works?"

"Yes, thank you." Phoebe marveled at her meek reply. "Meanwhile, I'd better return to the party." She started back.

"Wait, before you go."

Phoebe turned about to face him. "What?"

Color touched his cheeks. "Is anything bothering you? It seemed like it, earlier in the parlor."

Phoebe stepped backward. "I don't want to talk about it."

His face softened. "If you ever change your mind, let me know."

"Thank you." Phoebe left it at that. Confiding her jealous pangs to the man who invoked them was the last thing she planned to do. Even so, it warmed her to know that he'd cared enough to ask.

CHAPTER TWELVE

PHOEBE SLIPPED THROUGH THE COOLNESS OF early morning on her way to look out over the river. The sky lightened and blushed in anticipation of the sun peeking above the mountains. Its rays burst forth, and the barn cast long shadows onto the path at her feet. She emerged into golden light and stepped to the edge of the rise above the water. Birdsong from the trees along the shore swelled in greeting. A rooster crowed, adding a strident note to the wild chorus. She breathed in the fruity scent of willow leaves overladen by the pungency of river water. The aroma never failed to stir memories. She'd spent many happy hours in childhood wading in the shallows, clasping her arms around herself while waves lapped her legs. Watching the wash always made her dizzy, a fact she'd considered great fun.

Phoebe stretched. She'd slept well, which surprised her. Exhaustion must have taken its toll. She usually lay awake following a social event, turning over conversations in her mind. The same thing happened after an upset. She'd spent a bad night after arguing with Alton.

She pulled away from that topic before it consumed her thoughts. Condemnation from someone who professed to admire you took a little getting over.

So did Will, for that matter. He'd made his lack of intentions toward her clear. There was nothing to hold onto now except a dream of her own making. She'd tricked herself into hoping for change, but she could no longer do so. She needed to accept the truth, once and for all. Whatever Will decided about

Katerina, Phoebe needed to let him go.

She squeezed her eyes shut. *Dear God, help me find the strength.*

Her skin prickled, and she opened her eyes.

Footsteps crunched behind her.

Her mouth dry and her heart racing, she spun about. The breath choked from her.

A man strode toward her on the path. He was looking downward, his hat brim shading his face.

Phoebe tensed to run, but then the man raised his head. Morning sunlight bathed Will's face.

Phoebe stared at him in sudden relief. The old fear faded, leaving her shaken. Would she ever be free of it?

He scanned her face. "You look as if you've seen a ghost."

Phoebe clutched her middle. "You startled me."

"Sorry." He came to stand beside her. "You're up early."

"That's my habit."

"Mine, too." He nodded toward the river. "It's never the same."

"I know." She stood beside him in companionable silence, watching ducks float along the river's edge. The birds periodically dove beneath the surface, and then bobbed up again. Every so often, a duck took flight in a flurry of flapping wings.

Phoebe smiled. "I came down here as a child to wade in the shallows. Ma worried I'd fall in. I gave her fits, being so venturesome. She says that I often wandered off."

"That doesn't surprise me."

She glanced sideways at him. "What are you implying?"

The corners of his lips ticked upward. "Only that you have always been lively. You needed a strong hand as a child, from what Con told me. I'm afraid you did not find one."

She glanced at him in suspicion. "Are you saying that I'm spoiled, again?"

"I never called you that, Phoebe. I don't believe it's true. It's a shame your father wasn't present in your life. I'm sure your mother did her best to guide you, but it's hard for one parent to do the work of two."

His words made sense. She must have misunderstood him, before. Phoebe nodded. "I've thought the same, myself. I'm grateful that Rob married Ma and adopted me."

"I'm sure he makes a wonderful father."

"He does."

Silence stretched between them, so comfortable she hated for it to end. Maybe Will felt the same, because a long while passed before he spoke. "When I was a young boy, I used to catch pollywogs in the creek. I wanted to keep them in jars, but Ma made me let them go."

Phoebe smiled, remembering similar episodes with her own brothers. "How wise of her."

"I suppose they couldn't have lived in a glass jar very long."

"Pa taught me to skip stones."

"I learned from my older brother, Caleb. It takes a lot of patience."

Phoebe laughed. "Maybe that's why I wasn't very good at it."

"Caleb and I once threw a log across the creek and competed to see who could cross without falling in. We never expected Sophie to win." His eyes darkened, and he pressed his lips together.

"Is Sophie your sister?"

He glanced away. "No, a neighbor."

Why had mentioning Sophie brought on such a change in

Will? In the space of a heartbeat, he'd gone from relaxed and friendly to cold and distant. Instinct warned her not to question him further.

Some wounds cut deep, as she knew well enough. How could she expect Will to confide his sorrows while she refused him the same privilege? An image of herself crouched over her injury like a miser over gold arose in her mind. Exposing a wound to the air might hurt, and cleansing it certainly would. Freeing herself came at the cost of courage. She pulled in a breath. "When you walked up, I was a little more than startled."

He swung back to her. "I thought as much."

"I don't like to talk about it, but a Salish warrior tried to kidnap me when I was small. He almost carried me off, but two of my uncles stopped him."

"How terrible." Sympathy flooded his face. "Does it haunt you, still?"

"Sometimes. I never know when it will happen. I'll hear footsteps behind me or angry voices—even the smell of smoke from a chimney can bring it on."

"I'm sorry, Phoebe."

"Spukani—the man who tried to take me—he came back and carried off my mother." She wrapped her arms around herself, all at once cold. "I thought I'd lost my ma, but Pa rode out and brought her back. After that, I wondered if Spukani would come for me again."

"No wonder you're jumpy."

"It's been more than a decade. I should be over it." Eddies shimmering on the surface of the river caught her eye. A leaf spun about in the swirling water. "If Spukani wanted to take me, he would already have done so. I know this, but I can't quite convince myself it's true."

His gaze held hers. "Have you told anyone else?"

"No."

"I don't understand why you would carry such a burden all alone."

"I didn't want to trouble my parents, especially not Ma. Spukani has put her through enough."

He shook his head. "I'm certain she'd want to know. Any parent would."

"I never thought about it that way."

"Strength of mind is your virtue, but your independence sometimes gets the better of you."

That seemed true, but she didn't necessarily want Will pointing it out. "You seem particularly aware of my flaws."

"I'm only trying to help. I can't judge, especially in this case." He smiled. "It takes one to know one."

"You might help." She released a sigh. "I'm trying to be less prickly with you."

"I appreciate that. And I'll stop giving you unsolicited advice. Thanks for confiding in me. Why did you, though?"

"Maybe I realized I'm not the only one held captive by the past."

Will's eyes widened, and he glanced away.

She must have struck a nerve. It took no imagination to conclude that Sophie had broken his heart. The pain showed on his face whenever he spoke of her.

"There you are!" Fiona hailed them from the rear doorway of the barn.

"Good morning." Phoebe glanced at Will, who seemed less than pleased with the interruption.

Katerina stepped around Fiona and divided a gaze between Phoebe and Will. If she noticed anything unusual between them, she didn't remark on it. The skirt Katerina wore would require her to use a sidesaddle. How could she possibly expect to ride Diablo from such a precarious position? Phoebe resolved to recommend that she wear a split skirt for riding.

They entered the barn, and Fiona stopped at one of the stalls. What Phoebe took for a chestnut quarter horse pranced inside the box. ""I thought you could ride Sir Boss today. He needs the exercise."

"That's plain." Phoebe looked him over, warily. "Are you sure he's ready for the trail?"

Fiona smiled. "He's a little eager but sweet once he settles down. I'm sure you can handle him. Katerina, you'll ride Miss Buttons."

Phoebe smiled at the name of the mare. It hinted at a mild disposition, while the name of her own horse did not.

"Thank you." Katerina sounded confident, which spoke well for her. She must not fear riding, as Liberty had at first.

Phoebe saddled and bridled Sir Boss. She found Katerina saddling Miss Buttons. Phoebe checked that the cinch was tight. Otherwise, the saddle could slide off the horse's back, taking the rider with it. Katerina handled the horse well, another fact that weighed in her favor. Perhaps she would advance faster than Phoebe anticipated. Katerina needed to learn quickly if she intended to ride Diablo.

They emerged from the barn with the sun's rays slanting down in earnest. Scant clouds wisped across the sky, and a lone heron winged in the direction of the river.

Fiona tilted her face heavenward. "What a glorious day."

Phoebe could only agree. The sun had shaken free of the horizon, and the sky bloomed around its golden glow. Birds chattered all about, as if they too felt the excitement of simply being alive.

Will guided them down the trail along the river, but he didn't turn aside for the crossing that would deliver them onto the open range. No doubt, his concern about rustlers guided him. She didn't mind. It was joy enough to follow the path that wound along the river. Turning, it carried them beneath the forest canopy. They traveled through green half-light until they reached a clearing where bitterroot flowers peeked their purple faces from among the grasses. Bees buzzed in tall fireweed spikes, and a hummingbird feasted on the scarlet flowers of Indian paintbrush.

"Can we stop here?" Fiona called ahead to Will. "I want to gather wildflowers for my mother."

He nodded. "We can spare some time for that."

Phoebe dismounted to help Fiona gather flowers. She tried not to notice Will helping Katerina out of the saddle, or the brilliant smile she awarded him. Phoebe bent to her task while Fiona talked. She'd stopped listening to Fiona's chatter, but her happy voice washed over Phoebe in a pleasant tide. Fiona's loquaciousness became a double blessing. It distracted Phoebe from her own thoughts, and it kept her from listening in on Will and Katerina. Worrying about them forming an attachment would not keep it from happening. She shouldn't let the mere suspicion ruin a perfect day.

Phoebe gathered wildflowers with a lighter heart. The sun bathed her in warmth, a meadowlark rippled a sweet song, and the heady scent of the blossoms she held perfumed the air. A shadow fell across her, and Phoebe glanced up to discover Katerina standing between her and the sunlight.

"How pretty." Katerina pointed to a cluster of yellow blossoms at her feet.

"It's arrowleaf balsamroot, also known as Oregon sunflower. Like bitterroot, it provides food for the local Indians."

Will looked over Phoebe's shoulder. "We've used the roots in place of coffee out on the range. It's not bad."

Phoebe added some of the flowers to her posy. "You've made me curious to try it."

Will smiled. "I'll have to brew some for you."

Fiona joined them, her hands full. "I'd better stop gathering or I won't be able to carry them all, plus ride my horse."

"We should head back, anyway." Will turned toward the horses. "It's almost time for breakfast."

Phoebe started to follow, but Katerina touched her arm. "How am I doing?"

Phoebe stared at her without comprehension. "Doing?"

"At riding."

"Oh, yes." She'd nearly forgotten the reason for this expedition. She continued following Will. "Very well. You seem to have a natural ability."

Katerina smiled. "That's good to hear."

"You sit well in the saddle and have great posture. Just make sure not to hold the reins so high, and don't point your toes. Keep your heels down in the stirrups."

"Thanks for the advice." Katerina gazed up at her horse, looking a little lost. Will stepped up to boost her into the saddle.

"You're welcome." Phoebe mounted unassisted.

"I don't need help, thank you." Fiona shook her head at Will. "Except, would you please hold my bouquet while I get into the saddle?"

Once Fiona settled, Will handed the wildflowers to her with a flourish. "They are as lovely as their keeper."

"Thank you, kind sir." Fiona's eyes gleamed, and her cheeks flushed pink.

Will returned to his horse, smiling. Fiona set off, and he glanced backward. "Are you two coming?"

"Shortly." Katerina was still getting situated.

Phoebe nodded to him. "Go after Fiona. I'll bring up the rear with Katerina in a moment."

"I'll remind Fiona to slow down. She seems to have forgotten that some of us need more time." Will rode off.

Katerina glanced up from positioning her legs over and under the sidesaddle pommels. "You and Will seemed deep in conversation this morning."

"Oh, that?" Phoebe shrugged the subject off with a laugh. "I can be too intense at times." She didn't feel inclined to discuss personal matters with two people in one day. As for Will's troubles, revealing them was up to him.

"I'm glad to know it wasn't anything serious." Katerina gave her a questioning look. After a moment, she took up her reins. "I'm ready."

"Go ahead." Phoebe held back, allowing her to go first. The prickling sensation of someone watching crawled up her spine. Phoebe peered into the shadows but found no one there. The others leaving her behind, however briefly, must have triggered her uneasiness. Phoebe repressed the urge to barge after them, but she followed closely behind Katerina.

Phoebe spotted Will and Fiona waiting beside the trail. Katerina had almost reached them when a jackrabbit sprang from nowhere, bounded across Katerina's path, and narrowly missed Miss Buttons' hooves. The horse shied and Katerina screamed. Fiona gasped as Miss Buttons charged past her, and Will called for Katerina to hold on. Miss Buttons and her wailing rider disappeared down the path to the river.

Katerina gripped the sidesaddle pommels with her hands and legs, holding on for all she was worth. The wind chilled her damp cheeks and tugged her hair from its pins. Strands whipped it into her face, but Katerina couldn't free a hand to claw them away. She turned her head to clear her eyes. The horse's thumping of hooves and huffing breaths sounded loud in her ears. Miss Buttons swerved around a stump, and Katerina let out a yelp. She snapped her attention forward, grateful that by some miracle she hadn't fallen off yet. Katerina didn't know how much longer she could cling to the runaway horse. If she survived this ordeal and ever climbed back on a horse, she would ride astride, like Phoebe.

Please, God, help me. The silent prayer burst from her being. Images from her childhood in Germany flashed through her mind—a neighbor boy falling from his horse. His terrified screams still haunted her. She'd learned later that he had broken his neck.

Would she suffer a similar fate?

Katerina held on tighter, gritting her teeth against the pain that flared from her cramped hands and legs.

Breaking free of the trees, her horse rushed downhill. The river swung into view, straight ahead. A scream broke from Katerina. Water swirled around her legs and tugged at her skirts. Katerina canted sideways in the saddle, praying she wouldn't fall off and drown. Her head spun, and the world darkened around the edges. Black dots swam before her eyes. She tried to blink them away, but they remained.

All at once remembering to breathe, Katerina gasped in air. She clung to the saddle horn, fighting waves of dizziness. The mare swam with strong strokes to the opposite shore. Miss Buttons lurched as she stumbled on the riverbed. She found her footing and heaved upward, out of the water.

Katerina's hands slipped on the pommel. Her fingers were going numb, but she tightened her grip and held on. The mare bumped upward on what must be an animal trail. Katerina shifted backward on the steep incline. She sucked in a breath, certain she would slide downhill into the current. The river would sweep her away, never to be found.

Her father's face filled her mind. That was the look he'd given her after she'd tumbled out of their apple tree and sprained her shoulder. She might see him in heaven soon.

The mare crested the rise onto level ground. Katerina

pulled herself forward in the saddle. The ground rushed past at breakneck speed. She closed her eyes, swallowing against the need to vomit.

The pounding of other hooves rose in her ears. Katerina almost didn't dare hope for rescue. Disappointment would crush her. What else could it be, though? She could have wept at the sight of Phoebe and Will closing in behind her. Katerina pulled on the reins once more, to no avail. She'd heard of horses taking the bit between their teeth. That must be what Miss Buttons had done.

Will and Phoebe's hoofbeats grew louder. They split apart and came alongside the runaway horse. Will reached out and grasped Miss Button's bridle. The mare slowed and came to a shuddering halt.

Phoebe leaped down from her horse and caught Miss Button's bridle on the other side.

Will let go and dismounted. He reached up, and Katerina leaned down into his arms. He swung her to the ground.

"Are you all right?" His voice penetrated through the fog surrounding Katerina.

She summoned her voice. "Yes, thanks to both of you."

Phoebe embraced her. "Don't ever scare me like that again."

"Scare *you*?" Katerina could barely contain herself. "My life flashed before my eyes."

"It turned out well, thankfully." Will smiled. "Let's get you to the house."

Katerina eyed the mare shuddering beside her. "I'm not riding back on that horse."

"I'll take Miss Buttons and lead you on mine." Will spoke decisively.

"Thank you." Katerina accepted his offer, although she felt more like walking.

"Would you please pass the salt?" Phoebe asked the question more to divert the conversation than because her food needed seasoning. After the eventful morning, she could hardly believe they'd arrived at the ranch in time for breakfast. Katerina had declared her appetite lost but soothed herself with several cups of tea. Phoebe privately thought she was enjoying the attention, especially from Will. Fiona, who had ridden hard to summon help, ate with the gusto of a ranch hand. The sight might have distracted Phoebe more, if she hadn't been so hungry herself. She polished off quantities of toast, eggs, fried potatoes, and bacon.

"I'm grateful for what you did for me." Katerina bestowed a watery smile on Will, and then Phoebe.

"We only did what anyone else would have done," Phoebe protested.

"Without your intervention, I would have fallen." Katerina touched her napkin to the corners of her eyes. "I could have been injured, and maybe worse."

"I'm grateful you're safe." Phoebe glanced away from Katerina, embarrassed by her vociferous praise. Her parents were looking at her with identical awed expressions. They weren't alone. Aunt Elsa and Uncle Con couldn't have smiled any wider. Phoebe could swear she'd sprouted wings and grown a halo, from the way her family was acting. Will met her eyes and shrugged, smiling.

"I hope you won't let this mishap prevent you from riding again." That would be unfortunate. Katerina had a lot to learn, but she possessed the passion that would see her through.

Katerina made a face. "At the moment, I never want to see a horse again."

Phoebe laughed. "Maybe you'll feel differently tomorrow."

Katerina smiled. "It might take a day or two."

Aunt Elsa claimed Katerina's attention, coaxing her to eat a bite of toast. Katerina nibbled on the morsel, probably to humor her sister. Her face was drained of color, and she wrapped her arms around herself as if cold. It wasn't long before she excused herself to go lie down. Aunt Elsa climbed the stairs shortly afterwards, a towel draped over her arm and a steaming pitcher in her hands.

With breakfast over, those still gathered around the table pushed back their chairs and stood. Phoebe intercepted a secretive glance between her father and Uncle Con. She couldn't interpret it but wasn't surprised when the two walked off together in the direction of the library. Phoebe picked up her empty plate and reached for the serving bowl that contained the remnants of scrambled eggs.

Ma waved her off. "Go and put up your feet in the parlor with Fiona. You've both been through an ordeal."

Phoebe gave her a grateful smile and followed Fiona into the parlor. Phoebe sank into an overstuffed chair and stared absently out one of the tall windows. Beyond the mullioned panes, the garden basked in sunshine. Bees wreathed the lavender spikes and frequented sprays of tiny flowers on the tomato plants. A monarch butterfly swirled about on hidden currents before dropping into a stand of lupines outside the fence. What a pleasant day, but how quickly it had soured.

She might have lost Katerina today. Phoebe cradled her face in her hands. *I'm sorry for my jealousy, God. Please forgive me.*

"Are you all right?"

Phoebe dropped her hands. "Yes, but I wish I'd never suggested today's ride."

Fiona's eyebrows shot upward. "Surely you don't blame yourself."

"I know I shouldn't, but—"

"It was an accident, plain and simple. No one could foresee

what would go wrong. You and Will sprang into action quickly. If you hadn't, Katerina might have suffered harm. That's what you should remember."

Phoebe mustered a smile. "Don't leave yourself out. You went for help."

"Not that you needed any."

"If events had turned out differently, we'd have been glad of it."

"You and Will are the ones who forded a river." Fiona shook her head. "I'll never know what got into Miss Buttons. Why did she cross in that place when the ford was so close?"

"Who knows? She'd had a fright." Phoebe studied her. "Don't be hard on yourself for loaning Miss Buttons to Katerina."

Fiona's eyes widened. "How did you guess? I *do* feel guilty."

"Don't. You couldn't have known the horse would run away with her."

Fiona clutched a cushion against herself. "Thank the Lord Katerina wasn't hurt."

"I shall always be grateful for that." Phoebe leaned her head against the chair back.

The thump of boots preceded Pa into the room. "Phoebe? Uncle Con wants a word with you in the library, if you're not too tired."

"I'll go." Phoebe gave him a puzzled glance. "Did he say what he wants?"

"I'll let him speak for himself." Pa smiled. "He does that well enough."

Phoebe dragged to her feet and started down the corridor. She would rather lie down for an early nap, but curiosity would keep her from sleep. She couldn't imagine why Uncle Con had sent for her. The library door was open, and she paused at the threshold.

Uncle Con was seated behind his mahogany desk, which faced the doorway. "Phoebe." He stood up. "Come in and sit down."

Phoebe selected a harp-backed chair and waited while her uncle closed the door. The chair wasn't particularly comfortable, but moving would delay the satisfaction of her curiosity. "Why did you send for me?" she burst out the question as soon as Uncle Con sank down again.

He straightened a stack of papers, taking an unnecessarily long time, in her opinion. He then folded his hands on the desktop and cleared his throat. Finally, when Phoebe was sure she could bear the suspense no longer, he fixed his green gaze on her. "Your parents have changed their minds about your working at the ranch."

"What did you say?"

"They're in favor of my employing you."

She stared at him, hardly taking in his meaning. "But, you hired Mr. Malone in my stead."

"I hired him, yes." He grinned. "But no one could ever replace you."

"I don't understand."

He smiled. "I'd like to hire you as a ranch hand."

"You're sure?"

Laughter shook his shoulders. "You should see your face. Of course, I'm sure."

"But what about Mr. Malone?"

"I know a good worker when I see one. He can stay on. Well, *cailín*, what answer will you give? Do you want the job? I'll pay you the same as the others."

Phoebe summoned her powers of speech. "Yes."

"Wonderful. You can start right away. I imagine you'll want to collect your clothing and such first. You will, of course, stay in the ranch house with us."

Phoebe's mind spun with questions. She voiced the most important among them. "Does Will know about this?"

"I sounded him out briefly before he left. He's in favor of the idea."

"You're kidding." Phoebe blew out a breath. "I doubt today can hold any more surprises."

"Why?" He raised an eyebrow. "The two of you proved you can work together only this morning."

"Is that what persuaded him?"

"He didn't enlighten me, but it probably didn't hurt." Uncle Con smiled. "When may I expect your return?"

"As soon as possible."

"I thought as much." He leaned back in his chair, looking pleased with himself.

Phoebe jumped up and started for the door. "I can't wait to tell Fiona."

"I'm sure she'll be pleased. There's nothing more my daughter likes than company."

Phoebe paused with her hand on the knob. "Uncle Con, how did you persuade them?"

"Your parents?" A smile crept over his face. "A little bird may have suggested that you should get becoming a ranch hand out of your system."

CHAPTER THIRTEEN

PHOEBE BUCKLED HER VALISE AND FINGERED her initials, tooled into the leather. Ma had given the lightweight suitcase to her for Christmas several years ago. Phoebe might have guessed her mother's ambitions then, if she'd been paying attention. She shook off the thought. Ma had apologized and that's what mattered.

Phoebe plunked onto the bed beside her valise. She'd packed it with items she expected to need right away—her hairbrush and mirror, stockings and unmentionables, a toothbrush and dental powder, her Bible, and a copy of *Alice's Adventures in Wonderland*. Pa had brought the last item home after a trip to Helena. Since its publication last year, Lewis Carroll's fanciful story had taken the literary world by storm. Phoebe could see why. Although a children's book, it held her attention as an adult. She would finish reading the book at the ranch. She found that a comforting thought. With so many changes in her life, one thing would remain the same.

The trunk filled with her clothing waited beside the door. Soon, Pa and one of her brothers would carry it to the landau. She swallowed against a lump in her throat. Saying goodbye to her family wouldn't be easy. Her gaze ranged about the room that had belonged to her since she'd come to live at the ranch with her mother and brand-new father. Although she would return for visits, her room might not feel the same. Living elsewhere was bound to change her perspective. That was good in some ways but also sad. Today she would say goodbye not only to her room, but to the child who had once occupied it. On top of her dresser sat the whirligig Quinn had given her several years ago on her birthday. She'd begged Pa for the toy in the general store, but Quinn had bought it for her. She smiled up at the carved man driving a sulky. He didn't exercise his horse nearly enough anymore. Phoebe had lost interest in turning the handle to move the man's whip arm and the horse's legs. She'd given away her toys but kept this one out of sentiment.

"Phoebe?" Ma tapped at her door, which stood ajar.

"Come in."

Her mother walked in and stood at the foot of the bed. "Are you all packed?"

Phoebe nodded. "I think I remembered everything."

Ma's lips curved. "You can always come home for anything you forgot. We only live a short distance away."

"True." Phoebe didn't miss the reminder to come home. "Ma, thanks for not standing in my way on this."

"You're welcome. I love you and want the best for you. You might not like working with cattle, but you won't find that out unless you try it."

Phoebe detected Uncle Con's influence in Ma's thinking. *A little bird, indeed!* "I'm so glad you had a change of heart. I know I don't need your approval now that I'm an adult, but I would never go without it."

"Thank you, sweetheart." Ma sat next to her on the bed. "I wish I'd had your attitude toward my own parents. That I didn't, cost me dearly."

"I know." Images flashed through Phoebe's mind—horrible things a child should never see. An old woman lay unmoving in a strange place that smelled of bleach, flowers and decay. Ma wept at the woman's side. A red-faced man came in and screamed at her mother. He towered over Phoebe, but Ma thrust herself between them. Phoebe had been too young to fully understand what she'd witnessed but she'd pieced it all together later.

Ma put her arm around her. "I regret causing the rift in my family. With time and patience, my parents might have come around. I wonder sometimes what would have happened if they'd let me marry with their blessing. Avery and I might not have gone West. Our wagon wouldn't have tipped over in the Laramie River. You wouldn't have lost your father or your birthright."

Phoebe covered her mother's hand, which rested on her shoulder. She thought of the red-faced man. "I doubt your brother would have allowed that to happen. He'd have done anything to cut you out and inherit all their wealth."

"It's true, what the Bible says about the love of money being the root of all evil." Ma sighed. "I almost fell into that trap, myself. I thought I was doing the right thing, pushing you toward Alton Prescott. I didn't fully understand it, but I wanted you to have what I lost. Can you forgive me?"

"Ma, remember? I already did. More importantly, God has. Please don't reproach yourself any longer."

"Thank you, sweetheart. God is merciful. I'll always be grateful that He gave me you." Ma smiled, but her eyes shone suspiciously bright.

"Don't start crying on me." Phoebe spoke in sudden alarm.

Ma sniffed. "I'll miss you."

"I'm only going a couple of miles away."

"That doesn't matter. It's a mother's prerogative to grieve when her children leave the nest." Ma pulled a handkerchief out of her sleeve. "I came prepared."

Phoebe laughed. "Oh, Ma. I love you. I'll be back often, I'm sure."

"Don't mind me." Ma, mopping up, waved her free hand. "I don't know what you see in working cattle, but I'm glad you have an adventure ahead of you."

Will stood in the center of the corral, holding a pole tied with a red bandana at one end. He kept his face toward Diablo, who was trying to buck off an empty saddle. The mustang slowed, but Will waved the bandana at the horse's eye level, spurring him to renewed action.

Preparing a spirited horse for an inexperienced rider seemed a bad idea. Mere days ago, Katerina had proven herself incapable of handling even a mild-mannered horse. Will had explained to her at the outset that a wild mustang might never become a lady's saddlehorse. Although Katerina had conceded his point, she'd also promised to improve her riding skills so she could ride Diablo. Will shook his head. She seemed to have no concept of the challenge she was taking on.

Why Con encouraged her in this madness, he didn't know. Will couldn't believe he was blind to the situation. Will was beginning to suspect his boss had something other than horses in mind. Perhaps Con wanted his sister-in-law to remain at the ranch, for his wife's sake. From what Will understood, the family was drifting apart. He could sympathize with the desire for closeness, but it was best to be straightforward in such matters. Katerina and Elsa clearly enjoyed one another. He doubted they needed Con's help.

Despite his misgivings, Will meant to keep his word and break this horse. He wouldn't have promised to train the mustang if he'd fully understood the situation, though. The sooner he discharged his duty, the better. He'd never been good at detecting feminine wiles, but the glances Katerina gave him at times warned him away. He'd rather head off trouble before it arose. The quicker he broke Diablo, the faster the problem would end.

Diablo bucked with less enthusiasm now. His nostrils flared as he heaved in air. He was clearly tiring. Will seized the advantage and stepped into the saddle. He'd no sooner brought his weight down than Diablo took off bucking.

Will raised his arm for balance and held on tight. The mustang reared and twisted, jerking Will backwards and sideways. He held on and kept his seat.

Diablo circled the corral, and then ran at the fence. Will pulled his leg out of harm's way in time to save it from being crushed between the horse and rail. Will struggled to regain his balance, but the horse arched his back, launching him into the air. Will landed on his shoulder, rolled, and came up choking in a cloud of dust.

"I hope you're not injured." Phoebe called out of nowhere.

Will started, but then located her along the rail. "What are you doing here?" He returned his attention to Diablo. The mustang was circling the corral, bucking against his saddle.

"Showing up for work. I thought Uncle Con told you he hired me."

Will retrieved his hat and thumped it on his pant leg to remove the dust. "So, you decided to go through with it."

"Did you doubt me?"

Will waited until he'd hopped the fence to answer. "I wondered if you might change your mind."

"I'm reporting to work." She spoke with emphasis, as if to an inattentive child.

Will restrained a smile. He'd deserved that. He swept a glance over Phoebe's riding clothes, which consisted of a split skirt, jacket, and polished boots. "I see you came prepared."

She lifted her chin. "I thought it best."

"How long have you been here?"

"Pa brought me this morning."

Will could restrain his smile no longer. "While I commend your eagerness, I'm no slave driver. You can start tomorrow. Meet me in the barnyard at sun-up."

Her eyes lit. "I'll be there."

He watched Phoebe walk toward the house. She had quite a spring in her step. It would do her well to hang onto that enthusiasm. Miss Phoebe Walsh was in for a wild ride. He wondered how long she'd last.

Phoebe woke in the early hours, too excited to go back to sleep. She tossed and turned as long as she could endure, and then threw back the covers. Beating Will to their meeting place would be easier than she'd anticipated. Arriving first would give her time to collect herself before he appeared. Phoebe put on her riding clothes and settled in the chair at the window to wait. She drowsed a bit but came fully awake when the sky lightened toward morning.

After creeping downstairs, she let herself out the back door. The barn beckoned, but she continued along the path and rounded the rear corner. The burbling of water greeted her, loud in the stillness. Mist in shades of blue and gray softened the surface of the river. Rocks spilled from the banks into the flow, softened by the lush grass bending over them. Phoebe sat down, clasped her knees, and breathed in the cool morning air. Tinged with the scent of river water, it was the only tonic she needed.

"You look so peaceful, I almost hate to disturb you."

Phoebe opened her eyes a little reluctantly. Lack of sleep was catching up to her. Will stood silhouetted against the barn, his posture casual. She started to stand, but he lowered himself to the grass beside her.

"No rush. I came early." He tilted his head. "You didn't startle when I came up this time."

"There's no rhyme or reason to when it happens."

"Tell me—" He plucked a green blade and twirled it between his fingers. "What skills do you possess, other than riding, for working cattle?"

"Nothing specific, but I helped a bit at home."

"You're packing a pistol. How well can you shoot?"

"Very well. Pa made sure of it."

"Can you break a horse to saddle?"

"I've never tried."

"Do you know how to lasso a cow?"

"I've seen Pa and my brothers do it before."

Will shook his head. "That won't count when you're facing a Hereford steer."

To his credit, he didn't smirk, although her remark must seem ridiculous to a seasoned cowhand. "No, I suppose not." She glanced away, a little shame-faced. They both knew she'd landed her job because Con was her uncle. In the first blush of her enthusiasm, she'd somehow glossed over in her mind the difficulty of this undertaking. She'd never even considered the trouble Will would go to in training her.

"All right, we'll start with learning to lasso." Will stood up with a resigned air. "Let's get started."

They came around the barn, but Will didn't turn aside for their horses. "First, come and meet everyone."

The iron triangle outside the cookhouse began clanging.

"It's time for breakfast." Will grinned. "I hope you didn't think I was going to work you on an empty stomach. Or aren't you hungry?"

She smiled. "I could do with a hot cup of coffee."

"You'd better take more than that, if you expect to survive

without fainting."

Phoebe glanced at him. "That doesn't sound promising."

He laughed. "Learning to rope is hard work."

She considered herself warned. Murphy had tried to show her once, but her mercurial brother had lacked patience. What kind of teacher would Will make?

They reached the low-slung cookhouse at the same time as Matt. He tipped his hat. "Nice to see you, Miss Walsh."

She smiled. "Good morning."

Matt held the door for her. "Ladies first."

The cookhouse walls gleamed pristine white in the light that slanted through the tall windows. A kettle steamed on the pot-bellied stove in the center of one end-wall. Plates of flapjacks and eggs lined the two counters on either side of the stove.

Phoebe recognized the dark-hair and lean face of Brady Carrigan, Will's second-in-command, among those gathered around the stove. She'd seen the others about the ranch. Will introduced them to her, but there were too many to remember their names. Phoebe greeted each man and received a polite response in return. She couldn't tell if any of the ranch hands thought a woman had no business working cattle.

"And this is Cooky." Will gestured toward a bow-legged man with a drooping mustache stirring a steaming pot.

Cooky removed his hat with a flourish. "Good morning, ma'am. I hope you woke to birdsong as lovely as yourself."

Phoebe blinked. "Why thank you. That's a nice thing to say."

"Cooky has a way with words." Will grinned. "He's also the most important member of the crew. Ask anyone."

"I'll take your word for it." Phoebe inhaled the aroma of coffee, flapjacks with maple syrup, and fried eggs. "The food smells wonderful."

"I hope to shout, it is. I was up in the wee hours to wrestle it onto your plate."

Phoebe wondered if she'd offended the cook, but then he smiled.

"You're a sight for sore eyes—better to look at than even Sparky here." Cooky nodded toward a lanky fellow with flaming hair. It wasn't hard to guess how the man had come by his moniker.

Sparky smiled good-naturedly. "You're right about something, for once, Cooky. Neither me nor Davis would argue against you." He nudged the brown-haired man beside him.

Davis stared at his food, his face reddening.

Cooky filled a plate for Phoebe but left Will to fend for himself along with everyone else. She would rather not be treated differently, but she wasn't about to criticize the cook's kindness. Maybe he guessed how awkward she felt on her first day. Phoebe waited for Will to choose a place to sit. She didn't feel secure taking the initiative. What if she stole someone's cherished spot?

Phoebe slipped into the seat beside Will and bowed her head to say grace. Glancing up, she noticed others doing the same. Will brought the hot coffee Phoebe was craving. She waited for it to cool, and then took a sip. "This is really good."

Cooky smiled from across the table. "I'm glad you like it."

"What makes it so smooth?"

Will laughed. "You and everyone else wants to know."

Cooky's smile widened. "That's one of my secrets."

Matt chuckled beside the cook. "He has a lot of those."

"Well, it's delicious." Phoebe took another sip. She finished her coffee while Will cleaned his plate. After breakfast, the men dispersed to perform various tasks about the ranch while she and Will returned to the barn. He tossed her a pair of leather gloves before shouldering a coiled rope. "Come with me."

She followed him out of the barn and across the grass. He stopped within range of a tree stump on the far side of the barn. Unless she missed her guess, that would be her target. Unlike a real cow, it wouldn't move, but she had to start somewhere.

"First, you'll learn how to tie a lariat. Hold on a minute." Will removed the knots from his rope. "This is the way the Indians secure their bow strings. It's not complicated but can seem tricky at first."

Phoebe moved nearer to Will at the same time that he stepped toward her. His indrawn breath rasped in her ear.

He shifted away and cleared his throat. "You start an overhand knot partway down the rope—about here. Leave it loose." He demonstrated. "After that, you make a second overhand knot close to the short end. This one you tighten. Are you still with me?"

Phoebe nodded. "So far, so good."

"Here's the tricky part. You open a hole in the loose knot and pass the other knot through. Tighten the knot, and you have a small loop. Put the long end of the rope into this to form a second loop you can tighten. Got it?"

Phoebe stared at the lariat in puzzlement. "Could you show me again?"

He smiled. "You'll catch on."

Will demonstrated a second time while she focused intently.

He untied the knots and gave the coiled rope to her. "Your turn."

Phoebe managed to tie the two overhand knots, but then stood, staring at the rope "Sorry. I can't remember what to do next."

Will reached toward her, then paused. "May I?"

She nodded, thinking he meant to take the rope from her. Will's hands came down over hers. Phoebe caught her breath as warmth spread through her.

"You create an opening in the loose knot for the tight knot." Will's breath stirred her hair. "See?"

"I think so." Phoebe could feel his gaze. What would happen if she lifted her head? She wasn't ready to find out.

A moment went by, and then another. Will stepped away and cleared his throat. "Untie the rope and try again."

Phoebe's cheeks warmed. She fumbled with the knots but sighed in relief when she succeeded.

"Good. You'll want to practice on your own until it's second nature. I'll measure a rope for you to keep when we go back in. Meanwhile, you need to learn to coil a lariat."

Phoebe sighed. There was a lot to know about roping before she even started.

Will showed her how to flick her wrist to start the coils. After that, it was a matter of twisting the rope at every turn so it would lie neatly. Will made it look easy, but Phoebe added it to her list of necessary skills to practice. She had an uncomfortable feeling that, as the day progressed, the list would grow.

Will swung the rope above his head and lassoed the stump. Phoebe took a turn, but a loop wouldn't open.

"You're holding the rope wrong."

"Oh?" Phoebe glanced at him, forgetting to move her arm.

"Careful!"

The rope came around and smacked her in the eye. "Ouch!"

The distinct sound of snickering carried from the barn.

Will leaned over Phoebe while she cupped her watering eye. "Are you all right?"

"I think so."

"Wait here." He sounded grim.

Phoebe couldn't see him walk off, but she heard his boots thumping the ground in the direction of the barn.

"Might I ask what you think you're doing?" Will growled.

"Sorry, Boss." Sparky sounded sheepish. "I was just having fun."

"By spying on Miss Walsh while she tries to learn?"

"I don't mean to make trouble."

"Whatever you intended doesn't matter. You need to apologize."

"I reckon you're right."

The pain in her eye subsided, and Phoebe lowered her hand. She made out two blurry figures walking toward her.

"Sparky, here, has something to say." The one who sounded like Will thrust the other forward.

"I don't need no introduction, if it's all the same to you." Sparky belatedly removed his hat. "I know when I'm wrong. Miss Walsh, I made a mistake. I hope you'll take no harm from what I did."

He came into focus, and Phoebe could see remorse in his face. "I accept your apology."

"Thank you, ma'am." He returned his hat to his head, extinguishing its brightness.

"One moment, before you go."

Will's voice halted Sparky in his tracks.

"Since you've taken such an interest in Miss Walsh's education, perhaps you would be good enough to tell her what she did wrong."

"Sure." Sparky's posture relaxed. "That's easy. You don't want to swing a rope by its knot. The loop won't stay open when you throw it."

She nodded. "I'll bear that in mind."

A grin broke out over Sparky's face. "What you do is leave what's called a shank. That's a fancy name for the slack you grab with the loop. The rope should be doubled up in your hand. You want to keep your pointer finger down so you don't lose control."

"Thanks for the advice." Warming a little, Phoebe spoke in gentler tones.

"You're welcome. If you need any more tips, just ask me."

She smiled at his eagerness. "I will."

"I'd best finish cleaning out those stalls." He backed a couple of steps.

"Thanks, Sparky. You're a fine teacher." Will smiled. "You seem to have extra time on your hands today. After you're done with those stalls, go ahead and relieve Matt of guard duty."

His smile slipped. "Yes, Boss." He hurried off.

Will turned to Phoebe. "If you are fully recovered, let's continue our lesson. Did you understand everything Sparky told you?"

"I believe so."

"Well then, give it another try."

Phoebe soon tired of rotating her arm above her head.

"That's enough for one day." Will called a halt after several failed attempts.

Phoebe didn't want to stop, but her body did. She nodded, too emotional to speak. She wanted so badly to succeed but couldn't seem to acquire the knack. After coiling the rope a final time, she headed toward the tack room.

"Never mind, Phoebe." Will caught up to her. "You'll catch on."

"Thanks for saying that. I'm beginning to wonder if Uncle Con will get his money's worth out of me, after all."

"Don't worry about that. It's my job to make sure he does."

CHAPTER FOURTEEN

PHOEBE CAME UP GASPING FROM BENEATH the pump spout. She shook her head, and bright droplets scattered. Tendrils of dampened hair plastered to her face. She'd pinned up her curls this morning, but after a day of learning to rope and pitching hay, they were falling down. Her stomach rumbled with hunger, but Phoebe was so exhausted she wasn't sure she could eat. Besides that, she preferred not to let Uncle Con see her so dragged out. She didn't want him feeling sorry for her or interfering on her behalf. If she couldn't pull her own weight, she had no business working on the ranch.

Phoebe went into the house by the back door that led to the kitchen. She didn't have much time but wanted to change into clean clothing. She tried not to envy the other ranch hands, who didn't need to worry about such niceties. Cooky wouldn't object to honest dirt on their clothing, provided they washed their hands and scraped their boots before going inside the cookhouse. She crept up the stairs to her room and did her best to restore order to her appearance before joining her family in the dining room.

A tap came at the door. She opened it to find Fiona in the hallway.

Fiona scanned her face. "How are you doing?"

"I'm pretty tired."

Her cousin nodded. "That's not surprising. Are you coming down? We're waiting supper for you."

Phoebe groaned inwardly at the ordeal before her. "I'll be

right there."

In the dining room, Uncle Con greeted her with the same sort of look Fiona had given her.

She slipped onto her chair. "Sorry I'm late."

"That's all right, Phoebe." Aunt Elsa murmured. "I'm sure you had a good reason."

Uncle Con shook out his napkin. "How did your first day go?"

"I had no idea how much the ranch hands do around here."

Uncle Con smiled. "I appreciate each and every one of you."

"It sounds exciting." Richard's eyes gleamed.

Katerina glanced up from buttering bread. "What did you do today?"

Phoebe smiled. "I learned how difficult it is to rope a tree stump."

"I can imagine." Fiona shuddered.

"Don't worry." Uncle Con paused with a bite of noodles suspended on his fork. "I have no doubt you'll become an expert in no time."

"I hope you are right." Phoebe reached for her water glass and winced.

Aunt Elsa's eyes widened. "Have you hurt yourself?"

"It's my roping arm." Phoebe lifted the glass and drank, despite the pain lifting the glass had brought.

"I have some liniment you can rub into your muscles." Aunt Elsa salted her food. "I'll bring it up after supper."

"Thank you." Phoebe felt ridiculously like weeping.

"What's it like to work alongside Will?" Katerina sounded wistful.

"He's a good leader but tough to keep up with." Phoebe sliced into her chicken schnitzel, trying not to wince. "I watched him training your horse yesterday morning."

Katerina's face lit. "I'm so pleased."

"He handled Diablo well, but it might take a while."

"I'm not ready to ride my horse yet, anyway."

An image of Katerina's stricken face as Miss Buttons ran away with her rose before Phoebe. She chose her words carefully. "You should wait until you're feeling more confident."

The conversation shifted away from Phoebe, which was just fine. She was having enough trouble summoning the energy to eat. While the others made conversation, Phoebe plowed doggedly through the meal. Fortunately, the food was excellent. Otherwise, she'd have been hard put to finish. As soon as possible, Phoebe excused herself and dragged up the stairs to her room. She fell across her bed, fully clothed, telling herself she would only rest a minute. A rooster's crow woke her. Phoebe snuggled into the blanket someone must have put over her. A jar of liniment waited on her dresser. Phoebe flexed her throwing arm and winced. She'd better take it a little easier today.

Diablo's hooves thudded along as Will led him into the corral. After a glance at Phoebe this morning, he'd assigned her a lighter load. Presently, she was inspecting the fish traps. Phoebe didn't call attention to her pain, but he could tell she was suffering after yesterday and needed a break. For that matter, so did he—for a different reason. Training Phoebe was no hardship. In fact, he enjoyed it a little too much. Maybe breaking in a difficult horse would knock some sense into his head.

Diablo circled the corral while trying to buck off his saddle. Each time he slowed, Will prodded him to continue. After a long interlude, Diablo still showed no signs of tiring. Will had been too busy training Phoebe to take the mustang out yesterday. No doubt, he was full of pent-up energy.

"Are you planning to ride him?" Katerina sounded horrified at the idea.

Will spotted her leaning on the gate. Fresh-faced as always, she looked cool and beautiful in blue calico. "Not until he settles down."

"I admire your courage."

He shrugged, still driving Diablo around the corral. "It's all part of the job."

"Breaking a horse like Diablo is beyond your duties. I intend to pay you for your services, Mr. Canfield."

"I don't want your money. Con is allowing me to break your horse during working hours, which means that he's paying for it. Take it up with him."

"Are you always this stubborn?"

"Usually." He smiled.

"Thanks for the warning."

"Back away from the gate, if you would." Diablo was showing signs of weariness, and Will didn't want to risk an accident. He would have less control from the horse's back.

Moving swiftly, he put his foot in the stirrup and threw his leg across the saddle.

Diablo bucked with renewed vigor. Will wondered if he'd miscalculated. The mustang reared and twisted as before. Will kept his seat, but just barely. He held on as Diablo raced toward the rail. At the last minute, Will lifted his leg out of harm's way.

Katerina screamed, a piercing sound that seemed to spur Diablo. The mustang lowered his head and heaved against the saddle. Will's legs lost their grip. He bounced upward and fell. The ground rose to strike him, and he choked on dust churned by the mustang's hooves.

Will knew better than to linger on the ground. He rolled onto his side and shoved to his knees.

Katerina rushed to the corral rail nearest to him. "Will—

Mr. Canfield! Are you all right?"

"Yes and no." He jerked out the answer, still watching Diablo. After that display of temperament, Will was taking no chances. He jumped the fence and landed beside Katerina. His right leg buckled, but he grabbed the rail behind him. "I've been thrown before, but I landed a little harder this time."

She gazed at him from wide eyes. "I'm so sorry. Is there anything I can do?"

He nodded. "Help me to that straw bale over there." He pointed to the closest place he could find to sit and recover. He didn't want to walk much until the pain in his side eased. Also, the less he called upon Katerina's assistance, the better.

She moved to his side. "Lean on me."

Will tried to stand alone, but his legs felt weak. He put an arm across Katerina's shoulders and walked with her to the bale. He pulled away as soon as possible. "I can take it from here."

She stepped back, allowing him to take a seat without fussing over him.

He smiled up at her. "Thank you."

Katerina was looking past him.

Will turned his head and glimpsed Phoebe, ducking into the barn. She must have seen him leaning on Katerina. What had she thought they were doing?

Footsteps pounded from the direction of the cookhouse, where he'd left Matt patching the roof. Will picked up movement in his side vision— Matt running toward him.

"I saw you fall," Matt called. "Do you need the doctor?"

"Not me." Will shook his head. "But then, I never believe I do."

Matt stopped in front of him. "It looked pretty rough."

Will smiled. "Let's just say, I wouldn't want to repeat the experience anytime soon."

"Are you sure about no doctor?" Katerina frowned.

"I'm fairly certain, but I'll let you know if I change my mind."

"If it's all the same to you, I'll wait to see if that happens." Matt dropped onto the straw bale beside him.

"I'll go let Con know what happened." Katerina started toward the house.

"If you must." Will glanced at Matt. "So, did you finish that roof?"

"Nearly. The sight of you flying through the air interrupted me. Let me tell you—" Matt's voice trailed off as he watched Katerina hurry away.

"That doesn't seem to be your only distraction."

Matt grinned. "Miss Meier is attractive, but she's the kind of woman you settle down with."

"Are you against such a woman?"

"Not necessarily, but a man would need to provide a decent home, plus all the trappings." He shook his head. "That's a lot of responsibility to take on, especially for a drifter like me."

"Choose what you really want and the rest follows, or so I'm told." Will was not in a position to blame anyone else for shunning marriage, so he said nothing more on the subject.

Matt glanced sideways at him. "I've been meaning to ask if I can try my hand with Diablo. This seems a good time to ask."

"Does it now?"

"I expect you'll be laid up for a while."

"Don't count on it."

Matt raised his eyebrows. "You really should rest."

"I have too much to do."

"Well, then, let me take Diablo off your hands."

Will's laugh ended in a moan. "You're clever, I'll give you that. Why do you want to train Diablo?"

"My way of breaking a horse is different from most. Diablo responded well when I helped calm him on the way here. I guess that's when I got the itch to do it."

"Trying a different method is a splendid idea, considering how well I'm doing. It's up to Katerina." Will grinned at the consternation on Matt's face. It was gratifying to discover he wasn't the only one steering clear of a woman. "If you hurry, you can catch up to her."

Matt grinned. "You're enjoying this."

"I won't deny it." Will nodded Katerina's direction. "Go ahead. Ask her."

"What about you?"

"I'm fine."

Matt gave him a dubious look. "I'll be right back."

While Matt followed after Katerina's retreating figure, Will tested his aching muscles. He hauled to his feet, groaning. The pain demanded liniment, and he kept a tin for man or beast in the tack room. He hobbled toward the barn, telling himself he wasn't trying to find Phoebe.

Matt caught up to Katerina before she reached the house. "Hold on, would you?"

She turned around. "Is there something more wrong with Mr. Canfield?"

"Other than being thrown from a horse? No."

She pinned him with a glance. "That was my horse, Mr. Malone. I feel responsible."

He noted the creases in her forehead and the strain around her eyes. "I can see how you might, but try not to take it to heart. Will knew the risks, and he chose to take them."

"Do you think he'll be all right?"

"Will's pretty tough, and he's able to judge an injury. I'm sure he'll recover soon."

A smile flitted across her face. "Thank you for trying to comfort me. I'm not sure it's possible at the moment. If you'll excuse me, I should let Con know. Will is his employee, and he might want to overrule him and send for a doctor."

"Wait a moment." She didn't slow, but Matt kept pace with her. "I'm wondering if you'd like me to help break Diablo. Will is in favor of it. You'll recall that I did well with your horse when you broke down on the road to the ranch."

She slowed and cast a glance at him. "I suppose it's all right, but please be careful."

"I will." He stopped and let her hurry on without him. She seemed mighty concerned about Will, but that was none of his business. The important thing was that she'd agreed to let him work with her horse. He'd itched to train the mustang since encountering him on the road. Will's tactics worked with some horses, but he doubted Diablo would respond to them.

He walked toward the corral, where Diablo had finally stopped circling. There was no time like the present to reacquaint himself with his new student.

He spoke quietly while approaching the corral.

Diablo pricked his ears and rolled his eyes toward him.

Matt smiled at the subtle greeting. It wasn't much, but he would count it a beginning. Training the horse wouldn't be easy, but an even greater challenge lay ahead. Unless Katerina decided to sell Diablo, Matt would need to teach her how to ride him.

That would be the hardest part

Phoebe rubbed her hand down Nutmeg's neck and tried to forget what she'd seen. After checking the fish traps, she'd searched for Will to ask about her next task. She'd found him, all right, with his arm around Katerina. She could hardly credit he would do something so brazen. Didn't he care about Katerina's reputation? Didn't Katerina?

Ducking into the barn to avoid embarrassing them all had

seemed best. If she waited long enough, Will and Katerina might go somewhere else, and she could escape, undetected. Even if they came in, Phoebe could pretend nothing unusual had happened.

Nutmeg whickered, summoning Phoebe from her musings. The mare nudged her, and Phoebe smiled. "You would like me to keep petting you, I suppose." She resumed the neglected duty.

How ironic that this should happen right after she'd confessed her shortcoming in prayer. It was one thing to decide jealousy was unworthy of her, and quite another to face it down with a calm heart. She could at least learn something from wrestling with it. She doubted anything would come of her feelings for Will, but Uncle Con's assertion she should marry seemed true. Otherwise, why would she care so much about Will?

When Will had retreated into himself after mentioning Sophie, Phoebe had assumed he was afraid of being hurt again. She wasn't so sure of that anymore. What if he was amusing himself with Katerina, in the same way he'd dallied with her? She'd never told anyone but Liberty about Will kissing and then discarding her. However, Katerina deserved a warning. It didn't matter that Phoebe would loath giving her one.

Before she said anything, she needed to know Will's intentions toward Katerina. He might simply have fallen in love with her. In that case, Phoebe would wish them both well. If God was merciful, He would release her to love someone else. The Good Lord was able to do anything, even help a heartbroken spinster find love.

A shadow filled the barn doorway.

Phoebe squinted, but with the light behind him, she couldn't make out the man who entered. After a moment, he turned and headed for the tack room. That's when she recognized him. Through the light from the high windows, she caught a glimpse of Will's red-checked shirt.

Phoebe held back until he was thumping about in the tack room. He might hear the creak of the rear door, but she meant to walk softly enough for her departure to remain undetected. She'd almost reached the doorway when Will came out of the tack room. "There you are, Phoebe. I hoped to find you here May I have a word with you?"

"What do you want?" She hated how stiff she sounded.

"Well— You see—" He cleared his throat. "All right. I'm just going to come out with it. I believe you saw me leaning on Katerina earlier. I don't want you to get the wrong impression."

She glanced away. "I'm sure it's none of my business."

"Diablo threw me, and I needed— well, support."

She stared at him, taking in for the first time his hunched posture. "Are you injured?"

He shrugged. "It's not anything a tin of liniment and a little rest won't cure."

"When I saw you with Katerina, I thought—" She stopped herself, horrified at what she'd been about to confess.

"I knew how it might have looked. That's why I brought it up. I didn't want you to think I would take advantage of Katerina like—" He broke off and glanced away from her.

Like you did me? The words burned inside Phoebe, but letting them out would hurt them both.

"Like that."

"I'm glad no harm came from your mishap."

He nodded. "I think we'll skip your lesson today. Spend the time practicing roping and knot tying. If you tire of that, ask Brady for something to do."

"All right."

"Meanwhile, I need to return Diablo to his stall and take a load off my feet." He turned toward the doorway but halted with a groan.

Phoebe hurried to him. "Do you need help walking?"

"No, thank you. While having you pressed to my side would be delightful, it could lead to trouble."

Warmth rushed into her face. "I can find one of the men to assist you."

His jaw tightened. "I can manage under my own steam."

Phoebe stepped away from the stubborn man. "Your attitude is no different from a mule Pa once owned. He sold it after a week."

Will smiled. "I've been compared to that particular animal before."

Phoebe laughed, despite herself. "Perhaps you should take note. At least, let me deal with Diablo. I doubt you have the strength."

He shook his head. "I'd do it myself before sending you."

"I'm quite capable."

"No slight intended, but Diablo is a bit wild, even for you."

Phoebe doubted that but decided to let it go. Preventing him from handling a spirited horse while injured mattered more than her pride. "Then ask Brady to do it."

"I suppose I should."

Watching Will limp through the doorway tugged on her sympathies. They'd been at loggerheads for so long that it felt strange for him to take her advice. She wouldn't count on it as a sign of him softening toward her, though. Will's behavior had baffled her for a long time. If she'd figured anything out, it was that he was confused about romance.

Phoebe had once been as mixed-up as Will, but she now knew what she wanted. Only two choices remained. She could wait, with no guarantee anything would change, or embrace her heartbreak. Reckless as any gambler, while hope remained, she would choose the first option.

CHAPTER FIFTEEN

THE COOKHOUSE DOOR SWUNG OPEN, AND Phoebe dragged herself inside. With all her aches and pains, getting out of bed this morning hadn't been easy. All the ranch hands were bent over their plates. Cooky started up, but she waved him down with a smile. "I'm happy to serve myself."

After yesterday's mishap, she'd halfway expected Will to be absent, but he glanced up from beside Cooky with strain marking his face. What sort of night had he spent? Will gazed at her from narrowed eyes, as if shielding them against a bright light. Only faint rays found their way through the windows, however, and the lantern dangling above the table cast no more than a warm glow.

Phoebe helped herself to some of the fluffiest pancakes she'd ever seen. Abandoning all thought of ladylike portions, she crowded fried eggs and ham onto her plate. She needed to survive another tough day of proving how little she knew about ranching. At home, Pa had sheltered her from the worst of the work while letting her think she was a useful worker. Under Will's tutelage, she was beginning to understand how sheltered she'd been.

She carried her plate to the empty spot beside Will and turned back for coffee.

Cooky, carrying two steaming cups, nodded to her. "Sit yourself down. One of these belongs to you."

She surrendered to his kindness with a smile. "Thank you."

Phoebe bowed her head and said grace silently before

biting into a forkful of pancakes. "These are delicious."

A murmur of assent went round the table.

Cooky smiled. "It's because of my special ingredient."

"Another secret recipe?" Phoebe smiled. "How many do you have?"

He shook his head. "I've never counted."

"Most of them." Will lifted his cup. "We can't expect a man to give away his stock in trade, now."

"I suppose not." Phoebe blew on her coffee before risking a sip.

"It's the honey." Cooky nodded agreement with himself. "Yep, it is."

Laughter rang out around the table.

"Looks like Cooky has a favorite." Sparky chortled.

"I think you've made a conquest," Will murmured near her ear.

"Oh dear." Heat surged into Phoebe's face.

"It's harmless. Cooky's a confirmed old bachelor." Will put down his cup and rose slowly. "Soon as you're done, Brady will take you out riding. You've seen the range before, but not from a ranch hand's perspective. I'd take you myself, but I should stay off a horse for a while."

She frowned. "How are you this morning?"

"Stiff and sore, but otherwise fine." Will put on his hat and turned toward the doorway. The screen banged shut behind him.

Phoebe didn't linger over her meal, since Brady had nearly emptied his plate. She didn't want her tardiness to hold him up. After breakfast, they walked side-by-side to the barn. She thought he shortened his long-legged stride for her. Nutmeg whinnied a greeting, and Phoebe made short work of saddling her.

Brady met her in the barnyard on a paint horse. His dark clothing and black hat contrasted oddly with its chestnut coat mottled by white splashes. Brady glanced down at his horse. "Chance is acting a little frisky. I didn't ride him much yesterday."

She rubbed her horse's shoulder. "Nutmeg needs exercise, too."

He smiled, appearing younger than she'd thought him. "We can let them run a while, once we're on the range."

Phoebe followed Brady along the trail to the crossing. The scents of leather, warm grass, and perspiring horses wafted on the breeze. The river below them ran in shimmering tides. A pair of pheasants burst from the brush and took flight on whirring wings. Phoebe started, but Nutmeg took it in stride. The bird's croaking alarm cries punctuated the water's burbling. Phoebe's heartbeat slowed, and she relaxed in the saddle. Trees rose around them, casting dappled shade. Eventually, the trail dropped toward the river's edge, and the trees pulled back to reveal a place where the river fanned over a shallow bed. Nutmeg stepped into the ford behind Chance. The bright water slid above water-smoothed rocks in a mesmerizing display. In the center, the horses' knees vanished below the water. Phoebe lifted her gaze to the grassy banks where willows tossed their shaggy heads.

Nutmeg stepped onto dry ground, and Phoebe reined in beside Brady. "This seems an important location."

He nodded. "All the local ranchers cross here to access the open range. It's also one of the main places livestock and wildlife come to drink."

"Who owns it?"

"Your uncle. He wouldn't want to cut other ranchers off by fencing it in."

"I can't imagine him considering it."

"He may have to at some point, to protect his land from overgrazing." Brady shook his head. "That would be a crying shame."

She glanced about, trying to picture barbed wire intruding in this wild place. Fencing the range or not was a more complex question than she'd understood. She couldn't believe that her uncle would ever deny cattle, wild horses, buffalo, and other animals easy access to the cool, clear water they needed. Surely, he would find another solution.

The path climbed up from the river to a flatland. Brady nodded toward a group of cattle grazing in the soft sunlight. "The herd ranges mostly along the river. When the forage is good, your uncle's herd doesn't usually stray far from the water. That's not the case at the moment, and it makes keeping them together more challenging."

"I can see how that would complicate matters."

Brady nodded. "I expect we'll move to higher pasture before much more time passes."

"What do you do when riding herd?"

"Besides going after strays and rounding up cattle? We look after cows in any kind of trouble and watch for predators."

"Do you see many of those?"

He smirked. "Of the two-legged variety, sometimes we do. Rustlers can make a scourge of themselves. We also chase off bears, wolves, and coyotes."

Phoebe shuddered. "I hope I don't have to challenge a bear." She could recall finding telltale prints around the barn. The hair at the back of her neck bristled at the memory. For a while after Pa shot the intruder, the sensation of being hunted had remained with her.

Brady smiled. "Don't worry. Will won't give you more

than you can handle. Ready to gallop?"

She nodded, happy for the diversion.

Chance took off, and Phoebe urged her horse after the paint. The wind buffeted her, but she didn't care. She could tell that Nutmeg was pining for freedom. For that matter, so was she.

She could never have given up riding for Alton. It was the one activity that brought her most alive. Thankfully, Alton had revealed his true nature before she'd surrendered to him. He'd wanted to possess her, but no one could truly own another person. Alton might have crushed her until she didn't recognize herself. Never marrying would be better than to endure such a future. She couldn't live without love, although it might prove elusive.

She intercepted her thoughts, unwilling to dwell on depressing matters. On a glorious day like this, she should count the hues of green and tan in the grass, or maybe all the shades of blue in the sky. Each would be a wondrously impossible task, but worth the effort.

The cattle turned their faces toward them and lowed as they passed. Phoebe spotted Hereford, Shorthorn, and Angus breeds. She remembered a time when large herds of buffalo dotted the countryside, but the creatures were harder to find now.

They slowed on the climb into the foothills. In a particularly lovely meadow, Brady motioned her to stop. Phoebe obeyed, expecting him to suggest that they head back. Instead, he pressed one finger to his mouth. She frowned in puzzlement. Why would he gesture for silence? Something must be wrong.

The next instant, a feathered headdress caught the sunlight on the next hillside. A band of Salish warriors rode out of the shade. Phoebe's throat went dry. Their headdresses, clothing, and painted faces announced their readiness for battle.

Phoebe caught her breath. There'd been no time to hide. Exposed and vulnerable out in the open, they would be no match for so many. The old fear rose up to suffocate her. Phoebe's heart pounded, and her muscles tensed. It took all her will to stand, rooted to the spot. Provided the Indians moved away from them, they might escape, but if even one of the warriors looked back, they'd be found out.

Matt followed the sound of hooves striking wood into the barn. He wasn't surprised to find the mustang kicking his stall. The horse had been cooped up since yesterday's fiasco. Matt walked toward Diablo with a lead rope coiled across his shoulder. He kept his gait steady and his head high to communicate confidence. The horse watched him with softer eyes than before. "Hello, Thunder," Matt murmured in soothing tones. "I hope you're all right with my calling you that. We don't have to mention that other name. It doesn't suit you at all." Matt didn't want anything he said or did to remind the mustang of mistreatment he may have suffered in the past.

Diablo ventured forward from the rear of the stall, and Matt held still. The mustang reached over the gate and sniffed at his hair.

"You're not so fierce, after all." Matt pulled a sugar cube from his vest pocket. "Let's see if you have a sweet tooth." He held the dainty out, his palm flat.

Diablo sniffed the treat, and then crunched into it. He chewed with obvious pleasure. Matt took advantage of the moment to scratch behind the mustang's ears. He pulled out the end of the lead rope from the coil across his shoulder. "This won't hurt a bit." Swiftly, he fastened the bull snap to the mustang's halter.

Diablo jerked his head and started to back.

"It's all right," Matt soothed him. "We can stay here like this all day. Only, I thought you might like a little walk."

He waited for the mustang to settle down and then unlatched the stall door. Diablo quivered and eyed the opening. Matt kept the lead rope short to prevent him from bolting and led the mustang down the breezeway. The mustang's hooves clip-clopped on the barn floor, and then thudded in the barnyard dirt.

Matt blinked in the sudden sunlight. He turned away from the corral and led the horse toward the grassy area on the far side of the barn where he'd seen Phoebe practice roping. He continued around the rear of the barn before stopping. Diablo's nostrils quivered as he took in the sights and sounds of the river below them. The horse lowered his head and chomped the grass. Matt allowed him the pleasure, smiling as Diablo turned his ears sideways. "Feeling good, are you? That's what I like to see."

Matt let the horse graze for a little while before bringing his head up. "Come on, Thunder. We have other places to visit, but we'll come back, real soon."

They started off, and Matt smiled to himself. The horse's posture seemed more relaxed than before. Matt led him around the building, past the barnyard, and straight toward the corral. He brought the mustang up to the corral fence.

Diablo balked and backed.

"Easy, Thunder." Matt soothed the horse with his hands and voice. "You're all right."

The mustang quieted, but his relaxed posture didn't return.

Matt produced another sugar cube. "Good boy."

Diablo ate the treat and nudged him, clearly asking for more. "Oh ho!" Matt laughed. "None of that."

He led the mustang around the outside of the corral, glad to hear the even thumping of the horse's hooves. Matt rewarded him with a scratch behind the ears and met no resistance. After several more circuits, he judged it time to return the horse to his stall. Matt closed the gate behind him before unclipping the lead rope and removing Diablo's halter. He produced a final apple, which the mustang accepted without hesitation. "Thank you for a fine walk, Thunder. We'll do it again tomorrow."

Matt coiled the rope and hung it on a peg in the tack room. He walked into the barnyard with a lighter step. The outcome for the mustang should be favorable, provided no one interfered. His method didn't meld with the usual style of breaking a horse to saddle, but it worked. Some folks swore that a gently-broken horse performed better. Success depended, however, on the cooperation of others. Preconceived notions about how a horse should be broken sometimes hampered the process. Will seemed humble enough to let him try his own approach. Katerina could try to interfere, but she didn't know enough about horses to form much of an opinion.

"There you are. I was waiting for you to come out." Katerina peeled herself off the side of the barn, where she'd apparently been leaning.

Matt started. His thoughts might have summoned her. "I didn't see you there." Dressed in blue gingham, and with the sunlight in her hair, she seemed the very essence of summer.

"I saw you go into the barn with Diablo. I'm curious. How did your first attempt to train him go?"

"Very well."

"He didn't try to throw you?" She looked him up and down, but then her cheeks flamed.

Matt hid a smile. *So, she likes me, too.* "No, but that's because I didn't ride him."

Her brows drew together. "Why not?"

"He's not ready, in my opinion. Diablo needs to recover from the episode with Will, for one thing." Will pulled in a quick breath. "We're just getting to know one another, for another. Building trust takes time."

"That makes sense." She smiled, displaying pearly teeth. "You did say that your technique differs from most."

Matt nodded. "The average wrangler believes breaking in a horse is a battle between man and beast. I don't look at it that way. There's a difference between asserting natural authority and bending an animal to your will. Horses respond better when treated with kindness. In that, they are not unlike people."

"I agree with you." Approval shone from her face.

Matt smiled in relief. "I'm glad to hear it."

"Where did you learn to handle horses, if I may ask?"

"On my family ranch in Missouri."

"Why did you leave home to work elsewhere? Or is that too nosy a question?"

He smiled. "Maybe a little, but I'll answer it. My mother sold the place after my father died."

"Oh, I'm sorry." She put her hands to her cheeks. "I should never have asked."

"I don't mind." He smiled to ease her discomfort. "Ma moved to Boston to live with her sister. My own sisters stayed with her, but I didn't want to go. Neither did my brother. Caleb was bound and determined to mine for gold in Montana. I followed along. My brother succeeded, but I don't have the knack. I fell back on what I knew and hired out as a wrangler. It's called riding the grub train, drifting from one ranch to the next, filling temporary jobs."

"Is that what you're doing here?"

"Not this time. Con hired me for a permanent position, and

I aim to keep it."

"That worked out for both of you, I think. My brother-in-law is a generous employer, and I can tell you're a good worker."

He smiled. "I appreciate your vote of confidence. May I always prove worthy of it."

Her smile grew. "I have no doubt you will. Thanks again for helping with my horse. After your session, Diablo looked a lot better. I wonder if you'd allow me—" She glanced away. "I can pay for your services."

"There's no need."

"Are you certain? I can afford—"

He held up a hand. "I don't want your money. Helping a misunderstood horse find a good life is all the reward I need."

"If you do that, you'll have my undying thanks."

He gazed into her gleaming blue eyes, captivated despite himself. He glanced away from her, certain he shouldn't go down that path with his boss's relative. "I'll give it my all."

Phoebe started at every sound. A twig snapped, and she envisioned a moccasined warrior coming for her. A bird's trill became a hidden signal. The rustle of leaves warned of a captor, ready to leap.

"I think it's safe to go back, but quietly." Brady's whisper intruded into her thoughts.

Phoebe had to wait for her heartbeat to slow before climbing onto her horse. She turned downhill behind Brady, resisting the urge to send Nutmeg into a gallop. She wanted nothing more than to eat up the miles beneath her horse's hooves, but any sound might bring the Salish down upon them.

Brady pointed the way, as if aware of her panic. He allowed her to go first, and then fell in behind her. Phoebe would thank him later for his protective stance. His steadying presence calmed her enough to manage the fear that rode with her.

The trail dropped them to lower elevations more quickly than she'd anticipated. Why did riding out always seem farther than returning? Phoebe let herself hope that this nightmare would end soon. Nutmeg's head was sagging. How long had it been since they'd watered the horses? Phoebe reined in and waited for Brady to catch up. "I think my horse is thirsty." She spoke softly, although they were probably out of range for the Salish.

"There's a stream that way." He pointed. "It flows beneath those willows."

Phoebe followed the side path to the place where water tumbled beneath the trees. She let Nutmeg wade into the shallow edge of the stream and waited while her horse reached down to drink. Phoebe would normally enjoy the coolness brought by shade and rushing water. Today, she yearned to exchange it for the shadow under the rafters of Uncle Con's barn. She'd rather endure the heat of the trail to return to the safety of the ranch more quickly. When the horses lifted their heads, having drunk their fill, she sighed with relief.

The birds were singing in the flatland, as if nothing unusual had gone on. In their world, nothing had. Phoebe smiled at her thoughts, which bolstered her for the final stretch. She splashed across the ford and skirted the river on the path. In the place where the trees broke, a flock of geese winged into the sky. Their alarmed honking faded, replaced by a cow's bawling, which drifted to her from somewhere on the range. The next instant, the barn roof appeared. Ridiculous tears gathered in Phoebe's eyes, and a lump formed in her throat. She couldn't feel more grateful to come home.

After reaching the barn, Phoebe gave Nutmeg an extra

portion of oats. The mare had earned them today. She turned to go.

Brady opened the gate for her. "We should let the ranch manager know what we saw."

Phoebe would rather crawl under the covers in her bedroom than search for Will, but she nodded. "Yes."

They located him standing beside the bunkhouse with a pail of paint and a brush.

Brady hailed him, and Will waved back before returning to his job.

"I thought you were going to rest," Brady called when they came within earshot.

Will swiped white paint onto the bunkhouse wall. "This is restful."

Under other circumstances, Phoebe might argue with him. At present, she lacked the energy.

Will scanned her face. "Did you have a nice ride?"

"Yes, until we saw a band of Indians." She answered shortly, but from exhaustion rather than anger. "They were Bitterroot Salish--dressed for battle."

"Who knows what that means anymore." Brady rubbed his neck. "Raiding farms and stealing livestock?"

Will didn't seem to notice that his paintbrush was dripping. "What happened?"

"Nothing to us. We stayed out of sight until they left."

Phoebe was glad Brady answered, because she couldn't have sounded so calm. Hiding from the Indians hadn't felt like nothing to her.

Will squinted. "I wonder what they were up to."

Brady shrugged. "We may have found our rustlers."

Will laid his paintbrush down and reached for a rag. "I'd better tell Con."

Phoebe felt the need to speak. "It's hard to blame the tribe. The buffalo herd has shrunk, but they still have to eat."

"We don't know that they did anything." Will swept a gaze over her. "Go home, Phoebe."

She lifted her chin. "I can pull my own weight around here."

A faint smile played around Will's lips. "Yes of course, but not when you look so wrung out."

"Says the man who barely slows down after being thrown from a horse."

Will's smile grew. "I'll rest, if you will."

"All right." Phoebe peered at him in suspicion. "But I'll know if you don't."

"I am a man of my word, as I hope to prove to you."

Phoebe didn't know how to respond to Will's remark, so she said nothing more.

At the ranch house, Aunt Elsa fussed over her while Will and Brady spoke with Uncle Con in the library. The rumble of their voices carried to Phoebe in the kitchen while she ate several bowls of vegetable soup followed by gingersnaps warm from the oven.

Aunt Elsa sent her upstairs with warm wash water. Phoebe removed her dusty clothing and sponged the dirt from her skin. Once she was clean, she put on a lawn nightgown and turned down the bed covers. Light still shone through the window, but she didn't care to stay awake. Only when she slept would the fear leave her.

Phoebe tucked herself into bed and felt a little safer. She clutched her pillow and concentrated on breathing deeply. Exhaustion warred with her jumpy nerves but eventually won. Phoebe drifted into a quieter state of mind. Sounds faded to nothing…

Pressed against the back wall of a closet, Phoebe whimpered. The door burst open. A warrior with stripes painted on his face crouched in the opening, like a wolf ready to attack. Recognizing him, she gasped. Spukani glared at her, hatred marring his face. She screamed, but no sound came. Spukani caught her wrist with crushing fingers. He dragged her out of the closet and into her mother's kitchen. Darkness looked in through the windows. He bared his teeth in a silent snarl. Phoebe flinched, but instead of striking her, he hauled her out the open cabin door.

Phoebe cried out, her voice feeble.

No one came.

Spukani dragged her down the porch steps and thrust her onto the back of a pony, He leaped up behind her and carried her off into the night...

Phoebe startled awake and lay, panting.

A knock rattled the door.

For a panicked moment, Phoebe felt certain Spukani had stepped out of her dream. "Who is it?" Her voice quavered.

"Fiona."

Phoebe sat up in bed and shook her hair out of her face. "Come in."

Fiona opened the door and stood in the doorway, her clothes and hair neat as always. "Is everything all right in here? I could swear you screamed."

"I had a nightmare." Phoebe wrapped her arms around her knees.

Fiona swept into the room and settled onto the chair at the window. "Tell me."

"It was terrifying. I dreamed that Spukani made off with me."

"I'm sorry, *who*?"

Phoebe wasn't sure whether to laugh or weep at the

realization that Fiona had never heard of the man who had frightened her most of her life. "Spukani is the name of the Indian who kidnapped me as a child."

"And you still dream about him?"

"The memory troubles me at times." Phoebe didn't explain further. She could see no benefit to burdening her cousin with the depth of her fear.

"Have you told your parents this?"

She shook her head. "Bringing up Spukani would hurt Ma."

"I don't know much about such things." Fiona folded her hands in her lap. "Except..." She pressed her lips together.

"Except what?"

Fiona smiled. "Ma always says that the way to heal from your sorrows is to surrender them to God."

Had she looked to God for relief? Phoebe couldn't recall. That probably meant she hadn't. "Thank you. I should have seen the answer for myself."

"I'm glad to help." Fiona rose from the chair. "Why were you sleeping at this hour?"

"Will sent me home early. I was a little—upset."

"Did something happen?"

"I had to hide with another ranch hand from a band of Salish on the range today."

Fiona frowned. "Salish? We notice them around town sometimes. They seem quiet people."

Phoebe refrained from disclosing that the ones she'd avoided were dressed for battle. She didn't want to frighten Fiona. The warriors were probably raiding food or rustling cattle, as Brady had suggested, rather than going on the warpath. "It brought back memories."

"Of course, it would. How unsettling." Fiona bent and

embraced her. "I hope you are over it soon."

Phoebe managed to smile. "That makes two of us."

"Let me know if you want anything. I could bring your supper on a tray."

"It's nice of you to offer." Phoebe shook her head. "I wouldn't put you to the trouble."

"Don't be silly. You'd do the same for me."

"I'm more interested in sleeping than eating, but thank you."

Fiona studied her for a moment. "All right, but come to my room tonight if you can't sleep and want company."

"I will."

After Fiona left, Phoebe pulled the covers to her chin and closed her eyes. Sleep, like that stump she'd first tried to rope, eluded her. Fiona's wise words kept returning. The way to heal from her sorrows was to surrender them to God. She'd been holding onto her fear all these years. Maybe all she needed to do to escape was let go of it.

Phoebe slipped out of bed and knelt beside it. "Heavenly Father, I'm sorry for dwelling on my fears instead of giving them to You. Take them away, please. They're too heavy a burden for me, but not for You."

Phoebe stood up, feeling lighter. Whatever came, she refused to allow the past to hold her captive any longer.

CHAPTER SIXTEEN

PHOEBE RELEASED THE ROPE AND LET it uncoil through the air. The loop dropped over the tree stump with sweet precision. She tugged it tight and grinned at Will.

"Good." He gave a nod. "You can move up to roping from horseback. Saddle up and meet me in the corral."

Phoebe swallowed. "The corral? Do you mean, with real cattle?"

Will smiled. "You're not that far advanced yet. It's still the stump for you."

She did her best to conceal her relief. Only two days had passed since she'd hidden from the Salish warriors, and her nerves weren't up to another strain. "Why are we going to the corral, then?"

"Your horse needs to learn to rope, the same as you. We don't know how she'll react. It's better to start her in the corral, in case she spooks."

Phoebe almost asked why a stump would cause Nutmeg to shy. An hour later, after whirling a rope over her horse's head, touching it to her side, and dropping the lasso in front of her, Phoebe was glad she had held her tongue. Nutmeg did well, only shying the first time the lariat touched her flank. The mare even held her own when Will pulled on the rope as a lassoed cow would do.

"That's enough for today." Will picked up Phoebe's hat, which had fallen at some point. He dusted it off then handed it to her. "We'll practice again tomorrow."

Phoebe took her horse for a short ride around the ranch. It wasn't fair to saddle Nutmeg and not let her explore her new surroundings. Phoebe stayed away from the open range, displaying caution that would have gratified her mother. Ma might not rejoice to know, however, that she loved training to become a ranch hand. Phoebe couldn't say for certain that she would enjoy working as one. She had a lot to master before assuming her actual duties. Worse ordeals could lie in store for her.

Let them come. Working at the ranch gave her back some of the freedom she'd taken for granted as a child. The nameless yearning to do something that mattered was gone. She woke each morning to a feeling of adventure, not knowing what the day would bring. She could see how some people wouldn't like the uncertainty she lived with, but it made her feel alive.

Whether romance and marriage fit into all of that, she didn't know. It seemed unlikely. Maybe that was the reason so many ranch hands remained single.

Phoebe led Nutmeg into her stall before Cooky beat the iron triangle to announce the noon meal. She didn't want to show up late and walk in with all eyes upon her. The novelty of her presence should wear off soon--at least she hoped so. The men weren't unwelcoming, but she felt like an outsider. Apart from her days off, she took most of her meals in the cookhouse. Cleaning up in time for supper with the family had proven next to impossible. Aunt Elsa couldn't hide her relief at Phoebe's decision. It must have been hard for her aunt to wait dinner for a late houseguest every night. Phoebe didn't want special treatment, anyway. If she could get away with it, she'd ask for a cabin of her own. That way, she wouldn't disrupt the family in any way. Ma might worry about propriety, though.

Phoebe sighed as she removed Nutmeg's saddle. Those stuffy rules belonged in the East, where they'd come from in the first place. Living in Montana Territory called for a different code. She would continue to consider her mother's feelings, however, as a respectful daughter should.

A scuffling sound at the front of the barn raised the hair at the back of Phoebe's neck. She peered through the dimness, but nothing stirred. Phoebe hauled in a deep breath and let it out slowly. Her nerves were still on edge from yesterday's misadventure. After Fiona had left her room, Phoebe had slept surprisingly well.

A mouse must have rustled the hay, nothing more. Phoebe removed Nutmeg's tack.

The sound came again, and she pinpointed it in the hay mow. Phoebe crept toward the sound. She'd rather not surprise a nest of mice but wouldn't leave Nutmeg without making certain the barn was safe.

When it came to possible peril, Phoebe had learned long ago that her imagination could outstrip reality. She approached the hay mow with a lump in her throat and one hand on the gun in her holster.

A pair of eyes glowed from the shadows.

Phoebe stepped out of the light from the high windows. A beam fell across an orange tabby cat perched on top of a hay bale.

Phoebe let out her breath, recognizing one of the half-wild cats that exchanged shelter for mousing duties. Knowing better than to approach the feral creature, she backed away. Phoebe went back to feed Nutmeg, much relieved.

The cookhouse triangle rang as she emerged into the barnyard. Phoebe washed at the pump and hurried to join the others. The midday meal consisted of beans floating with salt pork. Phoebe carried her bowl and a thick slab of cornbread to the table. Some of the hands were riding herd and wouldn't come in until supper. She'd noticed them pocketing a biscuit and wrapping up extra bacon at breakfast. When her turn came, she planned to follow their example. Will had yet to assign her to guard duty. Despite the prospect of encounters with Indians or rustlers, she wanted to do her part. Next time she spoke to him, she'd ask about it.

Will whistled while he swiped a polishing cloth over his horse's saddle. He'd cracked a window in the tack room, but the pungency of neatsfoot oil clotted the air. Some of the hands hated the smell, but he didn't mind it. He rubbed the oil into the leather in a circular motion, careful to avoid the waxed linen threads. The oil could cause them to deteriorate, yet another reason others griped about it.

His pain had eased somewhat, but his injured muscles didn't much like constant movement. Phoebe would object to his continuing to work. Will smiled at the way she'd dogged him to spare himself. He couldn't forget the skeptical look on her face when he'd claimed to be a man of his word. Will couldn't recall giving her cause to doubt him—except once. If Phoebe ever forgave him for kissing, and then walking away from her, she'd accomplish something he had yet to do.

Will didn't count his present activity as breaking a promise. If he didn't occupy himself somehow, impatience would drive him into the saddle. He'd never been one to sit idle for long.

Once he finished, he'd sit down with a cup of coffee. That ought to appease Phoebe. At any rate, it would salve his conscience. The job took longer than he'd anticipated, since he had to keep stopping until the throbbing in his side let up.

Will capped the tin of neatsfoot oil and wiped his hands on a spare rag before leaving the tack room. In the barn doorway, he stepped back for Katerina. She seemed in a rush, but he'd noticed her that way so often it might be her normal state.

Will tipped his hat to her. "Good afternoon. Have you

come to see Diablo?"

"Yes."

Katerina's smile struck Will as a trifle nervous. He abandoned his intention to escape and leaned on the door jamb instead.

"How are you mending?" Katerina looked him up and down, a skeptical expression on her face.

"Well enough." He came up with a neutral answer. There was no point in two women nagging him to rest.

"I've been worried." She frowned. "I feel responsible."

"I can't imagine why."

"I shouldn't have asked you to train Diablo. He's too wild."

Will ignored the slight to his ego. "I wouldn't have agreed to do it unless I thought it possible."

"And do you still?"

She was giving him the chance to let himself out of his commitment. Honesty wouldn't allow him to take it. Although Diablo presented a challenge, Will felt certain that he could break the mustang. If all went well, Matt would save him the trouble. "I do."

She studied him for a moment before speaking. "Promise you'll let me know if you change your mind about that."

Women seemed bent on procuring promises from him lately. This one was at least easy to give. "I will."

"Thank you." Katerina smiled, but then she skittered a glance past him and through the doorway. The nervous expression returned to her face. "If you'll excuse me…" She set off down the breezeway toward Diablo's stall.

Will caught up to her. "I'm going this way, as it happens." He was, in fact, headed wherever she went. He intended to find out the reason for her jumpiness. "I haven't spoken with Matt today. How is he doing with Diablo?"

"I've been meaning to talk to you about that." Katerina

stopped and looked up to him. "I hope you aren't offended, but I prefer Mr. Malone's method."

She must have hated to tell him that. It explained her nervousness, anyway. "That's all right by me. Horses respond differently to individual people. From the way Matt talked about Diablo, I could tell they'd formed a bond."

She turned a concerned gaze on him. "Thanks for understanding. I would hate to hurt your feelings after you've been so nice to me."

"Don't worry about that." Will didn't mention his relief at being let off the hook. He would rather not climb back onto the horse that had given him the hardest fall he'd suffered in recent memory. Will was no coward, but he picked his battles. No, he didn't mind one bit. Best of all, he wouldn't need to engage in any more awkward conversations with Katerina. "If Matt can train Diablo with less bother for himself and the horse, I'm all for letting him."

She broke into a brilliant smile. "You're wonderful, did you know?"

A shadow reached to them from the doorway. Will turned his head as Matt came in. He stepped away from Katerina in a hurry.

Matt's eyebrows rose, but he made no comment.

"Hello, Matt." Will broke the uncomfortable silence.

Matt nodded to him. "It's good to see you on your feet."

Will smiled. "I expect the spring back in my step any day."

"You might wait a bit to dance." Matt removed his hat. "Good day, Miss Meier."

Katerina smiled. "Hello, Mr. Malone. Are you here to work with Diablo?"

"Yes, but I can come back later if it's not a good time."

"No, no. I intended to visit Diablo, but I forgot his carrot. You're welcome to work with him. I'll go and get his treat."

Katerina dashed toward the doorway.

Will grinned. "Do you always have that effect on women?"

Matt returned his hat to his head. "I wonder if you are the cause. You were standing mighty close to her when I came in."

"I'd be less than a gentleman, I suppose, to blame that on her."

"You'd be unforgivably obtuse." Matt adjusted his hat brim. "May I ask your intentions toward Miss Meier?"

"That's easy. I have none."

"I can scarcely believe you. She's a beautiful woman."

"I've told you the simple truth. Miss Meier is beautiful, and she can be sweet—yes. I also find her uninteresting, presumptuous, and more than a little annoying." Will shook his head. "No, thank you."

A yowl rang out, and a cat streaked out the door.

Katerina separated from the wall near the hay mow. "I'm afraid I stepped on its tail." She stared at Will with a stricken look before following the feline from the barn.

Will's unkind words rang in Katerina's mind, and she stifled a sob. She shouldn't have stayed to listen. Everyone knew that eavesdroppers always heard unfavorable opinions of themselves. If only he hadn't seen her. She could have pretended that nothing had happened. That wouldn't have changed anything, but it might have saved her embarrassment.

She stopped at the washing station outside the back door of the ranch house. The water she splashed into her face cooled her flaming cheeks. She couldn't do anything about her eyes, which ached so badly they must be bright red. Katerina opened the back door as quietly as possible, hoping against hope that she would meet no one.

Elsa stood stirring a steaming pot in front of the stove. She glanced up briefly, returned to her task, and then looked back again. "My goodness gracious. What's happened to you?"

Katerina's throat tightened, and the tears she'd held in check brimmed over.

"I don't have any handkerchiefs in here." Elsa glanced about, and then handed her a dishtowel. "Here."

Katerina hid her face in the white cotton towel and vented her emotions. She'd never felt so humiliated.

Elsa put her arm around Katerina and led her to a stool at the counter. "Sit down and take a deep breath."

Katerina plunked onto the stool, swiped her eyes with the cloth, and heaved a breath. She released it in a shuddering sigh. "I've made a complete idiot of myself."

Elsa patted her hand. "Tell me what happened."

"What you said about letting love find me?" Katerina sniffed. "I should have listened."

Elsa gave a swift nodded. "I'll make tea."

Katerina watched her sister fill the kettle and measure Earl Grey into a teapot embellished with roses. Elsa lifted the kettle from the stove and poured hot water into the pot. After returning the kettle to the stove, she turned with a smile for Katerina. "Circumstances are rarely so dark as we at first believe them."

"I wish that were true." Katerina shook her head. "I messed up pretty badly."

Elsa slid onto the stool beside her. "To venture a guess, this is about Will Canfield."

Katerina glanced away from her sister. "I all but threw myself at him."

"I'm sure you didn't." Elsa smiled. "You're too well-brought-up to do such a thing."

"It seemed like I did." Katerina cast back over the episode. "Maybe I was a little too admiring."

"That's entirely different—although still lamentable."

"Thanks." She sniffed. "I feel somehow better."

Elsa nodded and reached for the teapot. "Do you remember that advice I gave you when you were sixteen?"

"Which time?"

"What do you mean?" Elsa gave her a bemused glance. "I don't step in very often."

Katerina hid a smile. "Which advice did you mean?"

Elsa poured tea into matching rose-covered cups and slid one in front of Katerina before returning to her stool. "I simply suggested that you exhibit patience."

"Ah, yes. I remember." Katerina inhaled the aroma of the tea. "To be fair, I was young and headstrong at the time."

"Unless I'm mistaken, that cowboy will always be a drifter. I'm glad you gave up on him."

"Once Mutter heard about it, I could hardly do anything else." Katerina shook free of the memory. "That was a long time ago."

"The lesson I hope you learned holds doubly true for Will Canfield. Tread lightly, dear sister. I think Phoebe has his heart."

Katerina sucked in a breath. "I suspected something between them, but then told myself I was imagining things. Does she care for him?"

"I believe so." Elsa's spoon clinked as she stirred her tea.

"I would never have hinted to Will if I'd known. I love Phoebe."

"Don't let it trouble you." Elsa lifted her cup and blew on her tea. "I doubt you could change anything."

"That's plain enough." Katerina drew a deep breath. "I'm afraid I spied on Will—Mr. Canfield."

"I can scarcely believe that of you."

Katerina nodded. "I feel the same way."

"Where and why did this happen?"

"We were in the barn. It was after Mr. Malone interrupted

us."

Elsa's eyebrows shot upward. "Interrupted? What were you and Mr. Canfield doing?"

"Nothing much." Katerina shrugged. "Standing close to one another."

"I see."

"I suspected they would discuss me, so I hid in the shadows by the door. I wanted to know what Will thought of me." Fresh tears pressed Katerina's eyes. "I found out, all right."

Elsa slid her hand over Katerina's and said nothing.

"He detests me." Katerina's tears spilled over.

"That can't be true. Mr. Canfield doesn't know you well enough to detest you."

"Well—" Katerina sniffed. "He didn't use that word, exactly."

"I thought not. Your overwrought state of mind is playing tricks on you."

"Mr. Canfield knows I spied on him." Katerina wrapped her arms around herself. "I wish I hadn't done it."

"Give it time."

"I'm sure I don't need to." Katerina spoke with deep conviction. "I can never face either of them again."

Phoebe didn't bother dismounting before Nutmeg waded into the shallows at the ford. Her horse lowered her muzzle to drink, rippling the water in circles that widened until the current swept them away. Today, as she did every day after roping practice, Phoebe rewarded Nutmeg with a jaunt to the ford and back. She wouldn't venture onto the open range until Will assigned her to ride herd. That seemed a long time away though, and Nutmeg needed to run.

How strange that freedom should come at a cost. Phoebe would pay it, when the time came, for her mare's sake and her own. Restricting herself to the ranch made her feel like a caged bird batting at the bars of its cage. She couldn't imagine how Nutmeg felt. Her mare was used to a wider domain.

Phoebe returned to the barn to discover Matt walking Diablo around the corral. The progress he'd made with the mustang seemed nothing short of miraculous. Phoebe had breathed a sigh of relief after learning that Matt would train Diablo instead of Will. She'd wondered which would break first—Will or Diablo.

After removing her horse's saddle and tack, Phoebe left Nutmeg to munch her oats and headed to the cookhouse.

Cooky, his arm raised to ring the triangle, grinned at her. "You beat the bell today."

She laughed. "I'm hungry."

"Supper's hot." He nodded toward the cookhouse door. "Help yourself."

"You don't need to ask me twice." Phoebe hurried inside with the bell ringing in her ears.

Will stood up from one of the benches, an empty coffee cup in his hand. She nodded to him. "You look like you've been here a while."

"I need my rest, or so I'm told." He saluted her with his cup.

Phoebe's face warmed. "Rightly so, I'd say." She lifted a bowl from the stack on the table and turned to the steaming pot sending up a delicious fragrance.

Will waited behind her. "Are you over your ordeal?"

"I think the tide has turned for me." She scooped stew into her bowl.

"That sounds like good news."

"It is." She handed him the ladle. "I must thank Fiona. She helped me overcome my fear."

"How did she do that?"

"She told me that the way to heal any wound is to surrender it to God."

Will nodded. "You're not the only one who needs that reminder."

Phoebe couldn't read his expression, but his words sounded promising. She tamped down on the joy that welled within her. Hope could disappoint, if events didn't transpire the way she imagined they would. Whether or not Will changed his thinking lay between him and God. Nothing she did or said could change that.

Phoebe carried her bowl to one of the tables and sank onto the bench. Will claimed the spot beside her as the cookhouse began to fill up. Phoebe waited until after she said grace to ask the question pressing her mind. "When do you plan to assign me to ride herd?"

Will's eyes widened. "I can't believe you're asking me that. Didn't you go through enough the other day?"

"It's part of my job, right?"

His expression grew guarded. "That's my call."

"Well?"

He sighed. "I'm saying no, for the present."

Phoebe waited a moment before replying. "Why?"

"Sorry to say this, but you're still pretty green. You need to be comfortable with basic skills before I'd want to risk it. I also need to make sure you're not going to panic out there."

"What do you mean by that?"

"I think you know."

He'd spoken softly, but his words still hurt. "I shouldn't have told you."

"I'm glad you did."

"I did all right when Brady and I saw those Indians."

"Maybe, but you looked ready to faint afterwards." He took a bite of stew.

Phoebe paused to reflect. Much as she hated to admit it, he had a point. In his place, she might make the same decision. She squared her shoulders. "I understand that I need to prove myself, but what will that take?"

"Time, Phoebe." He smiled, his eyes warm. "I suspect we'll both know when you're ready. That doesn't mean that you can't work on the range with everyone else. I just don't want you riding herd until you're ready. Once you learn to rope well, I'll give you more to do."

"I'm glad to hear it. My horse needs exercise. She's not used to being cooped up."

"I'll take you out riding myself."

"Thank you." She managed to smile.

"Let's wait a while, though. I'd like to make sure that band of Salish has left the area."

Phoebe nodded and addressed her stew with more attention. Will had all but called her a greenhorn, and she supposed he was right. Phoebe could admit to a certain amount of relief at his decision. She didn't want to rush into anything that might jeopardize herself or others. Whatever she felt about Will's personal decisions, she trusted him as a ranch manager.

Phoebe didn't mind waiting a little while to ride out alone with Will. She wasn't quite ready for that, either.

Will polished off his bowl of stew and went back for a second helping. When he returned to the table, Phoebe excused herself and stood up. The sunlight slanting through the window picked out her tangled curls. Will's interest in food evaporated. He tried not to stare at her, but he couldn't seem to help himself. Phoebe's gaze settled on him, swept the room, and came back again. Faint color blossomed in her cheeks. She picked up her hat from the narrow table beneath the window. Her boots tapped across the plank floor, and the screen door banged shut behind her.

Will felt like he'd been kicked by a mule. He'd thought of Phoebe as slightly spoiled, but tonight she'd accepted his decisions with obvious humility. He shook his head. How could he have misjudged her so thoroughly? Phoebe was so passionate about life that it took his breath away. She could ride as well as any wrangler, shoot better than most, and dress up like a high-society lady to boot. A man didn't often come across the combination of beauty, spirit, and just plain gumption that made up Miss Phoebe Walsh.

Only a fool would try to change her. She'd shown Alton Prescott the door for trying. Will didn't blame her one bit. He hoped she wouldn't compromise for anyone—including himself.

Phoebe counted riches in a way that Sophie wouldn't have understood. His fiancée's desire for the trappings of wealth had broken them apart. Will was beginning to think that such a thing would never happen with Phoebe. In all the time he'd known her, she had never once shown an interest in material gain. Why hadn't he noticed that before?

Whoa, there. Will reined himself in at once. If he didn't watch out, he'd fall completely in love with her.

CHAPTER SEVENTEEN

MATT HALTED ON THE WAY TO Diablo's stall. Had he really heard a whickered greeting? The soft sound came again. He smiled at the sight of the mustang waiting at the stall gate. "Listen to you, Thunder. Anyone would think you're a saddle-horse, fit to carry a lady." He offered the mustang a carrot. Diablo held back for a moment, and then accepted the treat. Matt scratched him behind the ears, gratified when he didn't move away. "Dare I hope you'll let me ride you today?"

Diablo, busy chewing, watched him out of placid eyes. Matt clipped the lead rope to his halter, and the mustang didn't pull back. He saddled Diablo and brought him out of his stall. The routine he'd established never varied. He walked the horse around the outside of the barn twice, pausing each time at the rear of the barn. Afterwards, they circled the corral until Matt judged the mustang ready to venture inside. He then led Diablo around the open corral. After closing the gate, Matt lengthened the lead line to allow the horse to explore, unfettered.

He would take matters no farther until Diablo grew comfortable, even bored, with the routine. He waited while Diablo ran around the corral. When the mustang seemed to tire, Matt approached him from the left. He tugged on the pommel a couple of times, making the saddle move as it would when he mounted. "All right, Thunder. Let's see what kind of friends we are." He sucked in a breath, landed his boot in the stirrup, and lifted into the saddle.

Diablo shifted, taking his weight. He swung his head back

and sniffed Matt's leg, and then faced forward. Matt rubbed the mustang's shoulder and felt the horse tremble. He'd better take it slow. Diablo followed the corral fence around clockwise, and then took off in a sudden burst.

"Easy." Matt spoke to ease his own tension as much as to soothe Diablo.

The mustang slowed and backed to the fence, giving Matt—and probably himself—a respite. "You're doing fine." Matt rubbed the quivering shoulder again.

Diablo cut across the corral and traced the fence in the opposite direction. Matt guided him back around, to see how he would respond. Diablo turned neatly and headed clockwise again.

Matt took advantage of a quiet moment to swing down from the saddle. He rewarded the mustang with a sugar cube. "Well done, Thunder."

"I'm impressed."

Matt turned his head. Katerina stood watching him from behind the corral fence. He removed his hat. "Hello, Miss Meier. That's the first time he's let me ride him. I'm glad you got to see it."

"I couldn't help being curious. It looked so calm compared to when Will—Mr. Canfield tried to ride him."

Matt chose his words with care. "Nothing against Will. He breaks horses the usual way, but Diablo needs gentler treatment."

"I'm so glad you're working with him."

"Me, too. Thanks for the opportunity." Matt took a couple of steps toward her, ready to offer to train her to manage her horse.

Katerina backed away from the fence, a look of panic on her face. "I didn't mean to interrupt you. I should go."

"Please don't." He spoke softly, as he would to a frightened horse. "Not on my account, anyway."

"That's kind of you to say." She bit her lip. "I'm sorry for eavesdropping on you and Mr. Canfield. I feel dreadful about it."

"I appreciate that, but don't take it so much to heart." Matt smiled, trying to bolster her spirits.

"How can I avoid it?" She gazed at him with tears shining in her eyes. "My mother raised me better, I can assure you."

"I'm certain there was no flaw in your upbringing."

She sniffled. "I don't know what got into me."

"Look, I understand." He searched for words that would comfort her. "Maybe it wasn't the best thing to do, but you're only human."

A faint smile touched her lips. "You are kind."

"Have you spoken with Mr. Canfield?"

Katerina shook her head. "I'm not sure I should."

"If it were me, I'd want to clear the air."

"Of course, I do, but I'm not sure what he'll say."

"He's a little rough around the edges, but he's fair. Give it some thought."

"I will." She brushed away a tear.

The sudden desire to take her into his arms and shelter her from all harm seized him. Matt found himself at a loss for words, but it didn't matter.

She was already hurrying away.

Katerina rounded the corner of the ranch house and leaned against the back wall. She'd run the last part of the way to the house from the corral. Although it was early, warmth from the sun had already soaked into the clapboard. Katerina pressed one hand to her chest while she caught her breath. She let her eyelids droop downward, reducing the grass and sky to blurry lines of blue and green. Maybe, if she stayed like this long enough, she could forget everything but the feel of the sun on her face, the buzz of bees in the garden, and the calming scent of lavender.

After spotting Matt with Diablo, she'd almost stayed away from the corral. If she hadn't overcome her impulse to hide, she'd have missed seeing him ride her horse for the first time. That would have been disappointing. Matt's gracious response to her ill-mannered behavior spoke well for him. She didn't know if she felt better or not, though. He'd been so kind that she felt even more of a wretch for spying on him.

Matt's advice might be difficult to follow, but she would try. Not only did she need to ask Will for forgiveness, she should give it in return. Asking someone you'd wronged for mercy but failing to grant it to yourself would be prideful. She had to forgive herself as well. She wasn't sure which task would be harder. One thing she knew for certain. She could do none of them on her own.

Katerina closed her eyes fully. *Dear Lord, I'm sorry for trespassing into a conversation where I wasn't invited. I shouldn't have done it. Help me do better in the future.*

She pushed away from the wall, feeling much better. The weather was far too pleasant to go indoors. She'd noticed, when digging carrots for supper yesterday, that weeds were overrunning the garden. Katerina glanced down at her yellow calico dress. She should fetch an apron.

She started humming on her way to the house and walked with a lighter step. The back door banged shut behind her, and Elsa glanced up from kneading dough at the counter. "Good morning. Are you seized with the desire to help in the kitchen?"

"I wanted to tackle the weeding, but if you need help—"

"Not at all." Elsa smiled. "Don't let me keep you."

Katerina collected the cushion she knelt on while gardening, an apron, a pair of leather gloves, and a trowel from a shelf beside the door. She also retrieved the pail used for weeding.

The sun greeted her more strongly than before. She knelt in its warmth and dug out a dandelion nestled among the carrots. Katerina dropped the intruder into the bucket and dislodged another. A pine butterfly emerged from the trees crowding up to the garden and fluttered about on gossamer wings.

The rhythmic work soothed Katerina's knotted stomach. Tension sloughed from her shoulders, and her thoughts wandered in pleasant pathways. She would plant beans to run up the corn, the stalks were thick enough to support them. Maybe Elsa would like a row of lavender against the fence. A kitchen garden should be as functional as it was beautiful, in her opinion. Tomorrow, she would pull a carrot for Diablo. Visiting her horse early might help her avoid Will.

Katerina straightened and pushed wisps of hair out of her eyes with the back of her glove. Any peace she found would probably be short-lived until she resolved matters with Will. She pushed the uneasy thought to the back of her mind. After an hour in the sun, it was time for a drink of water.

She stripped off her gloves and folded them over the edge of the bucket. Once she cooled off, she would return. Coming in from the brightness outdoors made the kitchen seem dim.

Elsa stopped cutting tomatoes and wiped her hands on her apron. "Looks like some cooled tea would come in handy."

"That sounds lovely."

I'll stop for a moment and have some with you." Elsa poured two glassfuls from a blue willow pitcher.

Katerina sank onto a stool at the counter beside her sister.

She took a long pull of the soothing liquid. "Pulling weeds can be quite cathartic."

Elsa laughed. "I can imagine."

"I'm still smarting from Mr. Canfield's remarks. He said I'm uninteresting. Do you think I'm boring?" He'd also called her sweet, but that wasn't the part that rankled.

"Of course, not. To be fair, he didn't actually say you were boring."

Katerina blinked. "Aren't uninteresting and boring the same thing?"

"Not at all." Elsa sipped her tea. "You might not share the same enthusiasms as Mr. Canfield, but that doesn't make you boring."

Katerina glanced at her in suspicion. "If we want to split hairs, I suppose that's true. He also called me presumptuous."

"Well?" Elsa gave her a direct look. "Is he right?"

Katerina stared at her sister in horror. "Do you agree with him?"

"I never said that, but I'd call eavesdropping presumptuous. Wouldn't you?"

She averted her eyes. "Since you put it that way—yes."

"Have you done anything else that would lead to such an impression?"

Katerina felt considerably less peaceful than when she'd pulled weeds. "I'm beginning to suspect that Mr. Canfield is right."

Elsa nodded. "It hurts, I know, to realize your flaws."

"He also said that I'm annoying. Now that I think about it, I can see how he might feel that way." She put her hands to her cheeks. "I'm so ashamed."

"Katerina." Elsa shook her head, smiling. "None of us is perfect, not even Mr. Canfield."

"I need to apologize to him, but I'm scared of what he'll say."

"You can't control his reaction. All you can do is say you're sorry. The rest is up to him."

Diablo put his head over the stall gate, obviously waiting for a treat.

Matt chuckled. "All right, Thunder. You've earned this." He pulled a sugar cube from his vest pocket and held it out on his flattened hand. Diablo crunched into it at once.

"You're getting mighty tame, aren't you?" He coiled the lead rope, and then rubbed the mustang's neck a final time. "See you tomorrow."

Will's whistling reached him from the barnyard.

Matt decided to hold off on leaving.

Will strode through the doorway, appearing not to notice him. He made a beeline for the tack room. Matt needed to hang up Diablo's rope and halter, but that wasn't the main reason he followed him into the long room that housed an array of saddles, bridles, horse collars, harnesses, and other gear.

A square window at the far end occupied the wall above a work table. Matt spotted Will taking a bridle down from its peg. "Good morning."

Will nodded. "Morning."

"Going riding?"

"I am." Will flicked a glance to him, and then away.

Matt decided the man didn't need nagging, but a gentle reminder couldn't hurt. "I assume you're up to it."

Will smiled. "I'm ready as I'll ever be."

Matt didn't counter his opinion outright, but a hint might not go amiss. "Your recovery seems remarkably fast."

"If I'm making a mistake, I'll find out soon enough." Will

shrugged, and then winced.

"So you will." Matt slung the lead rope over its peg. "Where are you headed?"

"To check on the cattle."

Matt narrowed his eyes. "You have plenty of others to do that."

"All right." Will looked away. "I can't stand sitting around, and I'm aching to get back in the saddle."

"That, I do believe." Matt reached past him and slid the halter onto its peg. "I rode Diablo for the first time today."

Will swept a glance over him. "I'm glad to see you still in one piece."

Matt smiled. "It went well."

"I wish I'd been there. It must have been a sight to see."

"Miss Meier was watching, although I didn't know it at first."

"I'm not surprised." Will's voice took on a dry note.

"Meaning?"

"She's given to secrecy."

"I don't think you understand her correctly."

"I'm not sure how you can say that. She did make herself privy to our conversation."

Matt folded his arms. "Miss Meier apologized to me only an hour ago."

Will's eyes narrowed. "I hope she meant it."

The urge to protect her intruded on Matt once again. He kept his tone mild. "I have no reason to doubt her."

"Are you serious? She displayed a singular lack of character."

"Have you never made an error in judgment? She freely admits to wronging us. You have to give her credit for that."

"You defend her an awful lot."

"Maybe I shouldn't have to."

Will's expression softened. "Maybe not."

Matt chose his words with care. "Your words wounded Miss Meier, even though you never intended her to hear them. If it was me, I'd want to make things right."

"I do feel badly about criticizing her."

"Talk to Miss Meier, and I suspect you'll both feel better."

Will nodded. "Let me give it some thought."

Will held on as his horse splashed through the bright water at the ford. A small flock of ducks paddled away, whistling an alarm. Patches stepped over the bent grass and onto the bank. A crane fly whirred past, so near that the air its wings stirred touched his face. The appaloosa left the river behind, climbing the trail to a bench above the river. A meadowlark welcomed them with its warbling song. The tiny bird's yellow breast stood out against the leaves of a huckleberry bush.

The sun greeted them also, considerably warmer than in the riverbed. Will urged his horse onward, searching for cattle. The herd would be easier to spot before lying down in whatever shade they could find to wait out the heat. On the open range, the cattle fended for themselves. Will's main duty was to protect the ranch's livestock from danger. That took many forms. Lightning strikes could kill individual cows or panic the herd into stampeding. Grass fires sometimes broke out. Patches of locoweed tempted the cattle, who after eating the toxic plant grew listless and often died. Wolves, bears, and mountain lions might attack. Poachers were by far the worst predators, however. And of course, barbed wire posed a new peril to guard against.

Will urged his horse down an animal trail that cut through the grass. Pines, cottonwoods, and other trees cropped up, sheltering bunches of cattle beneath them. Strays from other ranches mixed in, competing with the herd for forage. The dark hides of the Angus set them apart among the reddish coats and white faces of Con's Herefords. Beyond that, the cattle were distinguishable by their brands. A lot more strays were mixed in with the herd than in previous years. Will wouldn't separate them out until the fall roundup. He wasn't certain the grass would sustain all the livestock until then.

Before much more time went by, it looked like he needed to move the herd to higher pastures. Going where the forage was harder to reach reduced competition, but it required him to establish a camp away from the ranch.

Will didn't envy Con, who was weighing whether to put up fencing after the fall roundup. It seemed harsh but, with the number of cattle on the range increasing yearly, might be the only way to save the herd.

Two men on horseback appeared in his line of sight. Recognizing Sparky's flaming hair and Davis's slouch, Will waved. He'd assigned them both to ride herd today. They returned his salute. Will sent Patches into a gallop that ate up the distance between them. Will reined in, and although Patches stopped, he fidgeted like a fresh colt. After days of confinement while he recovered, Will couldn't blame his horse for feeling antsy. "Good afternoon." He nodded to Sparky and Davis.

"Afternoon, boss." Sparky spoke while Davis maintained his usual silence. "I didn't expect to see you out here so soon."

"Nothing could keep me away." Will smiled. "Did you see anything out of the ordinary?"

Sparky screwed up one eye. "Some of our cattle have wandered afield."

"Better bring them in." Will restrained his restive horse. "Any sign of rustlers?"

Sparky shook his head. "Not today."

"All right." Will pulled down his hat brim to better shield him from the sunlight. "If you've nothing else to report, I'll leave you to your duty."

Sparky and Davis touched their hat brims and rode off.

Will rubbed his horse's shoulder and felt Patches quiver. He put the appaloosa through his paces in short order. Patches stretched his muscles with every appearance of delight. Will's back muscles protested, but he didn't have the heart to slow their speed.

The pain became a steady throb, and then sharpened. He reined in. The ache lessoned but didn't go away. Will brought his horse around. "Sorry Patches, but I need to go back."

Will had learned his lesson the hard way. From here on out, he would summon the patience to let himself heal. He should have listened to Phoebe in the first place. She would be gratified to know that he'd come to agree with her.

His thoughts wandered to Katerina, the other woman who had expressed interest in his health. From what Matt had said about her, she was also in pain, only of a different type. Will didn't like the idea of anyone suffering when he could prevent it.

By the time he reached the ranch, he'd decided to take Matt's suggestion and speak with her.

Will slid off his horse in the barnyard. Hooves thudded on the far side of the barn. Will smiled, despite his pain. It was probably Phoebe, who never let up on roping that stump.

He settled Patches in his stall and returned his gear to the tack room. All he wanted was to lie down. He went to check on Phoebe, anyway. Will rounded the corner to the sight of her lasso dropping over the stump with sweet precision. Nutmeg held firm while Phoebe tugged the loop tight, a look of triumph on her face.

"Good job." He limped her direction.

"Thank you." Phoebe stared down at him. "What have you done to yourself?"

"Patches needed to gallop, but I apparently didn't." He tried to make light of it, but she didn't seem amused.

"You promised to take it easier."

"I did. Only then I felt better and assumed I could do more."

"Honestly." Phoebe jumped down and freed the stump. "You need to learn patience."

Will couldn't argue with her. "It might please you to know that I'm acquiring that very virtue. There's no greater teacher than pain."

"I'm sorry you're hurting." Phoebe coiled her lariat with swift skill.

"I'll mend." His attempted smile fell flat. "You're ready for live roping, by the way. I'll need to recuperate for a day or two before we start."

Her eyes gleamed. "Only a day or two?"

"You never know." He winked at her. "It might even take a week."

CHAPTER EIGHTEEN

KATERINA CAUGHT HER BREATH AT THE sight of Diablo circling the corral with Matt on his back. Gone was the wild-eyed beast, and in his place walked a noble creature. Diablo held his head with regal grace, a proud mustang with an unbroken spirit. And yet, he bore Matt's weight without reproach. Matt seemed to belong on Diablo's back. He rode with a relaxed posture Katerina envied. It must take years to feel so at ease on a horse.

Matt turned his head and met her eyes. "He'll be ready to leave the corral soon."

She glanced away, suddenly shy. "You've worked wonders with him. I can't thank you enough."

"It's my pleasure."

She looked back at him. "I wish I knew how you manage horses so well."

"It's a gift." He shrugged. "Would you like me to teach you to ride?"

"Would you, really?" She beamed.

"Of course." Matt rubbed Diablo's shoulder. "You have a wonderful horse, and I want you to know how to handle him."

"I would absolutely love to learn from you."

"Then, it's agreed." Matt smiled. "We can start tomorrow morning, early, if that works."

"It's perfect."

"Good. I'll figure out something before then. Thunder is too fresh for you to ride while you're learning."

"What did you call him?"

Matt's face picked up color. "It's my pet name for him. I can't abide Diablo."

"I've been meaning to rename him." She smiled. "Thunder it is."

"I'm glad you like it. I was saying that I'll saddle another horse for you to learn on."

"Not Miss Buttons."

"Don't worry. I'll find a different one."

"Thank you." Katerina drew a deep breath. "I want to ride astride like Phoebe."

"All right." Matt's expression didn't change. "No sidesaddle. Come back an hour earlier than this tomorrow, and we'll begin."

"I can't wait." Katerina resisted the urge to jump for joy, something she hadn't done since she was a child. She would work hard and learn everything she needed to know. If she failed to ride her horse, it wouldn't be for lack of trying.

His smile grew. "I'll look forward to it."

Katerina left Matt and hurried to the ranch house. A detour through the garden for the joy of it seemed in order. *Thank you, God. I'm sure this is your doing.* She'd thought Will would help her, but Matt had stepped forward instead. Katerina had never expected the stranger who had soothed her horse to play a part in her life. Matt almost seemed heaven-sent.

Katerina burst into the kitchen. The aroma of huckleberries filled the air, and Elsa was stirring a pot on the stove. "You'll never guess."

"Mm?" Elsa didn't look up. "Sorry, this jam is about to gel. What can't I guess?"

"Mr. Malone is going to teach me to ride."

"The same Mr. Malone you never wanted to see again?"

Warmth seeped into Katerina's cheeks. "I regret saying

that."

"I'm glad to hear it." Elsa ladled jam into jars lined up on the counter. "He seems very nice."

"He was kind when I said I was sorry."

"So, you apologized?" Elsa wiped the jar rims with a dish towel.

"It wasn't easy, but I did it." Katerina hugged herself. "I still don't feel comfortable around Mr. Canfield, though."

"Did you apologize to him also?" Elsa ladled hot wax into a jar, sealing in the jam.

"No."

"That might be the place to start."

"But he insulted me."

Elsa added wax to another jar. "Not willingly. There's a difference."

"I guess so." Katerina didn't feel comforted, nor did she want her sister to be right. She couldn't deny the truth, however, while it stared her in the face.

Elsa finished sealing the jars and set the pan of melted wax on a folded dish towel. "When do you start your lessons?"

"Tomorrow."

"Excellent." Elsa's eyes gleamed. "That means you're free to help in the kitchen today."

Katerina feigned a sigh. "I suppose you want me to do the dishes."

Will rose early with more energy than his injured muscles could handle. Although he'd grounded himself from riding, he decided to make himself useful in other ways. He made his way to the barn, in search of something to do. The harnesses could use cleaning, for one thing. It had been a while since anyone had touched them. In the light from the tack room window, Will bent over a harness and massaged the leather with a cloth dipped in neatsfoot oil. He whistled while working, a childhood habit picked up from his father. Restoring suppleness to the leather also smoothed the rough edges of his impatience. He hardly minded the pain that dogged his movements.

This chore would take a while. Once finished, he could look for other tasks to distract him for a little while. He would soon have no excuse to avoid training Phoebe on live calves. He'd found teaching her tolerable, even amusing, so long as her target remained a stationary stump. Lassoing a living, breathing animal was a quite different matter. He didn't relish the task of keeping her safe. Roping accidents didn't happen all that often. When they did, the damage was usually bad. He'd seen unwary ropers lose fingers, horses cut by taut ropes, and calves bawling from broken bones.

Besides its dangers, roping was exhausting work. Phoebe didn't know what she was getting into. If she had any doubts about becoming a ranch hand, roping might help make up her mind on the matter. He'd never ask her to quit, but he almost wished she would. Quelling his protective instincts where she was concerned took a lot of effort.

A shadow fell across the open doorway, and Matt looked in. "I thought I heard you in here. You're up early."

"I figured I'd get a head start on the day."

"Is your back hurting you?"

"That's what woke me."

Matt nodded. "I know what it's like. I've been busted up a time or two."

Will poured more oil on his rag. "You're out and about earlier than usual yourself."

Matt leaned against the door jamb. "I'm waiting for Miss Meier. She's meeting me for riding lessons this morning."

"Good idea. From what I've seen, she needs them." Will ran his rag along another harness strap, gratified by its gleaming.

"If you're speaking of her mishap with Miss Buttons, that could have happened to anyone."

"True, but screaming made the situation much worse. If she'd shown more restraint, she might not have needed rescuing."

"No inexperienced rider acts self-possessed in the saddle, and especially not with a skittish horse."

"You make a good point." Will smoothed out a rough spot on the strap.

"I'll start her out with what to do in emergencies."

"That ought to bolster her confidence." Will shook his head. "Between you and me, I don't know why she wants to ride that brute of a horse she owns."

"I'll help her decide whether she should ride or sell him. By the way, her horse isn't such a brute any longer."

"I hope you can work the same miracle training Diablo's owner that you did with him. I'd love to hear how you broke him."

"I don't mind telling you, but I'd better not take the time this morning." Matt withdrew from the doorway, but he reappeared the next instant. "I forgot to ask. Did you decide to speak with Miss Meier?"

Will paused in his work. "I plan to, but I haven't come across her yet."

"She might be keeping out of your way from embarrassment."

"As well she might." The same thought had occurred to Will. Despite his abrupt remark, he didn't like the idea at all.

Matt jutted his chin. "At least she had the decency to admit she did wrong."

Will couldn't help smiling. "She has quite an advocate in you."

Matt shrugged. "Maybe."

"Thinking of settling down, by any chance?"

"Possibly."

Will cocked an eyebrow. "You're a regular fount of information, aren't you?"

Matt grinned. "All right, yes. Miss Katerina Meier has changed my mind about settling down. What about you? Are you going to let Cooky beat you to Miss Walsh?"

Will chortled. "Cooky is a confirmed bachelor."

Matt folded his arms and leaned against the door jamb, apparently forgetting the rush he was in. "Don't be so sure of that. Many a good man has fallen. You might even."

Will turned back to the harness he was oiling. "Being jilted at the altar changes a person's interest in marriage."

"I can understand how that might happen. I have one thing to say, and then I'll hold my peace."

"Only one?" Will somehow doubted Matt would stop offering him advice. He gave him his attention, though. Anyone who cared enough to intrude into his life deserved that much.

"If you're happy, fine and well." Matt gave the slightest shake of his head. "I wouldn't say you are, though."

Will frowned. "I haven't given it much thought."

"That's plain."

"I thought you were in a hurry."

Matt raised his hands, palm out. "All right. I'll stop meddling."

"Thank you." Will scrubbed at the harness leather with renewed vigor.

"Except to say that letting a past heartbreak destroy your

present happiness would be a crying shame."

The palomino mare watched Katerina from dark eyes while munching the carrot she'd offered her.

Matt placed a mounting block beside the horse. "Buttercup likes you."

Katerina cast a doubtful look at the mare. "I hope so." A horse could seem friendly—placid even—and then turn on you. Images of her ordeal with Miss Buttons had flashed across her mind all morning. She'd thought about calling off her lessons, but that would be quitting.

"I'm sure you'll get along."

Katerina nodded, not certain of that at all.

Matt seemed to know how difficult this was for her, for he didn't rush her. It took her a while to decide to climb the mounting block and step into the saddle. Her skirt, slit along its back seam, made sitting astride possible. She wore bloomers but couldn't get over feeling immodest. A couple of downward glances assured her that her ankles were decently covered. Sitting astride felt strange, but also more secure. No wonder Phoebe favored it.

Matt gazed up at her. "How are you doing?"

She nodded as much to reassure herself as him. "I'll be all right."

He gave her a questioning look, but then smiled.

Katerina listened intently while he showed her how to hold the reins. She already knew most of this, but she wanted him to cover it to fill in any gaps in her learning.

Matt adjusted the stirrups to the length of her leg, and then straightened. "I want to watch you ride Buttercup. Before you begin, let's make sure you have a thorough understanding of how to stop."

"Yes, thank you." Katerina managed a smile. "That was my problem with Miss Buttons."

He smiled. "From what I heard, she spooked and ran away with you. That could happen to any rider, no matter how well-schooled the horse."

"Really? I felt to blame."

"I doubt you could have prevented it. I'd like to teach you how to handle such situations better, should they arise."

She released a sigh. "That would help."

He nodded. "Knowing what to do might keep you from injury, even save your life. I don't want to deceive you, though. There's no guarantee you won't be injured. That's a risk every rider takes."

"How reassuring."

"Sorry." He smiled. "But knowing and accepting the danger can help you better deal with a crisis, should one arise. We'll begin with the best way to fall."

Katerina blinked. "There's a good way to fall?"

He laughed. "I wouldn't say that, but there are better ways to land. We'll go over what to do. Meanwhile, to stop a horse…"

Katerina tried to pay attention, but the way his face lit when he smiled distracted her. He paused, and she realized he was waiting for her to respond. She cleared her throat. "Would you please repeat the instructions?"

His gaze probed hers. "Am I going too fast?"

She shook her head. "No, I'm just a little overwhelmed." That was true enough. There was no need to explain why.

"Stopping is easy. Since you've ridden before, you must know to gently pull on the reins."

Katerina nodded, relieved that she hadn't missed much.

"I don't want to assume you understand the other ways to tell your horse you want to stop. Let's go over them, shall we?

You can push deeper into the saddle, stiffen your back, and squeeze the horse slightly with your legs. Understood?"

Katerina averted her eyes, her face warming at his mention of her legs. When Buttons took off with her, she'd tried all of that to no avail. "What if my horse ignores me?"

"Pull backward more firmly and say 'whoa.' Establish a good rapport in the first place, and the problem might not arise. The more you ride, the more self-assured you'll become. Your horse will sense your confidence and respond to your commands without protest."

"That makes sense." Katrina brightened, pleased to find something she could change, although it would take some doing. "It felt like Miss Buttons grew more fearful because of my nervousness."

"That's entirely possible." Matt beamed at her as if she'd won a prize.

"What a lot I've learned from that horrible episode."

"God turns all things to our good."

"Yes!" She gazed at him, becoming lost in his smile, as he explained how to tell if her horse had halted correctly.

"Did you catch all that?"

"What?" Katerina sat a little taller. "Yes."

He narrowed his eyes, looking unconvinced. "Repeat what I said, please."

She cast back in her memory, grateful to find that his words still lingered. "My horse, when she halts, should stand square with her nose down. If she flips her head up, I've pulled back too sharply. If she swings or turns, I'm probably holding the reins unevenly. Oh, and I shouldn't forget to breathe while remembering all that."

"Good." His eyes gleamed. "Ready to learn how to walk your horse?"

She really needed to pay better attention, but her work was cut out for her. His eyes were the most amazing shade of blue she'd ever seen.

Will hung up the last oiled and gleaming harness and flexed his aching back muscles. Time to stop. He wiped his hands with a clean rag before exchanging the fume-ridden tack room for the fresh outside air. His steps carried him to the high bank above the Bitterroot. Will stood for a long while, soaking in the sights and sounds. The rushing of water blended with the rattle of leaves. Geese set up a racket somewhere downriver. Their calls almost reminded him of hounds baying. Below him, the willows bending to the water like women washing their hair. The green shadows pooling below their feet spilled into the water, where they quenched shimmering tides. A fish jumped close to shore, sending bright circles to lap the bank.

The sun was nearing its peak, and the cookhouse iron would soon ring, but Will didn't budge. Nature sustained a man's soul the same as food nourished the body. It brought him closer to his Maker. Will would swear that he could listen to the wind soughing along the river and hear God whisper.

"It's beautiful, isn't it?" Phoebe murmured.

"Yes." Will didn't look around. Phoebe coming to stand beside him in this moment seemed as inevitable as the scent of the river. If he wanted to throw caution to the wind, he would say that she belonged at his side.

They stood without speaking. Out of the shadows below them, a crane winged across the river. The bird planted its feet in the shallows and fluffed its wings. Something swirling in the water caught Will's eye—a maple leaf, trapped in an eddy.

"Do you know how to fish, Phoebe?"

"Yes. I learned with my brothers. Murphy is better at it, but

I can hold my own."

Will smiled. "I'm not surprised."

"I thought the traps keep the ranch supplied."

"They mostly do, although they're too small for the larger species. If the forage runs out, we'll move the herd to higher pastures. Fishing comes in handy then. Sometimes we stop long enough to catch our supper during a cattle drive, too. How are you at hunting?"

"Murphy's better, but I can—"

"—hold your own?" He laughed. "I should have guessed. We hunt mainly in the fall and winter but sometimes at remote camps."

"Do you foresee going to higher ground this year?"

"I'm not quite sure." He watched the heron dip into the river—after a meal, no doubt. "I had to come back before fully assessing the range. In a couple of days, I'll ride out again."

"Take me with you? Remember, you said you would."

"I seem to recall saying something about it." Why had he made such a rash promise?

"Please—my horse needs the exercise, and I'm perishing for the chance."

He could think of no reason to deny her. "All right. We'll leave after breakfast, say in two days' time. You should bring any food you'll want, and don't forget your gun."

CHAPTER NINETEEN

PHOEBE EMERGED ONTO THE RANGE in time to surprise a herd of deer. She reined in behind Will as the herd bounded away. Phoebe had encountered deer many times but seeing the high-stepping creatures never failed to lift her spirits. An eagle spread its wings against a sky painted in the colors of sunrise. Soft light caressed the grass clumped in patches of green and brown. In places, it was cropped so short that it reminded her of the mown lawns at Prescott Manor.

Nutmeg pricked her ears, quivering and alert. Phoebe felt a certain anticipation herself at the prospect of a gallop. Neither she nor her horse could tolerate being cooped up at the ranch for weeks on end. Phoebe reminded herself that today's ride would differ from the ones at her parents' ranch. She was no longer free to indulge her whims but must allow her boss to lead. They should take Will's injury into consideration, which probably meant riding at a walk. Phoebe sighed. If only she could explain to Nutmeg why she had to hold her back.

Focusing on what she couldn't do was making her melancholy. A change of mindset was in order. She could be thankful that Will didn't seem seriously hurt. However reluctantly, he had brought her out with him. She would soon advance in her training, putting her closer to becoming a working ranch hand. All told, she had a lot to smile about.

Will's horse stomped and snorted. He laid a hand on Patches' shoulder, and the appaloosa quieted.

Nutmeg pranced, but Phoebe kept a firm grip on the reins.

"No running today, girl."

Will turned his head. "Why not?"

"I didn't think you could gallop."

"Maybe not for long, but I should hold up for a short while. I want to cover a lot of ground today, so we'll need to speed up once in a while."

She frowned. "That seems a lofty goal for someone on the mend."

"I hope you don't plan to brood over me." He smiled. "I learned my lesson the other day. Trust me to know whether I need to turn back."

"All right." Phoebe nodded, although she would find that difficult.

Will's smile widened. "As a matter of fact, this would be a good time to gallop—to settle the horses down, of course. Why don't we aim for that bench?" He pointed to a grassy shelf at the top of a rise. "It's one of the pastures we need to check for forage."

A knot formed in her throat. He couldn't have chosen a better destination. Riding through the flats would give both the horses and themselves a chance to warm up. She wished they weren't headed the same direction that she and Brady had gone when they'd encountered Indians, though. She would mention that to Will, but then he might guess her nervousness. Will was already leery of bringing her out here. What if he restricted her to the ranch indefinitely?

Phoebe scanned the bench and the surrounding area. Nothing moved. Maybe it was all right to stay silent.

Will moved sideways, allowing her the trail.

Phoebe pushed down her fear and loosened Nutmeg's reins. Her horse responded to her signal at once, needing little urging. Nutmeg went from a walk to a trot before moving into the rocking motion of a canter.

Phoebe bent forward to make galloping easier. The wind buffeted her ears, dulling the rhythm of Nutmeg's hooves striking the hard-baked trail. Dust rose in her wake. Will pulled up but didn't overtake her. The trail was wide enough on the flat for him to ride alongside. Even after it narrowed, he managed to keep pace. Once in a while, he vanished behind a tree, but he always found his way back to her.

The trail tilted upward, and Phoebe guided Nutmeg up and over swells. She slowed her horse as they climbed. Nutmeg was walking by the time they reached the bench.

Will reined in beside her. "The grass is shorter than I'd like here. There's another place I want to check. We'll need to go higher." He pointed to a second grassy shelf.

Phoebe sucked in a breath. "Wait."

He gave her a puzzled look. "What?"

She had to speak. "That's where Brady and I saw the Salish band."

"Why didn't you say something before?"

"I was afraid you would send me back."

He frowned. "You took the choice from me."

"I'm sorry."

He rubbed the back of his neck. "Never mind. At least you told me, in the end."

Will took a pair of field glasses from his saddlebag and lifted them to his eyes. "It doesn't look like anyone is still up there."

Phoebe nodded.

He held her gaze. "Are you up to this?"

"I think so." Her answer came out less firmly than she'd intended.

Will studied her for a moment. "Follow me, if you're

coming." He moved into the lead.

Phoebe's hands trembled on Nutmeg's reins, but she started after him.

The trail climbed steadily to the meadow where she'd hidden with Brady. As they approached, Phoebe searched about for threats. Drifts of wildflowers greeted her, their many-hued faces open to the sun. A meadowlark's melody rippled the air, and a bobolink added its chirping song.

Will raised his field glasses again. "It should be all right to go farther."

Phoebe's mouth went dry, but she didn't argue. They climbed steadily until they reached a third meadow.

"The grass is better here," Will declared.

Phoebe gazed about her. Stands of lupine, buttercup, blue flag, and wild rose waved in the sun. Pine trees circled the edges, dark sentinels that would guard those who sheltered here. Some of Phoebe's tension sloughed away. "This seems a better location altogether."

Will nodded. "We've used it before. Those trees act as a windbreak, and you can see for miles."

Phoebe looked out across the valley. The river glittered as it wended through stands of trees and grasses. A herd of horses broke into a run, manes tossing and tails flying. A reddish tide of cattle flowed beneath the trees. She frowned. "Isn't it too early for the cows to lie down in the shade?"

"Yes, as a matter of fact." Will pushed back his hat and turned his face toward the sky. "I don't like the shape of those clouds."

Phoebe looked upward. Fluffy clouds with flat tops and grey undersides loomed overhead. Shadows raced over the ground, and an ominous half-light blanketed the plain. The air fairly crackled with electricity. "Where did those clouds come from? The sky seemed clear a moment ago."

Will emitted a long whistle. "We're in for a thunder storm. Too bad. I wanted to check other pastures, but we should head back."

"Maybe it will blow over."

"We shouldn't count on that." Will swung his leg over Patches and landed on the ground. He untied a bundle behind his saddle. "Better put on your slicker. I doubt we'll make it back in time to avoid a drenching."

"Those clouds—" Phoebe dismounted also. "Shouldn't we seek shelter?"

"Our best protection is reaching lower ground. After that, yes. There's an old prospector's cabin we sometimes use when caught out in a storm."

"That place? I was scared of it as a child. Richard swore up and down it was haunted."

Will smiled. "He probably wanted it for himself. The only spirits I've met there were fumes from discarded liquor bottles."

"It sounds like a lovely spot to shelter."

"We've cleaned it up since then." Will returned to the saddle. "When you're ready—"

"One moment." Phoebe dropped her slicker over her shoulders. The oilskin cape rustled as she climbed back into the saddle. Will nodded for her to go first. She clucked to Nutmeg, who needed no other encouragement to set off down the trail. The mare's quivering warned of her uneasiness. "Easy, girl." Phoebe stroked her shoulder.

They'd almost returned to the first bench when lightning tore through the sky. Seconds later, thunder boomed. Rain drove into them.

The hair rose on Phoebe's nape. It was all she could do to suppress the urge to gallop. Even Nutmeg, who was normally steady as a rock, could give in to blind instinct. Phoebe didn't fancy clinging to a runaway horse in a thunderstorm. The cattle were bawling in the flats, and some milled about in fright. Her father didn't run nearly as many head as Uncle Con, but he always worried about a stampede. Phoebe remembered several. Thankfully, no one had gotten hurt, but Pa couldn't always locate the scattered cattle afterwards. When he did, they might be injured or dead.

Lightning flared again, and Phoebe counted the seconds before thunder rattled. She urged Nutmeg to go faster. The storm would overtake them soon.

Will glanced over his shoulder with a growing sense of dread. A jagged line of light split the sky. Thunder followed. He faced forward with more urgency, determined to reach shelter before the worst of the storm broke. Through the rain, he could make out Phoebe restraining her skittish horse. He could only admire her courage. He'd seen the fear on her face but also the determination to overcome it. Subduing a frightened horse while faced with her own panic couldn't be easy.

The rain pounded them in an unrelenting deluge. Patches stumbled with mud sucking at his hooves. Not much longer, and it would be too slick to go on. Will could hear cattle crying out in fear. One terrified cow could bolt all of them. The only way to stop a stampede was to surround the herd and turn it in on itself. That would slow the momentum and bring it to a stop. He reminded himself that the men riding herd were trained to prevent a stampede from starting in the first place. Hopefully, they could reach the cattle in time. He would hate to leave Phoebe, frightened and alone, to deal with a stampede.

Up ahead, the trail curved toward the crossing. A fainter track led to the right. Phoebe looked back as she neared the divide in the trail. From what she'd said, Phoebe had visited the cabin briefly in her childhood, perhaps only once. How remarkable that she remembered how to reach it. Will waved her forward, and she followed the fainter track. They passed through a stand of trees and reached a creek. The rough path continued on the opposite bank. Although water surged down the creek bed, Will waded Patches across behind Nutmeg. His horse slipped on the bank and stumbled before righting himself.

"Steady, boy." Will soothed him, although his own heart was racing. The sky darkened as clouds obscured the sun. Thunder shook the ground and rain lashed his eyes.

He barely recognized the cabin roof when it appeared. Halfway hidden in the deep shade beneath an overarching tree, it protected the bare-bones of the structure. The cabin might have fallen long ago, but for the ranch hands' efforts to keep it standing. It served a useful purpose, providing somewhere to shelter from wind, cold, and rain. A stove heated the cabin and allowed all comers to warm themselves and brew a cup of coffee before going back into the cold.

To the right of the cabin stood an even more derelict building, if it could be called by that name. A long, low structure listed to one side and might have fallen but for the timbers propping it in place. A small fenced enclosure gave away its use for livestock. He turned aside, dismounted, and opened the gate. They would call upon the makeshift stable to shelter their horses. The enclosure was too flimsy to hold a determined horse, but Will expected that Patches and Nutmeg would have the sense to remain beneath a dry roof. He threw hay to them as an inducement to stay put. He'd return to check on them once he had Phoebe settled.

The cabin door creaked open under Will's hand, and he entered behind Phoebe. The light outside was so dim that his eyes barely needed to adjust to the interior. He closed the door, shutting them in with rain pelting the windows. He glanced about, seeing the cabin with new eyes. The floor sloped at an odd angle, as if in sympathy with the stable. He checked for signs of rodents or other vermin. None appeared, thankfully. He turned his head and found Phoebe making a similar inspection. "The cabin isn't much."

A strained smile reached her lips. "It will do."

Will nodded toward one of the chairs at the scarred oak table. "Make yourself at home, and I'll see if I can scare up some heat."

After a brief inspection, Phoebe settled into one of the chairs.

The potbellied stove in the corner opened with a creak. Will bent to the pile of wood and kindling stacked beside it. He pulled a sulphur match from a tin safe and soon had a blaze going.

Will stood up. "I'd better take care of the horses." He found Patches and Nutmeg restive but calmer. Working the well pump in the rain was a chilling task, but he endured it for their sakes. After watering the horses, he spread straw for bedding. The familiar tasks seemed to calm them further.

He pumped a bucket of water and carried it inside the cabin. The aroma of coffee greeted him. "That smells good." Rather than dripping across the floor, he paused to hang up his slicker to dry beside Phoebe's on a peg by the door.

Phoebe smiled. "I found a jar of coffee and filled the pot from my canteen."

"It's not much of a kitchen, but we keep it stocked for emergencies." He ran his gaze over her face. Her eyes looked darker and wider than normal. "How are you holding up?"

She shrugged. "I'm grateful to be dry."

He wasn't fooled by her show of nonchalance. The storm had her rattled. "Have a seat." He gestured toward one of the ladderback chairs at the scarred table. "I'll look after the coffee."

Will took down tin cups from the shelf beside the stove while Phoebe sank down with a sigh. He glanced at her. She'd propped her elbows on the table and held her head in her hands. The wind howled outside the cabin, and he thought she winced.

In that moment, a fierce desire to shield her took hold of him. Feeling protective of Phoebe was nothing unusual for him, but this shook him. He wondered, not for the first time, how he would survive her working on the range.

He poured coffee and passed Phoebe's cup to her. As she accepted it, their fingertips touched. She glanced up with a startled expression. Will had felt it, too—a surge of energy that had nothing to do with the storm. He dropped into the chair across from her. Putting a table between them seemed a good idea.

Phoebe leaned forward. "How long will the storm last?"

She knew the answer as well as he did, Will felt certain. Even so, he would give it to allay the nervousness that must have prompted it. "There's no way of telling."

Phoebe nodded. "I guess we'll have to wait it out."

"I know we're in a compromising position, alone in the cabin like this." He drummed his fingers on the table. "I should have foreseen the possibility."

"You can't safeguard me against everything." She smiled. "I wish you wouldn't try so hard."

He firmed his jaw. "Don't ask me to go against my instincts."

"I wouldn't want to." She smiled. "I'm not as fragile as you think, though."

"Blame my mother, if you want. She taught me to protect females." He stroked his chin. "She wouldn't be happy with this situation."

"My mother wouldn't like it either, but she's old-fashioned." Phoebe shook her head. "I'd rather be safe than proper."

"Let's concentrate on both priorities, shall we?"

"Of course." Phoebe's dimples peeked from her cheeks. "After Alton offered to court me, Ma worried herself to distraction about propriety. Once I refused him, she settled back to normal." Phoebe sipped from her cup, and the steam curled around her eyelashes. She sighed. "I'm glad I don't have to bother about that anymore."

Will gulped a warm mouthful and let it slide down his throat. "So, you don't regret your decision?"

Phoebe shook her head. "Some women care about status and wealth, but I never have. I'm more interested in—" her cheeks went pink.

"What? Tell me what you care about, Phoebe." Will realized with a jolt how much he wanted to know.

She pressed her lips together as if determined not to speak, but then smiled. "Love. That's what matters most. It's true gold, not the fake kind. Finding it is worth more to me than anything Alton could offer."

Will nodded. "I know what you mean. I wish my Sophie had your attitude."

She studied him. "You've mentioned her before. Who is she?"

Will hesitated, not certain how much to divulge. "My fiancée. Sophie was the opposite of you. She wanted wealth I didn't have, but my brother could give her everything she wanted. She left me at the altar and ran off with him."

"How horrible." Phoebe stared at him with shock on her face. "I can't imagine what you suffered."

"At the time, it all but killed me." He smiled, despite his sadness. "I was young enough to believe love should turn out well."

"So it should. No one deserves such treatment."

"I figure that Sophie did me a favor. Otherwise, I'd have been bound to a woman who loved wealth more than me." He rubbed his thumbnail down a scar in the table. "Sounds like we've both had a narrow escape."

"Yes, it does. I've learned that there's life after heartbreak." She gazed at him with wide eyes. "That's worth knowing."

Will didn't like thinking that Alton had hurt Phoebe that much, but what else could she mean?

Phoebe stood at the cabin window, gazing at the lessening rain. The branches that had scraped the cabin through the worst of the storm must have lifted away. Lightning hadn't flashed for a while. She didn't want to leave. The warmth and coziness of the cabin felt preferable to suffering the discomfort of sodden clothing and stinging eyes on the ride back.

Will came to stand beside her. "We'll be able to return to the ranch soon."

Was it her imagination, or did he sound sad about the prospect of leaving?

She couldn't escape the fact that the invisible bond between them had strengthened. Phoebe had longed to talk intimately with Will. However, there were dangers in doing so. He'd already broken her heart once. She couldn't allow him to do it again. Although he'd told her about his painful experience with Sophie, revealing a hidden part of himself, she didn't trust the change in him. It was too new.

"Phoebe, I've never dishonored a woman." He paused, as if choosing his words. "Should there be any talk about our sheltering together, I wouldn't start with you."

"Thank you, but I doubt anyone at the ranch would gossip about us. If anyone did want to make it their business, they probably would, no matter what we did."

"I wish I'd thought twice about us coming out alone together. I've escorted you at the request of your uncle so many times, it seemed natural."

"Uncle Con put you up to accompanying me?"

"I thought you guessed."

Phoebe considered that idea. "Maybe I suspected."

"If there is gossip—" His jaw firmed. "I wouldn't let harm come to you in any way."

Phoebe smiled. "I appreciate that, but I don't believe in slavish devotion to the old restrictions. Certain things should remain between a person's conscience and God." Phoebe suspected what he was implying, but half of something with him wasn't good enough. When it came to Will, she wanted all or nothing.

He lifted her face with a finger under the chin and gazed into her eyes. "Never change, Phoebe."

She saw what was coming but couldn't summon the fortitude to escape it. Parting her lips in breathless anticipation, she waited while he lowered his mouth to hers. Although a featherweight kiss, it shook her to the core. Will pressed a hand to the small of her back, bringing her nearer. She leaned into him, offering her lips once more. He sealed her mouth with his own and stirred waves of desire that carried her closer to him.

Phoebe freed herself in sudden alarm. Today, she had revisited the place where she'd cowered from Indians with relative calmness. She'd avoided panicking despite the threat of lightning. But losing herself in Will terrified her more than anything else. Once she did, there would be no return to common sense.

CHAPTER TWENTY

WILL PASSED THE COOKHOUSE WITHOUT STOPPING and followed the path toward the barn. He couldn't summon an appetite for breakfast. Taking advantage of Phoebe after promising not to dishonor her couldn't be more reprehensible. He'd already spoken with God on the matter, but he also needed to ask Phoebe's forgiveness.

He rubbed his eyes, which ached from lack of sleep. He'd finally slept as dawn approached, only to be roused by the old nightmares about Sophie and his brother. Discussing the past must have summoned them. Will was glad he'd told Phoebe about Sophie, regardless. He'd been holding the pain in, like a child afraid to expose a wound for cleansing.

Will slowed at the side path to the ranch house. He could swear he'd seen—yes, there. Katerina knelt in the garden, her fair hair reflecting the morning sun. She brushed the back of her gloved hand across her forehead—the very picture of innocence. Will halted in his tracks. This seemed to be his day for apologies.

Birdsong greeted him as he neared the garden. The feathered creatures seemed obnoxious after his bad night. The heady perfume from the roses tumbling over the fence wafted to him. Katerina lifted her head as the gate squeaked open. Dirt smudged her cheek, and her hair wisped about her head. She gazed at him with guileless eyes. "Good morning."

"Hello." He nodded to her. "You're out working early."

"It's the best time in the garden."

"I can't argue with you there."

She put down her trowel. "I've been meaning to talk with you."

That was what he'd been about to say. "Oh?"

Katerina stood up and brushed off her skirt, lingering over the task a little longer than necessary. She faced him at last. "I'm sorry that I eavesdropped on you and Mr. Malone. Can you ever forgive me?"

It took Will a moment to switch from his own apology to hers. He *had* been pretty hard on her. "Yes, of course."

"Thank you." Relief shone from her eyes.

He rubbed a hand down his neck. "What I said about you was unforgivable."

Katerina's face reddened. "I won't say it didn't hurt."

"I'm sorry."

She glanced away. "I fear that some of your criticism was justified."

"Please don't trouble yourself. I'm the last person who should throw stones at anyone else. Am I forgiven for telling tales out of school?"

"Yes."

"Thank you. Why don't we put the whole thing behind us and start over?"

"I'd like that." Her face lit. "Shall we shake on it?"

"Agreed." He clasped her hand solemnly, but then broke into a smile. "I'm glad that's behind us."

"Me too."

She spoke with such relief that his conscience pricked him for taking so long to speak with her. He resolved not to repeat the same mistake with Phoebe. He would put matters right with her today.

Phoebe sliced into a fried egg, doing her best to ignore Will's absence in the cookhouse. It felt personal, after what had happened between them in the cabin. He seemed to be avoiding her company after yesterday. She couldn't pretend the possibility didn't hurt. After she'd broken off their kiss, he'd become moody and withdrawn. They'd ridden back in the last of the rain and parted afterwards in uncomfortable silence. She'd dragged herself upstairs to bed, feeling as dampened as her clothing. Sleep came quickly, but she'd awakened in the night, thinking of Will. What would she say to him the next time they met? She couldn't pretend nothing had happened between them.

The sensation of someone watching prickled her skin. She glanced up in time to catch Cooky's gaze on her. He smiled. "You're quiet this morning."

She nodded. "I'm still recovering from being caught out in the storm."

"No kidding." Sparky called from farther along the table. "It struck mighty quick. Me and Brady hunkered down but took quite a beating from the wind and rain."

Brady thumped his coffee cup on the table. "That weren't the worst of it, if you ask me. The lightning came so near that the hair on my arms stood right up. I thought we'd get struck for sure."

Matt looked across the table to an apple-faced ranch hand. "Davis and I got soaked talking the cattle around us out of stampeding."

Davis winced. "It was a near thing, but thank the Lord they took our advice."

Others spoke out on where they'd been and what they'd endured during the storm. After a few minutes, Phoebe stopped listening. She normally enjoyed the patter that broke out at the table, but this morning it grated on her nerves. Paying attention was too much of a strain, since her thoughts kept returning to Will.

Phoebe had dreamed of him looking at her the way he had in the cabin. She'd never imagined herself pulling out of his embrace afterwards. She hadn't felt safe in his arms. Too much remained unspoken between them. She wanted more than tender looks, sweet words, and passionate kisses. Her parents' love for one another sheltered the whole family. Phoebe's stubborn heart wouldn't let go of the hope that she could forge the same kind of bond with Will.

She looked up to discover Cooky watching her with a frown. His gaze skittered away. Phoebe sighed. The cook must guess the cause of her distraction. It was kind of him to worry about her, but she would rather save him the trouble. Time alone was what she needed this morning, anyway. Riding Nutmeg around the ranch might keep her thoughts from sliding back to Will. Nothing worked better to clear her head than being in nature. Fortunately, she could count exercising Nutmeg as part of her duties. Both she and her horse needed to stay in good condition.

Phoebe applied herself to breakfast, carried her dishes to the side board, and reached for her hat. She nodded a farewell to the cook.

Cooky's worried expression fled, and a smile spread across his face.

The screen door squeaked open and banged shut behind her. The breeze rushed over Phoebe, and she caught the scent of roses. The chattering of birds followed her along the path to the barn.

Voices carried from the garden as she neared the turn-off for the ranch house. She halted in her tracks. What were Will and Katerina talking about so intently in the garden? Far be it from

Phoebe to inquire. She almost succeeded in not looking their way.

Katerina and Will were facing one another with clasped hands and beatific smiles.

Phoebe sucked in a painful breath. Her stomach ached as if someone had kicked her. How humbling to discover that Will's absence from the cookhouse had nothing to do with her. Here he was, holding hands with Katerina, not twenty-four hours after kissing her in the cabin.

Phoebe hurried toward the barn. In its shadows, she could try to make sense of what she'd seen. She'd heard of women falling in love with men who proved themselves less than heroes. Hopefully, she hadn't become one of them. Her mind spun with possibilities, but only one made sense.

Will was making up to both her and Katerina.

Will walked with a lighter step on his way to the barn. The morning was turning out better than he'd anticipated. He'd never expected to find Katerina so willing to make peace. Hopefully, Phoebe's reaction would also surprise him. Despite his hopes, Will's gut tightened as he walked into the barn. The rush of air that followed him spun motes in the light slanting through the high windows. Some of the horses gazed at him over their stall gates. He would feed them, but first he needed to check whether Phoebe was inside.

He spotted her slinging a saddle on Nutmeg. He approached with caution, wary of the reception he would receive. He never quite knew where he stood with Phoebe. She'd responded to his kiss with fervor, only to push him away the next moment. Perhaps she'd come to her senses and recognized the compromising position she was in. Either that, or his kiss had repelled her. He couldn't bring himself to inquire. The riddle had occupied him, along with self-reproach, during the long painful ride to the ranch.

He removed his hat. "Phoebe?"

"Yes?" She delivered her response in frosty tones.

Will took a deep breath. "I want to talk with you. Do you have a moment?"

"I'm about to exercise Nutmeg." She kept her back to him.

He turned his hat in his hands and thought about giving up but squared his shoulders instead. "I won't keep you long."

She finished tightening the girth strap before facing him. "All right."

He chose his words with care. "I wasn't on my best behavior at the cabin. I shouldn't have—taken liberties."

She raised her chin. "No, you shouldn't have."

He winced. "I hope you can forgive me."

She glanced away from him, clearly searching for words. "I'll try."

"I mean it, Phoebe." He softened his voice. "I'm truly sorry."

She nodded, her face expressionless. "Is that all you wanted?"

Was it so hard to forgive him for desiring her? Will scolded himself for impatience. He should give Phoebe all the time she needed. "There's something else. You might want to know that I'm ready to teach you live roping. That is, provided you still want to learn."

"Why wouldn't I?" She frowned. "Of course, I do. When do we start?"

"Tomorrow morning, early. Saddle Nutmeg and meet me in the corral, ready to rope."

"I'll be there."

"Good. I'll give you some pointers on herding cattle. You'll need to know them soon."

"I will?"

The widening of her eyes was the first sign of animation she'd shown. The glimpse brought a pang, for it revealed how completely she had shuttered herself from him. Will cleared his throat, reminding himself to keep their conversation on business. "You can help drive the cattle to higher pastures."

A faint smile touched her lips. "I didn't expect to be included."

"You can't keep roping stumps forever." If he'd told her the same thing two days ago, she'd have jumped for joy. Will pulled his gaze from her wistful face and turned to go. He couldn't resist looking back from the doorway. Phoebe slipped a bridle over Nutmeg's head and fastened it. Intent on her work, she didn't appear to notice his continued presence, but her tense bearing spoke of strong emotion.

Will turned away. Phoebe remained a mystery he might never solve.

CHAPTER TWENTY-ONE

PHOEBE PULLED ON HER LEATHER GLOVES while Nutmeg shifted beneath her. The Hereford calf Will had called Daisy watched her from liquid eyes, her nose twitching. Will seemed to have selected the smallest cow in the herd for Phoebe to wrestle. That might not be the best idea. A younger calf could be easier to pin down, but it made a smaller target to lasso. Even so, she was glad the calf wasn't bigger. Lassoing a stump seemed a far shot from roping a living creature. She resolved to do everything in her power to avoid injuring Daisy, Nutmeg, or herself.

Will looked rough this morning, as if he hadn't slept well. He flicked a glance from her to the calf and back again. "Are you ready?"

Phoebe repressed the urge to say no. Delay would only prolong the agony. She needed to learn live roping in order to assume her full duties. She wanted Uncle Con to get his money's worth out of her. He shouldn't continue paying her handsomely to lasso a stump, do odd jobs, and ride around the ranch. She pulled in air. "Ready as ever was."

"All right." Will smiled. "Please confirm that your lariat is correctly coiled."

She checked for what must be the tenth time. "It's right."

"Mount your horse and take up your rope."

Phoebe followed his instructions, noticing that Nutmeg seemed a little skittish—probably due to the presence of the calf.

Will examined her hold on the reins and lariat. "Looks good. Now, remind me what comes next."

"I'll lasso one hind leg, dismount, flip Daisy onto her side, and tie her free hooves with a piggin' string."

Will peered at her from the shadow cast by the brim of his hat. "Why is it important to tie a calf's hooves?"

"To keep it from injury."

"Where do you hold the piggin' string?"

She grimaced. "Between my teeth."

He laughed. "It's the best way, Phoebe."

"Yes, I know. We've been through all that." She still didn't like the idea of clamping down on a piece of raw leather. Once she used a piggin' string to tie a calf, forget reusing it. She'd have to start new each time.

"What's next?"

She shook her head. "After that, I'll bring my horse forward a step or two to ease the tension on the rope."

"It sounds like you know what you're doing. Get ready." Will strode toward Daisy.

Phoebe expelled a tense breath, bit down on the rawhide cord, and swung her lariat. Daisy needed no prodding, but sprang past Will and ran her direction. Phoebe narrowed her eyes, the better to see the swiftly-moving legs. Choosing the right moment to release the loop wasn't easy. She took her best guess.

Daisy continued along the fence, kicking up her heels. The rope lay, crumpled in the dust, behind her.

"Once more." Will's practical tone cut through her shame.

Phoebe coiled her rope, resolving to do better.

Will started after the calf. Daisy leaped past him and charged toward Phoebe.

Phoebe barely got her lariat spinning before she had to release it.

"Better."

"You can't be serious."

Will grinned. "You came closer."

"The rope fell short."

"She didn't allow you much time."

Phoebe frowned. "This is harder than I realized."

"You have to get the feel for roping a calf. That takes practice. Speaking of which, let's give it another try."

Phoebe retrieved the rope, wishing she was anywhere else. She didn't enjoy failing repeatedly, and especially not in front of Will.

Daisy was trying to get at a patch of grass outside the corral. She gave Will a cautious glance but didn't budge.

He laughed. "She's getting wise to me already."

"It's your ingratiating personality." Phoebe twirled her lariat and waited.

Will waved his arms, and the calf sprang away from him at last.

Phoebe gauged the distances. The calf barreled past, and she threw her lasso. The rope bounced off Daisy's side and dropped to the ground.

Will returned to her, his eyes gleaming. "Not bad."

"What do you mean? I missed."

"At least the rope touched her this time."

Phoebe blew out a breath. "Tell me what I'm doing wrong."

"All right." Will sobered. "You're ruining your throw by tensing up. Relax, and I think you'll do better."

Phoebe gave him an incredulous look. "I'm trying to rope a running target, which is not exactly restful. And now you want me to relax."

He steadied her with a look. "You can do it, Phoebe."

She swallowed. "I'll try."

While Will charged toward the calf, Phoebe rolled her shoulders and did her best to calm the tension zinging through her body.

She set the rope spinning as Daisy launched out. Phoebe released the rope and watched it play out. The lasso settled over the calf's hind leg. Surprise froze Phoebe for a moment, but she pulled the rope snug in time and slid down from her horse. Nutmeg backed slightly, tightening the slack.

The calf was struggling to rise. Phoebe gripped her flank and laid her on her side. She whipped the piggin' string around the free feet, secured the rope with a hooey knot, and jumped upright. Phoebe brought Nutmeg forward to slacken the rope, and then returned to slip the loop off the calf's leg. Daisy lay still, bound by the piggin' string around her three hooves.

Will bent over Daisy, inspecting Phoebe's work. "Nice job." He untied the calf, and she ran off.

"Thanks." Phoebe waited to catch her breath before speaking again. "I didn't hurt her, did I?"

"What do you mean? That was the gentlest tie-down I've ever seen. You're the one who will likely be sore, not Daisy."

"I hope she's not terrified."

He smiled. "Does she look frightened to you?"

The calf was reaching for the grass outside the corral. Phoebe blew out a breath. "I'm probably worrying too much."

Will shrugged. "Daisy had her objections, but I don't think she'll hold it against you."

"I'm glad to hear it."

"You caught on awfully fast. I guess you have a knack for roping."

"It's all that practice with stumps." She began winding up the lariat.

"I suppose so." He ran his hand down his neck. "You look

beat. Let's call it quits, shall we?"

"All right." He wouldn't get an argument from her.

"We'll start up again tomorrow."

Phoebe summoned a smile, her best attempt at enthusiasm. What had she gotten herself into?

"You sent for me?" Will stood in the library threshold.

"I did." Con stood up from a chair by the fire and went to the window. "Close the door, if you would, and take a seat."

Will pushed the door to and lowered himself into a leather-cushioned chair across the hearth from the one his boss had vacated. "What's up?"

"I have news." Con began pacing. "A neighboring rancher sent word that he encountered a band of renegades in the area."

"I'm not surprised, after what Brady and Phoebe told me."

"They stole some chickens and several head of cattle."

"Hopefully, it won't go beyond that."

Con nodded. "By God's grace, it won't. Let me know if you notice anything amiss."

"Of course. Apart from the band Brady and Phoebe came across, we haven't seen any Indians. Hopefully, the renegades will move on."

"They may have already, but we can't count on that." Con paused in his pacing. "Have you noticed anything unusual at all?"

"We've noticed signs of rustlers." Will shrugged. "The scoundrels are impossible to avoid altogether."

"I wish more people understood it as stealing." Con commandeered a seat opposite him. "I also want to talk to you about Phoebe."

"Phoebe?" Will sat straighter.

"Yes. How is she working out?"

"Better than I thought she would. She's almost ready to help with the drive to higher pastures."

"That's good, but she's seemed unhappy lately." Con frowned. "Do you know the cause?"

Will would rather not mention his misstep with her, but he respected Con too much to withhold the truth. He cleared his throat. "That may be my fault."

Con studied him for a long moment. "Go on."

"I took her riding on the range, and a summer storm blew up."

Con settled into his seat. "I remember one a couple of days ago."

"That's when it happened. We didn't have time to return to the ranch before lightning struck. We were forced to shelter in that old prospector's cabin." Will steeled himself for Con's reaction to what he would say next. "I'm afraid I took advantage of the situation."

Con's eyes widened. "While I can understand something happening between you two, don't ask me to believe that you—well—"

"No, no." Will shook his head. "I kissed her. That's as far as it went. She hasn't acted the same toward me since. I don't blame her. I'm not happy with myself over it."

"Why is that?"

Will shook his head. "It wasn't fair to her—or me, for that matter. I don't expect to marry."

"Yes, well. You strike me as a bit confused about that."

"I won't quibble with you."

"Never mind." Con smiled. "I'm sure you two will sort yourselves out."

Will jumped up and began to pace. "I offered to make it right. Phoebe turned me down."

Con arched an eyebrow. "Did she, indeed?"

Will gave him a suspicious glance. Why did he seem to approve? "She said she doesn't care about the old restrictions."

Con grinned. "That sounds like Phoebe."

"I wish I knew what's going on in her head."

Con shook his head. "If I've learned anything about women, it's that they are hard to decipher. The only way you'll learn what Phoebe thinks is to ask her."

"Maybe not even then."

"It doesn't hurt to ask."

"There's where you're wrong." Will shook his head. "I don't want to make matters worse between us."

"From what you've said, I'm not sure that's possible."

"You may be right." Will dropped into his chair.

Con sat forward. "Might I suggest that you take time for reflection? Make peace with God and with yourself on whether to marry. Since you're confused about what you want, the Lord only knows what Phoebe believes."

The hues of sunrise bloomed bright against the darkened trees. The pines pointed skyward, catching fire at their tips. Phoebe looked away, blinking, from the sun burning at the horizon. She'd risen early and saddled Nutmeg for the drive to higher pastures. They needed to move the cattle before the heat made it hard on the livestock.

Phoebe looked about her. What had been a milling group of men and clumps of cattle had formed into a column, ready for the trail. A thrill of anticipation mixed with nervousness shot through her. She'd never herded cattle before, but she'd picked up live roping within a couple of weeks. Hopefully she could learn to herd as fast. She wanted to repay Uncle Con for putting faith in her.

"Miss Walsh," Matt called from the back of a chestnut horse. "Will wants you to help me."

"You? But you're the ranch wrangler. I thought I would work with cattle."

Matt drew up beside her. "Will tells me you're gifted with horses. I can use your assistance, to tell you the truth. Ralph usually drives the horses with me, but he's laid up with a sprained ankle."

Phoebe rallied. "Yes, of course." She could admit to relief at not needing to prove her mettle with cattle—at least not yet.

Matt smiled. "Come with me."

She turned Nutmeg and followed Matt's chestnut to the rear of the herd, where several hands were keeping the horses in line. Phoebe's enthusiasm dampened somewhat. The place in line ensured that she would breathe the maximum amount of dust kicked up by the cattle's hooves. Even so, she didn't really mind herding horses rather than cattle. At least, Will had included her in the drive. His logic in calling upon her to assist Matt made perfect sense. She knew a lot more about horses.

Whatever she felt toward Will personally, she respected his judgment as her boss. She had a lot to learn about roping. Although she could lasso a calf with relative accuracy most of the time, a grown cow was a different matter. She wouldn't dare try to lasso a steer by the horns, and she had yet to rope with another person.

She understood horses better but had never driven them either. Matt seemed a good teacher, though. As they started off, she soon learned that the instructions Will had given her worked equally well with horses.

Will and Brady rode in pointer positions near the front, and ranch hands flanked the herd at regular intervals on either side. No one actually led the column, however. That way, as Matt explained, the cows were less likely to suspect they were being guided along. The main duty of the cow hands was to keep the cattle moving while preventing them from wandering. They also fended off strays belonging to other ranchers from joining the herd.

Phoebe remembered Will saying that he loved ranch work, and she could see that in him today. She felt herself softening toward him but held back. She wasn't sure he felt about her the way she did about him. If she let herself succumb to his charm a third time, she would only have herself to blame.

A Bible verse sprang to mind. "Sufficient unto the day is the evil thereof." She embraced its wisdom. Each day brought its share of problems, and she lacked the ability to solve even one of them beforehand. It was hard enough to deal with those she faced today. It wouldn't hurt to focus on the delights and challenges before her and leave tomorrow's worries alone.

Phoebe sat a little taller in the saddle, glad for the morning sun warming her face. There would come a time when its warmth on her skin might not be so welcome, but she would deal with that when it happened.

They climbed steadily out of the valley and had to discourage the livestock from lingering at the first bench. The grass was longer there than in the valley but inadequate to sustain them for long. Phoebe could sympathize with their desire to graze, but they needed to reach their true destination before the afternoon heat.

They arrived at the second bench before noon. Cooky had gone ahead with the cook wagon. Excited voices and the bark of laughter rang across the meadow. As she neared, the delicious aromas of bacon, coffee, beans, and cornbread wafted to her. Her mouth watered in response.

The livestock milled about before lying down in the shade.

They would sleep away the soaring temperatures and rise to graze in the twilight hours. After watering the horses and leaving Nutmeg tearing the grass in the shade of a lodgepole pine, Phoebe joined the ranch hands gathered at the chuckwagon. She filled a plate along with everyone else but sat alone on a fallen log to eat. She didn't mean to seem standoffish, but sometimes she wanted quiet. No one remarked on her keeping to herself, but Will's gaze rested on her more than once.

After the meal, Will pulled a bundle from the back of the chuck wagon and brought it to her. "I thought you might like to use this."

Phoebe stared at the object in his hands. It looked like a bedroll, only bulkier. "What is it?"

"A tent." Will's eyes gleamed. "Con thought your mother might express concern about your privacy."

Phoebe smiled. "Thank you."

"You're welcome. Show me where you want it, and I'll set it up for you."

Phoebe stood up, feeling ridiculously like nothing had changed between them. "What about somewhere around here?"

"I don't know. I'm not sure I like you sleeping so close to the trail."

She eyed him. "Do you mention that for a particular reason?"

"Not really." He looked away from her.

She gave him a suspicious glance. Did he know something he wasn't telling her? "Too bad. I like this spot, and the ground is flatter here."

"I suppose it would work, provided you don't mind me laying out my bedroll within earshot."

"I'd like it best if you did." She smiled. "Sleeping alone in a tent at night can be scarier than lying out under the stars."

He laughed. "No need to be frightened. I'm a light sleeper. I'd hear anything that came near."

"Are you worried about animals on the trail?"

He shrugged. "They do roam them at night. Still want me to put the tent here?"

"You made that up to tease me!"

"No, it's true, but I've only ever seen deer."

"You could have told me that. My imagination doesn't need any outside help."

His gaze caressed her. "That happens to be one of my favorite things about you."

Phoebe attempted to steel herself against his charm and almost succeeded. She picked up her plate. "I'd better take this back to Cooky. He'll be doing the washing up soon."

She walked to the cook wagon with the distinct sensation of someone watching her. She couldn't say for certain that it was Will, because she refused to turn around and look.

Cooky pulled a frown when he saw her, even while his eyes sparkled. "You're just lucky I haven't started dishes yet."

She laughed. "I suppose I'd be washing my own plate."

He grinned. "I'm glad to see you'll have a tent. A cattle camp is a rough place for a young lady."

"I could sleep out like everyone else."

"I'm sure you would, but it's good that you won't need to."

She nodded. "My uncle thought so, and Will is doing his bidding."

He peered at her. "Don't you want a tent?"

"I don't like special treatment."

"Now, there you have a problem."

"I do?"

Cooky nodded sagely. "Because you are special."

Phoebe smiled. "Why couldn't I fall in love with someone

like you instead of—" She broke off, horrified at what she'd been about to let slip.

"Will?" Cooky gave her a sympathetic look. "Do you think I don't know?"

"Promise you won't breathe a word."

He chuckled. "I wouldn't divulge a lady's secret, but I think you'll find we all suspect what's going on between you two."

"How humiliating."

"Don't be embarrassed. I can't think of anyone more suited than you and Will. You work together beautifully."

"Do we?" She'd paid more attention to their personal spats. "I guess I missed that."

He nodded. "Sometimes, dear friend, we miss the truth that's right in front of us."

She left Cooky in lighter spirits. Maybe things would work out after all. In her absence, Will had set up the tent with the door facing into the meadow. He was nowhere in sight, but she heard him murmuring somewhere close at hand. Matt replied, but she couldn't make out what he was saying—not that she cared to eavesdrop. They could be discussing anything. There was no reason to think Will was checking on how well she'd herded the horses. She could hold her head high in that regard, and Matt would be fair enough to say so. Phoebe opened the tent flap and discovered her bedroll, waiting inside. Although she would rather be treated like everyone else, having a shelter made her feel safer. Sleeping under the stars had its risks. A rattlesnake might intrude on her sleeping self. After a hot day, the fearsome creatures sometimes slithered out at night. She didn't want to think about bears, cougars, or other predators. There was safety in numbers, she reminded herself. The others wouldn't sleep far away from her, and Will would be closest of all.

Phoebe joined the men swapping stories around the campfire. She was content to let them talk, especially when the topic turned to the recent thunder storm. She caught Will watching her from across the fire. Warmth flooded her cheeks, and she glanced away.

The heat eased up after dark, much to Phoebe's relief. Finished drowsing, the cows lumbered to their feet and lowered their muzzles to graze. The wind picked up, still warm from the day, but at least the air was moving. The sun glowed crimson. She shielded her eyes and looked toward the horizon where sunset hues bathed the shoulders of the mountains. Overhead, the sky shone the same deep blue she'd seen at the heart of flames. The babbling of the creek winding through the meadow grew louder, and crickets began to chirp.

Phoebe left the campfire. She wanted to lay out her blankets and prepare for bed before darkness made it difficult. Dark shapes loomed in the dimness, and her throat clogged with the old panic. She narrowed her eyes, peering through the twilight at the dark shapes of men on horseback.

She hurried over to Will, who was laying out his bedroll. "Who are they?"

"Don't be alarmed." He straightened. "Those are our ranch hands. They're riding night herd."

"Night herd?"

"Yes. The cattle sleep off and on during the day and do the bulk of their grazing at night. We need to keep an eye on them, so they don't wander off or fall prey to predators."

A low, melodious humming floated to her. Phoebe tilted her head. "Is that—singing?"

"I forget this is all new to you." Amusement tinged his voice. "Your ears aren't deceiving you. We call it singing the cattle. It goes on through the night."

"Why?"

"It reminds the herd that the riders are nothing to fear. They find human voices comforting, and we want to keep them calm at all costs. A stampede is a horrible event."

"Wait, listen. That tune reminds me of a hymn I know."

"I wouldn't be surprised." He laughed, a pleasant sound that warmed her. "I imagine the lyrics would surprise a preacher or two, though."

"Oh my. Should I stop my ears?"

"Most likely, not. The men know a woman is in camp."

"Will *I* ever ride night herd?"

"We'll see." Will gazed at her in the fading light. "It's not easy for me to let you, I must admit, but I don't want to hold you back because of my own fears."

"Thank you." It came as news that Will feared for her. She'd thought his reluctance was due to her lack of ability. Weariness washed over her, reminding her it had been a long day. "I'd better hurry to turn in. I'd rather do it before nightfall."

He nodded. "If you get scared or need anything, remember that I'm right here."

"I will."

Phoebe shut herself into her tent and crawled into her bedroll before the last rays fled the sky. She lay still, trying to sleep, but the excitement of the day kept coming back to stir her. Despite this, she smiled to herself, soothed by the voices of those riding night herd. As time progressed, their words dwindled into humming. Phoebe drifted to sleep on a raft of harmonious melody.

She woke near dawn with an urgent need to relieve herself. Phoebe pulled on her outer clothing, fastened her shoes, and opened her tent flap. She could still hear humming voices, although they sounded sleepier than before. It comforted her to know that if threatened, she could call for help.

She paused to savor the beauty of the sleeping meadow. Lights shone all about, startling her until she realized they were reflections of the moonlight in the eyes of the grazing cattle. The full moon brightened the landscape enough for her to reach a nearby stand of trees. Phoebe dealt with her need, and then hurried out of the shadows. She rushed toward the hulk of her tent, only slowing when she neared it. Phoebe breathed a sigh of relief and reached for her tent flap.

A scuffling sound came from behind her.

Phoebe looked over her shoulder, but nothing seemed amiss. The sky was lightening above the horizon. It wouldn't be long before dawn. She pulled in a deep breath of cool air and turned to go into her tent.

A hand clamped over her mouth, and an arm hauled her backwards.

Phoebe struggled, but her captor overpowered her. If the hand over her mouth hadn't kept her from screaming, her breathless panic would have. All she managed was a weak moan, quickly squelched when the hand moved up to cover her nose also. She fought to breathe, and an odor she recognized filled her nostrils. The Salish used bear grease in their hair. She'd smelled it often in the Indian school.

Dizziness made her head spin, and she felt herself slipping into darkness. The hand moved away before she succumbed, but a gag whipped over her mouth in its place. Phoebe felt herself lifted, and her cheek grazed what felt like leather.

She was all at once a child of three again, being kidnapped by Spukani.

CHAPTER TWENTY-TWO

PHOEBE PULLED HER GAZE FROM THE headdress of the warrior leading her horse behind his. Watching its feathers flutter in the wind was becoming hypnotic.

What does he want with me?

Her head spun with questions. Why had this happened? She couldn't put it together. The warrior had appeared out of nowhere, for no apparent reason. His actions seemed more than impulsive. He'd abducted her in silence, and with restraints ready. Why wait until dawn, though? Wouldn't the dark of night have made pursuit less imminent? Maybe he hadn't planned her kidnap, but had taken advantage of the opportunity.

The Indian pony swayed beneath her. She pulled, yet again, at the cords binding her wrists and feet. Phoebe winced from the chafing pain. Her stomach heaved, and she fought the urge to wretch. Vomiting would be a disaster. The gag pressed the corners of her mouth and restricted her air. Tears gathered in her eyes, but she held back her emotions. Crying would only make matters worse.

Three Salish warriors on horseback waited beside the trail, half-hidden beneath a stand of larch trees. They rode painted ponies and wore feathers in their hair. The renegades dressed like one another in canvas pants, boots, and vests of fringed leather. One sat taller than the others in his saddle, and his legs extended lower. The broad black stripe on the upper part of his face gave the impression of an outlaw's mask. Another must have cupped his chin with a red-painted hand. The third had a red face, except for a white stripe across his eyes and forehead.

The warriors nodded to her captor but exchanged no other greeting.

Phoebe couldn't make out her kidnapper's features beneath the black-and-white stripes covering his face. He was much too young to be Spukani, but he might show himself every bit as terrifying. Phoebe closed her eyes. *God, I know You notice when a sparrow falls and that You care about me. My life is in Your hands*

Her captor continued along the trail. Although bound and gagged, Phoebe held her head high. While riding by the two warriors, she felt their gazes pierce her. Phoebe shivered as they closed in behind her. The band of Indians stole down the trail, making little noise. Phoebe caught only the faint thud of hooves. Her heartbeat, thumping in her ears, sounded louder.

The camp faded into the distance as dawn spread its wings across the sky. After leaving the trail, the Salish picked up speed. Striking out across the terrain slowed their progress, but it also concealed them. Fresh tears sprang to Phoebe's eyes as her hopes of rescue faded.

Leaving the path would work out for the best, she decided. She wouldn't want the renegades surprising any unsuspecting traveler they might meet. Not that they were likely to come across many on the remote trail they'd forsaken. The thought comforted her, regardless.

The journey went on without relief for miles. Phoebe's existence distilled to the thud of horse hooves, brutal heat, and the constant struggle to breathe. She slipped into a strange state halfway between waking and sleeping. Terrors chased across her mind. She jerked upright in the saddle, escaping them. Only then did she realize that the nightmare went on.

How much time went by before the horses stopped, Phoebe couldn't say. They halted in the shade of a rocky bluff. A spring wept down one side, pooled at its feet, and overflowed into a narrow rill that cut through the lush grass.

Phoebe's captor untied her feet and dragged her from her

horse. She clutched his leather vest to keep from falling. He jerked the gag from her mouth, and Phoebe hauled in air. The world spun, and her stomach churned, but at least she could breathe.

She gritted her teeth against the tingling pain in her feet as feeling returned. Her captor shoved her away before she could stand. Without thinking, Phoebe rolled as if thrown by a horse, softening the impact of her fall. She pushed to hands and knees, sat up, and lifted her head. No good would come of cowering before her captor.

His face came into clear view. Younger than she'd thought him, her captor watched her from dark-fringed eyes. Without the paint, he might have been handsome, although a certain hardness marred his features. Braids hung on either side of his head. Strings of beads dangled from his neck, and metal bands encircled his upper arms. A feather headdress rose above his beaded headband and fanned out behind him.

"What do you want with me?" She challenged him in Salish.

He seemed unsurprised, although she had addressed him in his native tongue. "Do you not know me?" He spoke in a throaty voice.

Phoebe couldn't place him, but he did look familiar….

Another face rose in her mind's eye. She gasped and shrank from him. "Who are you? Why do you resemble Spukani?"

"You remember my uncle but not me."

"You are Spukani's nephew?" Phoebe cast back in memory and grasped the hazy image of a young boy. It slipped away, fading like a specter. She shook her head. "I've forgotten."

He frowned. "We went to school together, but you do not remember me."

"I don't recall—"

"I stopped coming." His face hardened. "I didn't want to anymore after your mother killed my cousin, Rain."

"She didn't," Phoebe snapped, sick to death of this

accusation. "Spukani believed that my mother could control the measles. She was unable to convince him otherwise. My mother did her best to save Rain from a disease your people had no defense against."

"Be quiet!" His nostrils flared. "Or I'll cover your mouth again."

"I'm telling you the truth."

"You speak lies, like your mother before you."

She sighed and blinked back tears. "I wish you would believe me."

"I grow weary of talking. Go watch the horses. You are good with them, I know."

She narrowed her eyes. "Why do you say that?"

A smile lifted his lips. "I've seen you."

Tension uncurled inside her, like a snake uncoiling. "You spied on me."

"Yes."

Phoebe stared at him in horror. She'd felt someone watching her, off and on, for years. Attributing the sensation to her early trauma had hidden the truth from her. "For how long?"

"Most of my life, whenever I could get away." His smile was more like a grimace. "You never knew I was there."

"Which way did they go?" Will reined in at the trail fork and stared at the tracks leading off in both directions. "It's impossible to tell."

"I've seen this sort of thing before." Matt spoke from beside him. "It's a tactic the Indians use to avoid pursuit."

Will fought against a rising wave of despair. The first thing he'd seen this morning was Phoebe's tent gaping open. There'd been no sign of her anywhere. Tracks around her tent indicated a scuffle. Facing a gun usually caused a person to comply, not struggle. Whoever had kidnapped Phoebe must have gagged and overpowered her rather than threatening her with a firearm. That didn't mean her abductor didn't have a weapon, though. A gunshot would have roused the camp and sent a pack of ranch hands swarming after them like angry bees. Few women possessed Phoebe's strength. She'd been raised to do ranch chores. He'd worried about her wrestling down calves during roping practice, but she'd managed it. Her captor must be a man, and he hadn't been alone. Marks made by unshod horse hooves marked the trail a short distance from camp.

Will couldn't assemble a group to ride after her fast enough. He'd had no shortage of volunteers, but he wouldn't call on those who were falling asleep on their feet after riding night herd. Nor would he ask anyone assigned to the next shift. From those remaining, he'd chosen three—Brady, Matt, and Sparky. They'd ridden hard, only to come to a crossroads where the Indians must have scrambled their tracks.

Will rubbed a hand down his neck. If he hadn't slept through the disturbance, this morning would be a different story. Why he had remained a mystery. Staying vigilant while he drove the cattle all morning must have tired him more than he'd known, but he often slept with one eye open. It would take a stealthy individual to avoid waking him. The Indians were known for soft-footedness. They also rode unshod horses. The picture seemed clear.

Phoebe's captors obviously wanted her alive. Will might take comfort from that if it didn't raise terrifying possibilities. He hated to imagine what Phoebe was going through. The situation seemed a twist of irony. She'd overcome her fear of Spukani, only to be kidnapped by Indians.

Please, God, let Phoebe be all right.

Will eyed Brady, who jumped down from his horse and squatted beside Sparky to examine one of the hoof marks.

"They're fairly fresh."

Sparky nodded. "I noticed that, too."

Brady straightened. "We must be right on their heels."

"My guess is that they've gone that way." Will pointed down the south fork of the trail. "Logic tells me renegades would seek out wilder parts, especially with a captive in tow."

"I don't know." Brady straightened. "They might guess we'd think that and head north."

Matt shook his head. "I doubt they'd go that direction. It's more settled, and they wouldn't want to risk being caught on the trail."

"I think Brady is right." Sparky climbed onto his horse.

"There's only one way of telling." Will tightened the reins to quiet his restive horse. "We need to split up and follow both forks. Matt and I can head south. Why don't you ride north with Brady?"

"Be happy to." Sparky smiled. "Don't tell her, but I kind of fancy that little filly. I'd hate for any harm to come her way."

Will smirked at the thought of Phoebe's reaction to Sparky calling her a little filly. He didn't blame Sparky. Phoebe seemed to collect hearts wherever she went. She'd gained his as well. "Whichever group runs out of trail will double back and catch up with the others. Agreed?"

"Naturally." Sparky gathered his reins.

Brady gave a brief nod. "Count me in."

"Splitting up makes sense." Matt frowned. "Except, we'd divide our strength."

"I know, but if we stay together but go the wrong direction, we'll lose time." He firmed his jaw. "We can't let that happen."

Phoebe watched over the ponies wading into the shallows. As they drank, ripples circled out from their muzzles and spread to the bank. Phoebe stole a glance at her captors, lounging in the shade of a maple tree. Her mouth was parched from the wretched gag they'd forced her to wear until they'd left the trail. They must have worried that someone who chanced along might hear if she called for help. Waiting to drink was torture, but finally the horses moved off to graze. Having discharged her duty to the horses, Phoebe bent to slake her own thirst. Soothing mouthfuls eased the dryness in her throat. She paused to splash her heated face and neck, but then continued drinking. After Phoebe had consumed her fill, she sank down in the shade.

Spukani's nephew didn't seem to care that her feet were unbound. He must guess at her weakness. Shock, exposure, and exertion all dragged at her. Riding in the sun wasn't easy without a hat. If the evening hours could bring peace, she might yearn for their coolness. She had no idea what would befall her then.

The trickling water formed a gentle backdrop to the drone of voices. Phoebe's eyelids drifted shut. The thump of a hoof recalled her, but only for a moment.

A foot struck her side, jerking her awake. Phoebe sat up, heart racing.

Spukani's nephew loomed above her. "Get the horses."

Phoebe scrambled to her feet. She would rather stand than allow him to tower over her, nor did she want to risk another kick.

He stepped closer. "I used to watch you at the Indian school. You never even noticed."

"I rarely paid attention to such things." She spoke the truth out of mercy, although he didn't deserve it. She'd been more concerned with chasing butterflies and weaving stories in her mind than childhood crushes.

He shook his head, disbelief on his face. "I was only one of the many Salish your mother taught."

"You can't have attended school for long or wouldn't have forgotten you."

He thrust a hand beneath her chin and lifted her face. "My name is Elk Hunter. Remember it."

She pulled away from his touch. "My uncle won't stand for this. Return me to our camp, and I will ask him to let you go in peace."

"Do you think I fear your uncle?" He jerked her close. "My people are being driven from our home. The big chiefs in Washington tricked our chief into signing away our land. They promised we could hunt buffalo and gather berries in this valley forever. They did not speak of fencing the land. They said nothing about shooting the buffalo we need to live. They hid their plan to build a railroad through our hunting ground. My people go hungry. If I find food for them, I am a thief." He shoved her away. "And you think I am afraid of your uncle."

Phoebe stumbled backward. "I'm sorry for what happened to the Salish—truly. Neither I, nor my uncle, mean you harm."

From the corner of her eye, she noticed some of his companions tilt their heads, as if listening.

He glared at her. "Why should I believe the daughter of the woman who killed Rain?"

She took a deep breath. "I can't change what you think about that. I won't waste my time trying."

"I saw when my uncle left the tribe in disgrace because your mother deceived our chief. I promised him that one day I would make things right."

A shudder ran over her. "What do you mean to do?"

"You will replace Rain. Many years have passed since she died, but my uncle still needs a daughter."

CHAPTER TWENTY-THREE

THE HORSE SWAYED IN A GENTLE rhythm, following a trail Phoebe saw only faintly. The waning moon cast a silver glow over the rocks and trees around her. The wind fanned her hair, which had fallen from its pins, over her face. With her hands bound, she couldn't claw it away but tossed her head to dislodge it.

She had no idea how long they'd ridden. Apart from watering the horses, her captors did not rest. They seemed ready to ride through the night. Phoebe was no stranger to spending long hours in the saddle, but she kept catching herself nodding off. Even so, she didn't know whether to hope they would stop. She had no idea what might befall her when they did. Continuing would keep her ahead of rescue, however. She had no doubt Will would follow, along with some of the others. What would happen when he caught up to her captors didn't bear thinking on.

She pulled her mind from the possibility of bloodshed and focused instead on Elk Hunter's headdress. The eagle feathers rose and fell with the motion of his horse. She could barely see the black tips of the vanes, but their fluffy bases gleamed white. The breeze tossed the feathers in a sudden flurry. Phoebe watched their gyrations until her eyelids drifted shut. She felt herself slump in the saddle. Time ebbed and flowed like the wash of a river.

Phoebe started awake as her horse stumbled. She jerked upright. How long had she slept? Her surroundings seemed the same. She'd drowsed in the saddle many times, but today she wasn't riding Nutmeg across her family's ranch. The Indian pony seemed docile enough, but the situation warranted vigilance.

Willing herself to remain awake, Phoebe rode on through the night. The moon sailed across the sky, nearly completing its arc before Elk Hunter paused their long march. A stream glimmered in the darkness, reflecting the fitful moonlight. Phoebe could make out the curve of the horses' flanks and the darker outlines of the renegades.

Elk Hunter untied her feet and lifted her down. He'd bound her feet more loosely last time, and she was able to stand. She stood blinking while he freed her wrists. He gave her a slight push. "Go and see to the horses, and make sure you hobble them. We can't have them wandering off." He emphasized the last sentence before following the other renegades upstream.

The horses waded into the water and lowered their muzzles to drink. The poor creatures must be exhausted. Phoebe doubted they would wander far, but she hobbled them with the leather straps Elk Hunter had given her. It took quite a while in the darkness. Leaving the horses to graze the grassy bank, Phoebe returned to the stream. She bent and scooped handfuls of silken water to her mouth.

Phoebe came up from the stream to find Elk Hunter watching. She'd been too weary to think of escape, but he would have seen if she'd tried.

"You come," he commanded.

Phoebe walked toward him, heart pounding.

He pointed to a spot in the grass with a pile of wooden stakes beside it. "Sit down."

Phoebe wished she'd tried to escape.

"Do as you are told." He pushed her down.

She didn't know what he had in mind, but he'd already proven himself a bully.

Elk Hunter picked up a stake from the pile and pounded it into the ground with a rock. He grasped one of her wrists and wrapped it with cord, and then tied it to the stake. He repeated the action with her other wrist, and then secured her feet in the same way.

He stood, with his face in darkness. "You sleep." He turned and walked away.

Relief rushed through Phoebe. She was still lying helpless in the night, but Elk Hunter had gone away. Phoebe doubted she could sleep but closed her eyes. Waves of exhaustion rocked her, and she floated in their wash.

The sun on her face woke her, followed by a shadow. Phoebe kept her eyes closed, not willing to reveal she was awake. When fingers worked at her bonds, she opened her eyes to discover Elk Hunter bent over her. After freeing her, he reached into a pouch tied at his waist, and tossed a portion of food to her. "You eat."

Phoebe stared at the conglomeration of fat and bits of unknown items. Her stomach was growling, and she needed to eat. She bit off a chunk but gagged from the unfamiliar taste and texture.

Elk Hunter snatched back the rest of her food, shrugged, and took a bite. Mouth full, he nodded toward the stream. "Go get the horses."

Phoebe found the ponies much recovered. In fact, they eluded her with such vigor that she despaired of catching them. She brought them eventually, roped and saddled, to the renegades.

They resumed their journey and climbed into the foothills at the base of towering mountains. The sky shone blue, but gossamer wisps of cloud snagged in the treetops. The green shadows of a forest closed in about them. Overhead branches shut out the sky, bringing blessed coolness. The swishing of the leaves lulled Phoebe, and she caught herself nodding off. Her eyelids felt so heavy that they must surely close. She shook her head and sat taller to rouse herself.

"At last, we are here." Elk Hunter called out in Salish.

Between the trees stood a cabin with smoke curling from the chimney. The glint of water revealed a creek running behind the building.

Phoebe wet her lips. "Where is this?"

Elk Hunter glanced back at her, triumph on his face. "I have brought you to my uncle's house."

Phoebe stared at him, speechless. Her every fear had come true.

Elk Hunter bared his teeth in a smile. "Come, Teacher's daughter." He led her horse into the cabin's yard. For once, he didn't command her to take care of the horses. After untying her, he grasped her wrist and hurried her toward the cabin. The sagging porch boards rang hollow beneath their feet, and then they were inside the dark interior.

Phoebe could see nothing at first, but then her eyes adjusted. A man huddled on a wooden bench at the window, watching her with a blank stare. Phoebe started, recognizing his rugged features. The malevolent being who had haunted her dreams was nowhere in evidence. Spukani had shrunk to a broken shell of the strong warrior he had once been.

Phoebe pulled in a breath. The man she had feared most of her life had little in common with this frail creature. Almost, she could pity him, for he seemed lost in his own home.

Elk Hunter shoved her forward. "Uncle, I've brought you a gift."

The old man tilted his head, reminding Phoebe of a baby bird waiting for a worm. He slid his gaze over her. "Who is this?"

Elk Hunter's smile faded. "Do you not know Phoebe? She is grown but doesn't look much different from the child you once took."

Phoebe lifted her head under Spukani's stare. She thought awareness flickered in his eyes, but the light of recognition faded. He thrust out his chin, displaying a touch of the belligerence she remembered. "I don't know this woman."

"She is Teacher's daughter."

Spukani's nostrils flared, and his eyes narrowed until they glittered. He rose to his feet. "Teacher's daughter, you say?"

Elk Hunter smiled. "You remember."

Spukani advanced on Phoebe. She turned as he circled her, never leaving her back to him. Swift as a bird's claw, Spukani caught her face in his hands, his dry fingernails scraping her skin. His scowl loomed in her vision. "I know you." Spukani's breath misted her cheeks.

A shudder ran over Phoebe. What would he do to her?

Will reined in as the tracks they'd followed turned in at a log cabin. Through the trees, he could see horses tied up outside. Phoebe must be inside.

He glanced at Matt beside him. By unspoken agreement, they backtracked to the trail before leaving it for the shade beneath a grove of cottonwoods. The birds singing in the branches ceased abruptly. He hoped no one in the cabin would notice.

"What now?" Matt murmured.

Will kept his voice low, although tension thrummed through him. "We rescue Phoebe." Having her so near, and yet out of reach tore at him.

"I wish Brady and Sparky would catch up to us." Matt looked toward the trail, as if half-expecting them to appear.

He seemed nervous, but Will didn't blame him. His own heart was beating in quick time. He drew a steadying breath. "We haven't given them much chance."

"Maybe we should wait for them to come along." Matt spoke hesitantly, clearly not convinced of his own suggestion.

"That's a bad idea." Will's voice came out more sharply than he'd intended.

"I didn't think you'd like it." Matt shrugged. "How you feel about Phoebe is plain."

Will softened his tone. "I'll thank you to leave my feelings out of this."

"Fair enough." Matt smiled faintly. "Let's talk logically then. I spotted four horses tied up outside the cabin and another grazing while hobbled. Even subtracting the one Phoebe probably rode, we're outnumbered."

"I know, but we can't wait."

"We don't know how many people are actually inside the cabin. There could be more horses in the stable." Matt shook his head. "I'm no coward, but I'd rather not rush in where angels fear to tread."

Will rubbed his neck. "Who knows what Phoebe might be going through."

Matt's gaze slid away. "Let's come up with a plan, at least."

"That's a fair request. We should leave our horses here and approach on foot. I don't think any dogs are around to announce us. None barked earlier."

Matt nodded. "Any idea of what to do once we reach the cabin?"

"There's a lot we can't know in advance."

Matt frowned. "Listening at the windows could help us figure out how many we'd face."

"Good idea."

"We might also learn how quickly we need to act."

Will's jaw tightened. "There's no question about that."

"I only meant that if Phoebe isn't in immediate peril, we could watch for them to come out again. No one leaves horses tied up unless they mean to leave again."

"I like your thinking. We'd have a better chance of surprising them when they come through the doorway." Will swung his leg over the saddle and stepped down from his horse. "I'm not sure we'll be able to wait, though. If Phoebe sounds the least bit distressed, I'll want to go in."

"I understand." Matt dismounted. "What should we do if we run into trouble? Go in with guns drawn?"

"Maybe, but that might get Phoebe hurt. Let's figure it out when the time comes."

Will led the way. Following the stream allowed them to stay off the trail. It wasn't long before the cabin reared ahead of them. Constructed of stacked logs daubed with mortar, it seemed a formidable fortress. Will shut out all thoughts of failure and stepped over a clump of bunchgrass. His doubts could become self-fulfilling, if he gave them rein.

The neighing of horses came from the cottonwood grove. Will exchanged glances with Matt. Whoever was inside must have heard.

Will rushed toward the cabin. Matt came with him, apparently with the same thought in mind. They needed to hide before anyone came out to investigate. They'd barely made it into the shadow at the side of the building when the door burst open.

Will flattened himself against the wall beside Matt.

Two Indians strode into view.

Will held his breath. If either looked back, he and Matt would be in plain sight.

The Indians hurried down the trail in the direction of the horses.

Will released his breath. The situation answered the question of whether to delay. They had only a short window of time to rescue Phoebe before the pair returned.

Matt peeled off the wall and crept toward the cottonwood grove along the stream.

Will stared after him. So much for their plan. If they lived, he would have a word with Matt about teamwork. The unexpected move left Will with a choice to make. He could either go and help Matt take on the two men or try to save Phoebe on his own.

Feeble light filtered through the cabin's few windows as Phoebe served the trout she'd been forced to cook alongside a bread she'd fried from flour and water. The aroma of the food taunted her, reminding her that she hadn't eaten in more than a day. She returned to the kitchen area and picked at the leavings in the cast iron frying pan.

She should have kept a little back for herself. Elk Hunter and Spukani, seated together on the bench at the window, ate hearty helpings. She'd cooked enough for the two renegades, but their plates sat cooling while they investigated the neighing of horses. The two had called back from the window before going outside that their horses were accounted for.

Phoebe didn't dare hope that the horses that had neighed belonged to rescuers. If they turned out to be strays or wild mustangs, the disappointment would crush her. On the other hand, if Will was out there, he and anyone with him were in grave danger.

"Why have you brought this woman to me?" Spukani demanded.

Elk Hunter flitted a questioning glance at his uncle. "She will be your daughter in place of Rain. Isn't that what you wanted, all those years ago?"

Spukani scowled "You should have asked me before you did this."

"But why, Uncle? I don't understand."

"Is it so hard to see?" Spukani shook his head. "She only reminds me of all I've lost."

"But—I waited a long time to bring her to you."

"I don't want her. Take her away."

Phoebe released a sigh. She wouldn't have to spend her future waiting on Spukani in this wretched hovel.

Elk Hunter slashed his arm in an angry gesture. "It is not right to let her go."

"You should not have taken her in the first place." Spukani's eyes crinkled at the corners. "Do you think I want the soldiers to come?"

"Are you so afraid of them?" Elk Hunter shook his head. "This is not the warrior I once knew."

Spukani bowed his head. "Perhaps I have learned wisdom."

Elk Hunter's nostrils flared. "Since you will not keep her, she must die to avenge Rain."

Phoebe backed toward the door.

"No!" Spukani shouted, the veins standing out on his neck.

Phoebe remembered to breathe. The room swung, and she caught hold of the wall. In her wildest dreams, she'd never imagined Spukani would become her champion.

"The soldiers would shoot us both for such a thing."

Elk Hunter jumped to his feet and towered over the older man. "I don't fear the soldiers."

"Then, you are a fool."

Elk Hunter's face went red. "I am ashamed of you."

"Leave me!" Spukani's shoulders shook. "And take Teacher's daughter with you. Kill her, and you will pay the price."

Elk Hunter rushed toward Phoebe, but she shrank from him. His fingers bit into her upper arm, and he hauled her across the room. Upon reaching the door, he kicked it open and thrust her into blinding sunlight.

Phoebe blinked rapidly, desperately trying to see. "If you murder me, my uncle will hunt you down."

"If he comes, he will also taste death."

Phoebe's vision cleared as a blade flashed. Rage in every line of his bearing, Elk Hunter raised the knife in his fist. Phoebe trembled, certain it would fall on her.

He glared at her for several long moments, but then lowered his arm. Elk Hunter shoved her with a hand to her back. "Go water the horses."

Phoebe stumbled away from him. It took a long time for her fingers, clumsy from fear, to untie the ropes. The image of Elk Hunter with his knife raised kept returning. Why had he changed his mind about killing her? Maybe he hadn't. He might only have decided to postpone the deed, for his uncle's sake. Spukani, who wanted nothing to do with her death, would probably object to her blood soaking his porch.

Her legs felt rubbery as she led the ponies to the stream, but she did her best to walk strongly. Any show of weakness seemed a bad idea.

While the ponies stood in the stream and gathered mouthfuls of the bright water, Elk Hunter kept his gaze on

Phoebe. She could swear that he guessed her intention. She lingered at the stream, hoping that Elk Hunter would relax his vigilance. At last, he turned his head and peered down the trail. He must be watching for his two companions to return.

Phoebe saw her moment and took it. With more speed than grace, she climbed onto the back of her pony and rode for the trail.

Elk Hunter shouted behind her.

Phoebe urged her horse faster, knowing that Elk Hunter could easily overtake her. She could only hope, as Pa often did, that God would smile upon her.

CHAPTER TWENTY-FOUR

"Don't even think about riding after her." Will stepped out from cover, his gun aimed at the stocky Indian.

The man spun about, and his eyes widened. "Don't shoot me."

"Cooperate, and I won't." Will noted with interest the knife in the man's hand. "I can shoot faster than you can throw."

The Indian froze.

"Drop the knife and put up your hands." He kept his voice even with difficulty after witnessing this man's treatment of Phoebe. Not long ago, he'd been seconds away from shooting the knife out of his hand.

Glaring, the man obeyed. "You are foolish."

"Is that so?" Will kicked the knife out of reach.

"Kill me, and others will hunt you down." His nostrils flared. "They won't stop until you are dead."

"I have no intention of killing you." Will pulled a piggin' string out of his vest pocket. The flexible strip of rawhide could tie more than a calf's feet. One end was already looped and secured with a Turk's head knot. "Turn around and put your hands behind your back."

The Indian sneered and didn't budge.

Will cocked his gun. "Do it."

He received better results, this time.

Will eased off on the trigger. Working one-handed, he slipped the loop over one of his captive's wrists. Will then wrapped the tail of the piggin' string around the Indian's other hand before pulling the end back through the loop. Will tugged the knot tight, certain that, if a calf couldn't get out of it, a man never would. He glanced about. No one had come out to investigate. Preferring to keep it that way, he jerked the bandana from around his own neck and holstered his gun long enough to gag the Indian. He pressed the barrel of his gun to his captive's back to discourage any ideas about running off.

"It's a mite hot out here. Let's sit you down against the trunk of that cottonwood." Will guided the man into the deep shade of the large tree closest to the cabin. He made quick work of binding his captive's ankles and stepped back to survey his handiwork. "I hate leaving any man trussed and helpless, but it's no less than you deserve." Ignoring the furious glare he received, he turned away.

Hopefully Matt would return and find the prisoner in a moment. He couldn't wait to find out. Phoebe could ride like the wind. Although his own skill with a horse matched hers, delaying any longer would mean never catching her.

He commandeered the strongest-looking painted pony and headed south, the direction Phoebe had taken. Riding on one of the Indian's high-pommeled saddles felt strange. Forcing himself to allow the horse to warm up took all his strength of will. He'd seen the fear in Phoebe's face before she'd ridden off. The thought of her careening down hillsides in a blind panic tore at him. Alone and unprotected in the wilderness, she might suffer all sorts of mishaps. When he could stand it no more, Will pressed the pony to go faster.

The world reduced to the sounds of beating hooves and huffing breaths. Will concentrated on staying in unison with a horse traveling at a pace that even Patches rarely obtained. The fresh hoof tracks revealed that Phoebe had so far kept to the trail. Maybe he worried too much about her. He had, in fact, never known anyone as clear-eyed or level-headed. Nor had he come across a woman more beautiful, inside and out.

Careful, there. Next, you'll be admitting that you love her more than life.

Hoofbeats from another horse rang out, and the forest fell away as he entered the plain. Will could see Phoebe clearly ahead of him, her hair streaming behind her. The distance was too great to call to her. Determined to close the gap between them, Will spurred the pony to fresh exertions.

A realization settled over him with the warmth of a worn blanket, comfortable from much use. The truth had crept in on him over time, until he couldn't imagine anything else.

If they got out of this alive, he had a few things to say to Miss Phoebe Walsh.

Phoebe held on while the Indian pony leaped into the air, praying the horse hadn't miscalculated. The fallen log passed below them, and the horse's front hooves thumped the ground. Phoebe blew out her breath, glad to have kept her seat. She stayed upright in the saddle but ducked almost at once to avoid low-hanging branches.

She guided the pony back onto the trail. Desperation to put distance between herself and Elk Hunter had prompted her to take that shortcut. Detouring was far too risky in forested terrain. Elk Hunter hadn't followed, at least not right away. Something must have prevented him from riding after her. He would, if he could. Of that she had no doubt.

More pressing than possible capture was the growing suspicion that she was going the wrong way. She'd arrived at the cabin while drowsing in the saddle and couldn't remember which direction they'd turned onto the property. She should be headed north, toward Uncle Con's cabin, but the sun was shining on the wrong side of her.

Phoebe reined in for a moment, uncertain what to do. Continuing south would carry her into a vast wilderness. Retracing the trail could land her in Elk Hunter's hands. At the least, she would pass by Spukani's cabin. The prospect of losing herself in the wilderness was daunting, but so was the possibility of running into Elk Hunter.

The tattoo of distant hooves intruded. Phoebe's heart pounded, and she swiveled her head to peer down the trail. The hoofbeats grew louder. She broke into a cold sweat. It had to be Elk Hunter, coming after her.

Phoebe sent her horse southward. She shouldn't have stopped for anything. The trail broke free of the trees and cut across a meadow. Phoebe kept herself from looking down at the ground sliding by in a dizzying rush. Exhaustion dragged at her, but she couldn't surrender to it.

Phoebe urged her horse faster, but to no avail. If anything, the pony slowed. She must be driving it too hard. Her breath caught in her throat, and a sob escaped her. This time, Elk Hunter would kill her for sure.

"Phoebe!" Will's cry reverberated through the air.

Phoebe could hardly believe her ears. Was she hallucinating? She glanced back twice before daring to trust her eyes, but she would know the way Will sat in a saddle anywhere. Phoebe slowed her horse and turned to meet him.

He drew up beside her, his face tense.

Tears ran down her cheeks and a lump clogged her throat, but she managed to speak. "You came for me."

"Of course, I did." A smile touched his lips. "I couldn't stay away."

"Thank you." She hiccupped on a sob.

"Don't cry, Phoebe." His forehead creased. "Are you all

right?"

"Mostly." Phoebe scrubbed tears from her cheeks with the back of her hand. "We shouldn't stop and talk. There's a Salish warrior who wants to kill me coming after me."

"I doubt that."

Why did he seem so calm? "You wouldn't say that if you knew Elk Hunter."

"I've made his acquaintance."

She stared at him. What was he saying? "When?"

"Not long ago, in fact." Will's eyes took on a steely glint. "He won't trouble you again—not if I have anything to say about it."

She shivered. "I don't want to know what you've done to him."

"Let's just say, I doubt he'll come along anytime soon."

She peered down the road, not quite ready to trust his assessment, but Elk Hunter was nowhere in sight. "Even so, I'd feel better finding a place to hide."

He frowned. "I hate to say this, but we have to return to that cabin. Matt is there, and I can't desert one of my men."

Phoebe pulled in air, which seemed all at once in short supply. "I wouldn't want you to, but I wish we didn't have to go back. I'm not sure I have enough gumption."

"You don't need to. In fact, I'd rather you didn't. I'll concentrate better without worrying about you."

Her mind spun, too exhausted to draw conclusions. "But, what—"

"We'll find somewhere close by for you to wait. You can look after the horses while I go to the cabin on foot. How does that sound?"

"Better, except for the last part. Please be careful." She shoved at her hair, but gave up on trying to restore order. A more pressing matter clamored for her attention. "Do you have any food?"

He reached into his vest pocket and pulled out a sourdough biscuit that had seen better days. "Sorry, but this is all I can offer at the moment."

"It will do." She bit into the stale biscuit and chewed with relish. When the morsel was gone, she licked her dry lips. "I could use a drink of water."

"We'll find a stream." Will pulled a gun out of his boot. He extended it to her, handle first. "I'd feel better if you had this."

"You and me both." Phoebe tucked the weapon into her waistband.

He smiled. "I keep forgetting how proficient you are with firearms."

"I'd rather not use one on a person, though." The thought made her shudder.

Will wheeled his horse about. "Let's hope it doesn't come to that."

Will dragged his gaze from Phoebe's upturned face. "Sorry, but I'm not taking any chances where you're concerned."

"I'm not excited about going back to the cabin, but I'd rather stay with you than hide like this."

"I need you to keep an eye on the horses. We might have to ride away quickly."

She glanced around the small meadow well back from the trail. "Waiting here, not knowing what is happening, would drive me to distraction."

"That's a poor reason to risk your life." He shook his head. "Don't ask me to go along with it."

She glared at him, her eyes stormy. "Why are you so stubborn?"

"You can call it that, if you want." He shrugged. "I know my own mind, same as you."

Surprise washed over her face. "Fair enough."

"I can't force you to hide here, but it's in your best interests."

"I know."

He studied her. "Do you mean that?"

She gave him a wounded look. "Are you accusing me of insincerity?"

"A quick change of heart seems out of character for you. That's all."

She folded her arms. "I meant it."

Will nodded. He wasn't entirely convinced she would stay put, but he shouldn't delay going after Matt any longer. "I'll try to come back soon."

She glanced away from him. "All right."

He hesitated, but it had to be said. "Should I fail to return before morning, go back to camp without me."

Her gaze flew to his. "You want me to abandon you?"

"Not exactly."

"I couldn't do that."

Will thought fast. "You might be good with a gun, but you're only one person. You'd help me more by sending others after me."

Will strode off before she could argue any further, but he glanced back from the edge of the meadow. Phoebe was standing where he'd left her, watching him go. He forced himself to turn away from her. He should have chosen a hiding place more distant from the cabin. Only a fool would think that he'd won her agreement to stay put. Phoebe had a mind of her own. Her reluctance to cross paths with Spukani and Elk Hunter might guide her decisions, but he'd better make this quick.

He couldn't let himself dwell on everything that might go wrong if she followed him. Even if she didn't, Phoebe could suffer a mishap while alone in the meadow. Since she'd come to work at the ranch, he'd done his utmost to look after her. It was galling to realize that, despite his overprotectiveness, he could still lose her.

Keep her safe, Lord, where I cannot. The plea wrenched from him.

Will met no one on the way to the cabin. Elk Hunter was either still tied up or had decided not to follow them. He wouldn't have gone by on the trail while they were in the meadow. Will had done his best to hide signs of their passage, but he doubted an Indian would have missed them.

He parted the shrubs in front of the cabin. Elk Hunter was missing from beneath the cottonwood tree. Matt might have moved him, but Will wouldn't count on that. The cabin door stood gaping, giving the place a derelict look. Will flattened himself against the outside wall. He couldn't see anything from this position, but he could listen.

No sound came from inside, but a twig snapped behind him.

The hair on the back of Will's neck bristled. He looked toward the sound.

The clicking of a gun being cocked stopped him.

"Where's Phoebe?" A most unwelcome voice snarled in his ear.

"I thought I left you tied up." Will spoke without turning his head.

"Answer my question."

"Do you think I would betray Phoebe and tell you?"

"You will."

The smugness of Elk Hunter's voice rasped on Will's

nerves. He tried not to imagine the tactics the renegade might employ. "Harm me, and my men will see that you pay."

Elk Hunter laughed. "Do you mean the ones tied up in the cabin?"

Dismay surged through Will. Brady and Sparky must have shown up, unfortunately. Will summoned all the bravado he could muster. "For each of them, five others will ride after you."

Cold metal pressed behind his ear. "Shut your mouth."

"Why? I'd think you would want to know."

"You lie!"

"Are you sure of that?"

"Be quiet, and throw down your gun."

Will hesitated. Letting go of his weapon would make him defenseless. If only he could find a way to avoid it.

"Do it!" The gun barrel pressed more firmly behind his ear.

Will removed his six-shooter from its holster and dropped it to the ground. Elk Hunter withdrew the gun. Will's side vision showed him Elk Hunter bending to retrieve his own weapon. Acting on impulse. Will spun about, flanked the Indian, and flipped him like a calf. Elk Hunter's gun discharged, and blood spattered.

Elk Hunter clutched his stomach, moaning.

CHAPTER TWENTY-FIVE

WHATEVER ELK HUNTER HAD DONE, WILL couldn't leave him to bleed to death. He eyed the open doorway. No one came to investigate. That made sense if those inside were tied up, although he had to wonder where Spukani might be. Elk Hunter moaned again, and Will gave up on figuring it out. After ripping cloth from his own sleeve. Will knelt beside the stricken man and applied pressure to his wound. "Hold that in place."

Elk Hunter's fingers grazed Will's as he took the cloth. "Why help an Indian?"

"Our skin may be different, but we're both people."

Elk Hunter gritted his teeth. "Tell my uncle that he was right."

"Your uncle? Is he inside?"

"Tell him—I should not have stolen Teacher's daughter." The Indian's cough ended on a gasping breath.

"Lie still, if you can." Will rose and collected his gun. The other pistol glinted where it had fallen, identical to one he'd seen Matt use. He claimed it, too. Will looked back to Elk Hunter and discovered that his chest no longer moved. He spared a moment to close the man's staring eyes.

Will stepped onto the porch, making little sound. Inside the cabin, he could see Matt, Brady, and Sparky sitting, bound and gagged, against one wall. Beyond them, a man rocked to-and-fro on a wooden bench. Light from the window behind him picked out the gray in his long braids. Since he held no weapon, Will didn't raise the gun in his hand. "Are you Spukani?"

"That is my name."

"Your nephew's gun went off by accident. He's dead."

Spukani nodded. "I heard. I saw."

"I'm sorry."

Spukani tilted his head upward, and tears glinted in the seams of his face. "Revenge is the thief that banished me from my people. I regret what I did to Teacher and her daughter. If I had explained that better to Elk Hunter, it might not have destroyed him."

A gasp came from behind Will. He swung about, gun leveled. Phoebe stood in the doorway, pointing the pistol he'd given her at Spukani.

Phoebe could hardly credit what she'd heard. In all her imaginings, she'd never considered that remorse could change Spukani from the angry man she remembered.

The Indian rose with quiet dignity. "I am not afraid to die, but let me do so on my feet."

"I heard what you said." Her voice shook as badly as her gun. "I'm glad."

His expression lightened. "Then maybe you would put away your weapon."

Phoebe lowered the gun. "I didn't come to shoot you, only to help my friend." She nodded toward Will as she spoke.

"I am no threat to him, or to you." Spukani waved a hand. "Or to these men, either. Go away, all of you, and let me mourn my nephew in peace."

"Phoebe, get out of the doorway." Will pulled her to one side. Outside the cabin, nothing moved. "We'll go, but first answer one question. Where are the other two Salish?"

"I don't know." Spukani glanced outside, as if expecting them to appear. "They went to investigate some noises and never came back."

"I think he's telling the truth." Phoebe cast back in memory. The incident seemed a long time ago. "I was here when they left. They should have come back hours ago."

Will shook his head. "Something doesn't make sense. Matt went after them, but here he is." He peered at Spukani. "Who tied up these men?"

"Elk Hunter, alone." Spukani scowled. "I told him not to do it, but he didn't listen to me."

Will caught Phoebe's gaze. "Keep watch, will you?"

No wonder Will had warned her away from the doorway. She crept back to it, but looked out from close to the wall. A glance into the room revealed Will removing Matt's gag.

Matt smiled a little stiffly. "I'm glad to see you."

"Likewise." Will gave a swift nod. "Lend a hand with Sparky, and I'll free Brady."

Soon, the cords that had restrained the men littered the floor. Phoebe stepped back as her companions neared the doorway, allowing them to go out. She met Spukani's eyes. "Thank you."

He seemed to flinch, but then a faint smile touched his lips. "Go home, child."

Phoebe couldn't muster a smile but nodded before going outside. Elk Hunter lay sprawled below the porch. She looked away from his body as she skirted it. Will turned back toward her, and she hurried to his side.

"I wish you hadn't seen him," Will put his arm around her shoulders. "I did ask you to stay away."

She leaned into his side, drawing strength from him. "I never promised I would."

Will gave her the half-exasperated, half-amused look she knew well. "We'll talk later." He turned to Matt. "Any idea where the other Indians are?"

"Tied up." Matt touched his cut lip. "It took a while."

"I can imagine.," Will spoke in dry tones. "I suppose that's how you came by that black eye."

"Let's say I was glad when Brady and Sparky showed up."

Phoebe noticed that the two ranch hands seemed in much the same state as Matt.

Will released her and turned to Sparky and Brady. "And where have you two been, might I ask?"

"Nearly to Stevensville and back." Brady shook his head. "We were tricked, good and proper. What we thought was a group of renegades turned out to be a single Indian leading two riderless horses down the trail."

Sparky nodded. "If he hadn't finally slowed down, we might have followed him clear to Hell Gate."

"It worked out for the best," Will murmured. "You showed up right when Matt needed you."

"It was a rare fight, I must say. We finished by hogtying the pair of them." Matt gave Phoebe a sheepish look. "Begging your pardon, Miss Walsh. I forgot your presence or I wouldn't have been so forthcoming."

She smiled faintly. "I'm sure I'd hear the tale around the campfire, anyway." By the time she did, Phoebe had no doubt that it would be much embroidered. "You won't soon forget the experience."

"That's the truth, and no less." Matt glanced toward Elk Hunter. "We had the matter in hand, only then this fellow ambushed me from behind. He took my gun."

"Speaking of which—I have it." Will pulled a pistol from his vest pocket. He extended it to Matt, handle first.

Matt glanced from the gun to Elk Hunter, and then back at Will. "I guess you do."

Phoebe shuddered. "We should get out of here."

Brady looked up from murmuring with Sparky. "We'll bury the body before we go."

"It's the least we can do for the old man," Sparky added. "After he stood up for us."

"All right, but let me take Phoebe out of here first." Will turned to Phoebe. "Where are the Indian ponies?"

"Back in the meadow."

"We'll retrieve them after I get Patches from where I left him A couple of Indian ponies will come in handy to carry the renegades to the sheriff."

Phoebe shrugged. "The ponies belong to them, anyway."

"I assume the horses are in the cottonwood grove where we left them?" Will addressed his question to Matt. "No one seems to stay put these days."

"They were there, last time I saw them—along with two tied-up Indians." Matt holstered his gun.

Will started down the trail. "Why didn't Elk Hunter free them when he captured you?"

Matt fell in beside him. "He was a little busy marching the three of us to the cabin at gunpoint. I think he was going back for them when you arrived."

Will's eyes widened. "It's a good thing I didn't come along any later. I'd have had three to contend with." He shook his head. "Events might have gone very differently."

"But they didn't." Phoebe quickened her steps to keep up with the men's longer strides. "God smiled on us."

Phoebe spotted the two Indians, crumpled on the ground in the shade beneath the cottonwoods. A pang of sympathy went through her. She'd recently suffered in the same manner. Their bonds looked more humane than hers had been, but their eyes revealed the same helpless fear that she'd experienced. Phoebe pictured the two warriors as they had looked when she'd first seen them, sitting proudly on their painted ponies. "Must we turn them in?"

Will swung to face her. "I'd think you would be the first to want justice."

Matt kept going toward the horses, which were grazing along the stream bank.

Phoebe squinted against the lowering sun. "Justice, yes, but not revenge. I'm afraid they would receive harsher treatment than they deserve."

Will's jaw firmed. "They kidnapped you."

"I don't think they meant to. They simply happened to be with Elk Hunter at the time."

"They didn't have to go along with it."

"That's true, but if left to themselves, I doubt they would have taken me."

"Just what do you propose?" Will rubbed the back of his neck. "Surely, you're not suggesting letting them get away with what they did?"

"I don't know." The murmur of water rose to fill the silence between them. "What would be best?" Certainly not giving them over to the sheriff or soldiers. During the present tension between the settlers and the Indians, it might result in their hangings. She didn't want that. How strange to find herself in agreement with Spukani, who only wanted to live in peace. Thinking of him sparked an idea. "Couldn't we give them into Spukani's keeping and ask him to make sure the tribe deals with them?"

"That's a fair solution, provided Spukani agrees." Will sighed. "I'll go ask him."

Will went to carry out his errand while Phoebe kept an eye

on the prisoners. The light softened, and a gentle wind stirred the cottonwood branches, weaving shadows across the grass. Matt's voice carried downstream as he spoke to the horses.

If Spukani wouldn't take responsibility for the captives, she would ask Will to free them. The realization arrived with a feeling of finality, as if dropped into her spirit from the judge who sat on heaven's throne. She refused to nurture bitterness, which would only grow and destroy its host. She had only to look at Spukani to see proof of that.

Will returned with Brady and Sparky. He caught Phoebe's eyes. "Spukani has agreed to take in the renegades."

Phoebe smiled. "God seems to be giving the old man a chance to redeem himself with his people."

"I hope it works out that way for him. Sparky and Brady, take the prisoners to the cabin. Matt, you can stay with our horses while Phoebe and I collect the Indian ponies. I've never stolen a horse, and I don't intend to start now. I'll return the Indian pony I borrowed, but we'll need to keep one for Phoebe a little longer, or she'll have no way home."

Sparky and Brady were already untying the prisoners' feet.

"Please, take off their gags, as well." Phoebe called to them.

"Must we?" Sparky appealed to Will, one eye closed against the sun.

"Do it." Will took Patches' reins from Matt. "And give them water."

A pained expression crossed Brady's face. "They'll make our ears ring all the way to the cabin."

Will led Patches nearer to Phoebe. "We'll need to ride double to go after the ponies."

She nodded. "I want a word with the prisoners before we go."

Will gave her a questioning look. "Are you sure?"

"Never more so." She went to stand before the prisoners, who were rubbing their cheeks where the gags had been. "I want you to know something." She spoke in their native tongue. "Helping Elk Hunter steal me from my people was wrong. It brought me much fear and suffering."

They each looked away from her. Neither answered.

"You may not be sorry for what you did, but I have decided to forgive you anyway. I am the one who asked to free you."

She had their attention, for two sets of dark eyes turned to her. She drew a deep breath. "Elk Hunter is dead. His hatred killed him. I hope you won't let that be your story, too."

They looked away again, but with chastised expressions.

She returned to Will, who mounted his horse and reached down to pull her up behind him. Phoebe circled her arms around his waist, beyond caring if the others saw her lean against him. She loved this man to distraction, and there was no use pretending she didn't.

Patches swayed down the trail. The horse had spent long hours grazing a lush stream bank, and it showed in his lazy gait. Will let him amble until they passed the cabin, and then quickened his pace. With the first blush of sunset staining the sky, Phoebe understood the need to hurry. Although she'd hobbled the Indian ponies, they still needed to be located, after which, she and Will would rejoin the others. She couldn't imagine that any of them might want to camp so close to Spukani's cabin. That meant having to travel the few hours remaining before full dark fell. They should find the ponies quickly to allow more time. Even so, Patches brought them to the meadow too soon.

She could appreciate its beauty better now, with Lupine waving like flags beneath the spruce trees at the edge of the meadow. Bitterroot flowers threaded the grass, although their daisy-like purple faces would close soon. A stream glinted back the faint sunset hues washing the sky.

Phoebe sang out when she spotted the ponies half-hidden by the shade under a clump of lodgepole pines. Will dismounted and reached up for her. Phoebe no longer needed to prove her independence. She leaned down to him and felt his arms enclose her. They rocked together for a sweet moment. The urgency of their errand, her desire for food, even time itself fell away.

Phoebe pulled away first, but only to gaze up at him. "I can't thank you enough for coming after me."

"As I mentioned, I couldn't stay away." He touched her cheek. "I don't think I've made it clear how much you mean to me. With your permission, I'd like to do that from here on out."

Phoebe gaped at him, speechless. She'd dreamed of him saying such words, but not while she was half-starved and in need of a bath.

He rushed on before she could speak. "I'm sorry, but I've been a complete idiot where you're concerned."

"You have?"

"I'll admit it every day for the rest of my life, if you'll only give me the chance."

"You will?"

He smiled. "Phoebe, don't look so shocked. I love you more than life. Can I dare to hope that you love me, too?"

"Of course, I do. Didn't you guess?" Phoebe adopted a matter-of-fact tone, but her pulse picked up. "I've been waiting for you to figure out what you want. At first, I thought that was no woman. You seemed so averse to them. But then, I thought Katerina changed your mind."

"Katerina?" He raised his eyebrows. "Where on earth did you get that impression?"

"But—I saw you holding hands in the garden."

"You *what?*" Will stared at her, but then his eyes glinted. "You must have seen us shake on an agreement we made."

"An agreement?"

"It's a long story and somewhat private."

"Sorry. I shouldn't have asked."

"No need to apologize. You gained the right to ask about my affairs, the first time I kissed you. I should have done right by you then. I hope you can forgive me."

"I already did, long ago." Phoebe stuck out her chin. "That doesn't mean I didn't give in to frustration a time or two."

"Ah, yes." He grinned. "I recall the tongue-lashings you gave me vividly."

Phoebe's face heated. "I believe I've apologized for them."

"I deserved worse, to be honest. All I can say in my defense is that after being left at the altar, I was terrified of being hurt again."

"I figured that out."

"That's all behind me now, Phoebe. After Elk Hunter kidnapped you, I realized how deeply I love you."

"Are you sure of that?"

"I couldn't be more certain."

She gave him an arch look. "Then I suppose you'll stop trying to marry me off to other men."

His face went red. "I did do that."

"You did."

"I'm sorry."

"As you should be." She stepped out of his arms. "You also apologized for kissing me—twice. That's hardly flattering."

"But, I dishonored you."

"That would only be true if you weren't serious, as you tried to convince me. Apparently, you *were* serious, as you have now explained." Phoebe glanced sideways at him. "If I may ask, what are your true intentions?"

He smiled. "They are purely honorable, I assure you. Your uncle would have my hide for anything less."

She tilted her face upward. "Then you may kiss me again."

"Oh, I can, can I?" Will caught her to him, laughing. He took possession of her mouth, his lips caressing hers in a melodious rhythm they alone could hear. Phoebe yielded to his touch in a sweet surrender that felt victorious.

He ended the kiss and rested his forehead on hers. "Why did I fight this for so long?"

"Shh…" She hushed him with her lips.

Will's eyes gleamed. "Keep that up and we'll need to find a preacher right away."

Phoebe laughed. "I can recommend one in particular."

"I'm sure we'll wind up standing before your Uncle Shane." He caught her into his arms. "But let's start at the beginning, shall we? I want to savor every moment of courting you."

A thrill went through Phoebe at the prospect of being cherished by Will. It would be a very different courtship than Alton had envisioned. She was glad she'd refused him and followed her heart, instead. Alton wanted to possess her, whereas Will had sacrificed to free her. She could see plainly that selfishness inflicted wounds, but love healed them.

Phoebe lifted her lips for Will's kiss, grateful that she'd held out for love.

EPILOGUE

"Hurry!" Fiona pushed Phoebe through the cabin doorway and right into Liberty.

"Ouch!" Liberty balanced on one foot.

"Sorry." Phoebe steadied her with a hand on her elbow. "Did I stomp your toe?"

"Yes." Liberty laughed.

Phoebe gave her a puzzled glance. "What's so funny?"

Liberty's eyes widened. "Oh no! I can't get the giggles on my wedding day."

"Yes, you can." Katie grinned. "It's entirely possible, as you are proving."

"Don't tease me." Liberty choked back laughter. "You'll make it worse."

Aunt America glanced up from laying bouquets on the table. "Take a deep breath."

Ma paused while carrying a box of pins. "Try drinking some water."

"That was close." Katie pulled the door shut with a decided click.

"I'll say." Will's sister, Alice, grinned. The diminutive woman had the same brown hair, dimpled chin, and blue eyes as her brother. She'd arrived only two days ago, having traveled from Philadelphia with her husband and two children. Phoebe already loved her.

"Come and I'll do your hair, Phoebe." Ma pulled out one of the ladderback kitchen chairs, which scraped across the floorboards with a familiar sound.

Phoebe sat down and steeled herself for the trial she would endure. She'd always been tender-headed. Ma did not share this affliction, which must make it hard to be sympathetic, although she tried. Ma brushed and parted and tugged until tears filled Phoebe's eyes. When Phoebe looked at herself in the mirror, however, she smiled. "You've done it, Ma. It looks just like the picture." Her mother had wound and braided her hair into a becoming hairstyle from Godey's Lady's Book, the magazine Phoebe had enjoyed reading since she was small. The result, she decided, was worth the pain.

Most of the other bridesmaids arrived, tittering with excitement. They'd dressed at the Hayes house. The scents of lavender and roses from the ribbon-bedecked bouquets filled the cabin. Phoebe, Liberty and their bridesmaids would carry them down the aisle before long. Two veils draped the front room chairs in clouds of gauze and lace. A thrill went through Phoebe at the sight. This was really happening. The day of their double wedding had taken forever to arrive, but now the morning was speeding by. In no time at all, she would exchange vows with Will, and Liberty would marry Jake.

"Here they come again." Fiona spoke from her station at the kitchen window. "Will and Jake are walking toward the church this time."

"He came." Phoebe breathed the words at the same time as Liberty. "How do they look?" They spoke in unison again.

Fiona's eyes sparkled. "Jittery but so handsome."

Katie, who had been helping Aunt America dress Liberty's hair, chuckled. "I'm not sure which of you makes the most nervous bride."

Phoebe pictured Katie, white-faced and trembling, at her own wedding. "And you weren't one?"

"I never said that." A grin spread across Katie's face. "I'll admit to fretting. I couldn't help but wonder why Eustace wanted to marry a woman with Cheyenne blood."

"How could that possibly matter?" Liberty waved a white-gloved hand. "The man couldn't be more in love with you."

"He's made that clear, ever since." Katie's face took on a smug expression. "But it took me time to accept the truth. Until I met Eustace, remember, I was preparing to become a spinster."

"How could we forget?" Tears sprang to Phoebe's eyes, but she blinked them away. "I know what it feels like to contemplate such a future."

Katie engulfed her in a rush of blue taffeta. "I'm thankful God had other plans for us both."

"Uncle Con felt that God had called me to marry, and that Will was my husband. I doubted him at the time, but he was right." Phoebe smiled. "Maybe I should tell him that."

Liberty laughed. "I'm sure there's no need. Uncle Con is certain to announce it all day long."

A tap came at the door. Fiona hurried to open it. "I was about to ask after you. Come in."

Liberty's two sisters rushed into the cabin in a flurry of satin, pearls, and lace. Aisling, the older of the two at eighteen, had her red-gold hair gathered into a jeweled comb from which it cascaded in ringlets. She put a hand to her chest while catching her breath. "Sorry to take so long. Shannon couldn't find one of her gloves."

Sixteen-year-old Shannon shook her dark head, which was pinned up and threaded with yellow grosgrain ribbon. "Could I help it that it fell behind my dresser?"

"Honestly." Aisling rolled her eyes. "If you would take better care of your belongings, it wouldn't have fallen."

Aunt America frowned. "Let's not quarrel, ladies. We don't

want anything to spoil this special day."

Aisling crossed her arms and raised a delicate eyebrow. "Sorry."

Shannon nodded. "Me, too."

"Never mind." Liberty smiled at her sisters. "You came before we left for the church, and that's what matters."

"Speaking of which, we'd better not dally." Aunt America turned into the front room. "Come with me, Liberty, and let's put on your veil."

"You, too." Ma beckoned to Phoebe.

A short while and several pin jabs later, Ma nodded her approval. "You'll do."

"You make beautiful brides." Fiona beamed at Phoebe and Liberty in turn. "Just think, next year it will be my turn."

This statement might have alarmed Phoebe if she didn't approve of her cousin's match. She'd feared that Fiona's longing to marry might lead her astray, but she had surprised them all by falling in love with one of their most sensible neighbors. Timothy Walton had a knack for fixing things. Everyone in the community had called upon his skills at one time or another. Picturing flighty Fiona married to practical Timothy made Phoebe smile. "I'm sure you will be very happy."

Aunt America finished pinning Liberty's veil into place. "Is everyone ready? It's time to go."

Katie gave Phoebe and Liberty their bouquets. "Don't worry about anything. Just enjoy yourself."

"I'll always treasure sharing this special day with you." Liberty spoke softly from behind her veil.

"So will I." Moisture gathered in Phoebe's eyes.

"Here." Ma gave her a scrap of linen and lace. "Tuck this into your sleeve."

Phoebe touched the raised golden letters, her initials

embroidered lovingly into the cloth. "Thanks, Ma." She was beginning to understand why people cried at weddings.

Cold sweat beaded Will's upper lip, and his stomach churned. Throwing up seemed likely. What had he gotten himself into? If a second woman left him at the altar, the heartache would crush him.

Pa had always taught him that the only way out of a problem was straight through to the other side. He'd forgotten that particular bit of wisdom, but there was no better time to grasp it. He could only endure this torture because of his love for Phoebe.

If anyone failed to show up for this wedding, it would not be him.

Jake fidgeted beside Will. "I don't think I've ever been so nervous."

Jake's brother and best man, Gideon, clasped his back for a bracing moment. "Everything will go well."

Will mustered a smile for Jake and didn't point out that Gideon couldn't possibly know such a thing. Life was full of risks, but you had to take them.

Matt, on Will's other side, gave him a bolstering smile, and the sick feeling settled down some. It helped that Matt was the very image of a happily married man. He and Katerina had tied the knot after a brief courtship last year.

It meant a lot that Matt had stepped in to be his best man since none of his brothers were available to fill the position, and certainly not Caleb. He'd learned from Alice that Sophie had left Caleb for a wealthier man. Hearing of his brother's sorrows did not bring Will joy. Sophie had taken more from Caleb than she had Will, but she'd stolen most of all from his family. Maybe someday he and his brother could reconcile, and they all could heal. Meanwhile, only his mother and one sister had made it to his wedding.

He would count it a start.

Liberty's father, wearing a dark suit and clerical collar, joined them at the side door to the sanctuary. "Ready gentlemen?"

Will nodded, and Jake murmured his assent.

Reverend Hayes cracked open the side door and peeked out. Will caught a glimpse of the mothers of the brides standing together inside the rear door of the church.

"The wedding party is lined up and waiting," Reverend Hayes whispered. "It's time for me to go escort my daughter. Do you remember what to do?"

Jake nodded. "After the ushers seat both mothers, we'll go through the door and onto the platform."

"Good. I'll see you at the altar." Reverend Hayes included Will in his smile.

A few minutes later, the organist struck the wedding march.

Will met Jake's eyes, blew out a breath, and opened the door. He concentrated on the simple mechanics of walking, and made it onto the dais without a hitch. Matt and Gideon took their places also.

The flower girls started the processional. Con and Elsa's five-year-old daughter, Meg, strewed rose petals with intense concentration. Lisbet, Alice's four-year-old, clutched her basket with all the fervor of a dog guarding a bone and refused to part with a single petal.

The music swelled, and the attendees rose in unison. Liberty came through the rear doorway on Reverend Hayes' arm. Will heard Jake suck in his breath. Liberty gazed unwaveringly at her groom as she advanced toward him. Reverend Hayes continued onto the platform, leaving his daughter standing below it. Jake came down and held out his hand to her. Liberty placed her own hand into his, and they climbed the steps together. Reverend Hayes had suggested this variation, and Will had to admit it was beautiful. When it was his turn, he hoped he wouldn't trip and mess it up.

Phoebe appeared then, and he forgot to breathe. Walking toward him in a gown of flowing white silk, she looked like a princess, but the gleam in her eyes reminded him that she was still strong-minded. He wouldn't want her any other way. Will gazed at the woman he loved with all his heart and lost all desire to flee.

The look her bridegroom gave her made Phoebe's face heat. She lowered her own gaze but couldn't look away for long. Will's smile anchored her, and her nervousness vanished. Phoebe gave him back glance for glance, reveling in this sacred moment. She held her head high in the knowledge that this fine day, she would pledge herself to Will before God and man.

Beloved faces stood out as Phoebe walked down the aisle. Liberty, her brothers, and many of her cousins beamed at her from the platform. Katerina smiled while Phoebe passed, glowing as befitted an expectant mother. She'd confided her news to Phoebe earlier. Mr. and Mrs. Daly couldn't have seemed more joyful. All her aunts and uncles looked happy, and Uncle Con winked. In the front pew, Ma and Aunt America dabbed at their eyes with handkerchiefs, but they were both smiling.

Phoebe and her father stopped below the dais. "Go on, then, girl," he whispered. Phoebe squeezed his arm, and he kissed the back of her gloved hand before leaving her.

And then there was only Will. He came down the steps and offered her his hand, watching her with such love that Phoebe caught her breath.

She curled her hand into Will's, more certain than ever that her future belonged with him.

Author's Note

The Whispering Wind, like all the Montana Gold books, is a blend of fact and fiction. Most of the characters sprang to life in my imagination, but a few are an educated guess at the personalities of actual historical figures. I hope any living descendants will forgive my audacity in including Marcus and Margaret Daly in my story.

Marcus Daly was one of three men known as "copper kings" due to the incredible fortunes they made in mining. (William A. Clark and F. Augustus Heinze were the other two.) Marcus was a geologist, engineer, and astute businessman. As a gifted geologist, Marcus could tell that areas around Butte, Montana contained rich lodes of copper ore. An astute businessman, he foresaw that Thomas Edison's invention of the lightbulb would lead to a copper boom.

Marcus purchased the Anaconda, a failing silver mine, and several others near Butte with the intention of mining them for copper. He used his skill as an engineer to launch the Anaconda Mining Company. Despite achieving tremendous success, Marcus appears to have remained humble. He is remembered as a generous patron, a good boss, and a wonderful family man. Marcus dearly loved his wife, Margaret—his "Maggie." Their romance began in 1872 when Marcus worked as a foreman for the Walker Brothers banking and mining syndicate of Salt Lake City. A miner named Zenas Evans accompanied Marcus to inspect a new mine. Evans' 18-year-old daughter, Margaret, came along. While touring the mine, Margaret slipped, but Marcus caught her. He could make her blush, ever afterwards, by remarking that his wife literally fell into his arms. They were married later that year.

A historical figure mentioned in this book is Margaret Heffernan Borland. Born of Irish immigrant parents, she became the first female trail boss. Despite being widowed three times and losing four of her seven children, Margaret retained the starch to drive a thousand longhorn cattle from her ranch in south Texas to Wichita, Kansas. She followed the Chisholm Trail—taking her three living children and one grandchild along. Sadly, Margaret died of trail fever shortly afterward.

Harriett "Hattie" Louise Standefer Cluck was another female Texas pioneer who traveled the Chisholm trail with children in tow. Hattie was three months pregnant when the drive began.

Calamity Jane is a well-known historical figure who scouted for the army, rode for the Pony Express, and ran her own cattle ranch. She often wore men's clothing, which were far more practical for these activities.

The love story between President Grover Cleveland and the much-younger Frances Folsom, mentioned briefly in the story, did scandalize some people. A wider age gap than we are used to today wasn't uncommon between spouses at the time. Perhaps the shock was due to speculation that paired Cleveland with Frances's mother, Emma Folsom, who often visited the White House with her daughter.

I hope you've enjoyed the Montana Gold series as much as I have. I wrote it to honor the Irish who immigrated to America and stuck it out despite many hardships. They were a resourceful people, and equal to the challenges of the Wild West.

Book Club Questions

1. What were some of the restrictions imposed on Phoebe, and how did she overcome them? Did you feel they were fair for that time period, or too harsh/not harsh enough?

2. Was Phoebe spoiled or lively? Have you met someone like Phoebe? Did she rub you the wrong way or did you see beneath the outer layer to understand the depths beneath?

3. What was Will's greatest fear, and how did he overcome it? Did you ever need to overcome fear to receive a blessing?

4. Phoebe waited for Will to be ready to marry, and it worked out well for her. Are there times when it is foolish to put your life on hold for someone else?

5. Have you had to wait a long time, as Phoebe did, for an answered prayer? What pulled you through?

6. Why did Katerina and Will decide to apologize to one another? If you have struggled with a similar situation, what did you do to resolve it?

7. In what ways did Will see himself in Diablo? Have you dealt with being mischaracterized?

8. Phoebe encountered pressure to conform to societal expectations of women. How have those expectations changed? Would you rather live in Phoebe's time or in the modern world?

9. How did facing her fear of Spukani cause Phoebe to overcome it? Have you ever felt overwhelmed by fear of something that turned out to be a lot less scary than you'd thought?

10. How did the desire for revenge lead Elk Hunter astray? When called upon to forgive someone else, how have you broken through your reluctance?